Burn Notice: Subnet Echo Directive Seven-Two

Burn Notice: Subnet Echo Directive Seven-Two

By
Angel Giacomo

1st Battalion
Publishing

Copyright ©

First publication in 2025 by 1st Battalion Publishing
1stbattalionpublishing@gmail.com

ISBN 979-8-9874744-5-7

Library of Congress Control Number: 2025910969

Printed in the United States of America

First Edition: 2025

DEDICATION

This book is dedicated to all who have served in every branch of the military. I write it with extreme humility. It is intended to honor the veterans of the United States who have fought in our conflicts—past, present, and future.

"The task of the leader is to get his people from where they are to where they have not been. In the realm of intelligence, this means understanding not only the current landscape but also anticipating future threats and opportunities, often through the lens of secrecy and strategic foresight." – Henry Kissinger

"If you know the enemy and know yourself, you need not fear the result of a hundred battles." – Sun Tzu

"The world is very different now. For man holds in his mortal hands the power to abolish all forms of human poverty and all forms of human life." - President John F. Kennedy

"The very word 'secrecy' is repugnant in a free and open society." – President John F. Kennedy

"We'll know our disinformation program is complete when everything the American public believes is false." - William Casey (Director of the CIA 1981-1987)

"The world is not enough." – Ian Flemming (James Bond novels)

"In a time of deceit telling the truth is a revolutionary act." – George Orwell

"And ye shall know the truth, and the truth shall make you free." – CIA Motto

ACKNOWLEDGMENT

Thank you to those who believed in me.

A special thank you to:
Dr. Russell W. Ramsey, Lt. Colonel (1935-2023) - U.S. Army (retired) USMA 1957 - 8th Regiment, 1st Cavalry Division – Vietnam – 1965-66. Thank you for being my friend. Hooah! I will miss you always. Go Army! Beat Navy!

Robert A. Soles – Specialist 4th Class, U.S. Army, 14th Inventory Control Company – Vietnam, March 1966-67.

YN2 Paul C. Giacomo (1940-2017), U.S. Navy – U.S.S. Valley Forge (LPH 8) – Vietnam (U.S. Navy - 1959-1970, SSGT, 445th MP Company, Oklahoma National Guard 1976-1992).

INSPIRATION

Lieutenant Colonel Rachel Merrit, a fictional character in this novel, draws inspiration from the trailblazing journeys of Captain (later Colonel) Elizabeth R. Smith and Captain (later Colonel) Judith A. McGowan, the first female Judge Advocate General (JAG) officers in the U.S. Army.

Commissioned in 1972, Elizabeth Smith and Judith McGowan shattered major barriers in a male-dominated field, embodying resilience and determination as they paved the way for future generations of women in military law.

Through Rachel's character, the narrative explores the challenges and triumphs faced by women in the JAG Corps, celebrating their contributions to the military justice system while honoring the legacy of those who paved the way.

CHAPTER 1

0710 Hours
January 15, 1984
Spring Lake, NC

The road curved sharply past the tree line, and Colonel Theodore "Teddy" Roosevelt IV took it without slowing down, shuffle steering to maintain control. The old primer-gray Dodge Charger bucked once on the gravel shoulder before settling again, its tires gripping the loose stones like a knife dragged across bone. He didn't look back. Not yet.

The sun hadn't risen yet, but the sky bled gray at the edges, lightening with each passing second. A winter storm was trying to push through the hills behind him, fat snowflakes swirling in the twin beams of the Charger's headlights. The woods flanked both sides of the road, thick with shadows and frost. North Carolina farm country on the outskirts of Spring Lake—quiet, elegant, and never as empty as it seemed.

The driver's side mirror flashed once, then again.

A tail car was behind him, completely blacked out with government plates.

He hit the gas. The Charger responded like a thoroughbred with a bayonet stuck in its flank. The engine roared, tires spitting gravel into the darkness. Ahead, the road forked, one path leading straight into town while the other veered toward a nearby ridge. Teddy took the left, heading toward the ridge and an old furniture warehouse just beyond the county line, which had served as an illegal distillery and bootlegging hideout during Prohibition. He knew the land—had scouted it years ago when Ghost needed a dead drop cleared for package retrieval. Back when they were still in the government's shadows, not hunted by them.

Teddy gripped the steering wheel tighter, feeling the pain in his left side, a leftover from the last time someone tried to solve a problem with a bullet. The scar wasn't fully healed. Neither was the betrayal by someone he trusted.

The radio crackled—an old CB unit wired directly into the dashboard, no external antenna, just a short magnetic one glued to the back package tray. Static followed, then a clipped voice.

"You've got three units trailing. Helicopter lifting off from Bragg. You've got maybe eight minutes before they box you in," said Captain

1

Jack Stratton, his friend, call sign Ghost for his ability to vanish into civilian populations and assume roles flawlessly.

Teddy didn't answer. He reached across the seat and flipped open the glove box. His sidearm was there, a standard military-issue M1911A1 Colt .45 caliber pistol. So was the compact field map—a coded overlay of old staging areas and fallback points from the Laos years. Not all of them were still useful. However, the one ahead—marked with a faint grease-pencil cross—had that old warehouse and a storm cellar, useful only when the weather turned bad since it was full of venomous snakes. The best tactical feature of the warehouse was its line of sight in three directions.

He took another curve at high speed. The Charger swayed from side to side but stayed on the gravel road. The black Chevy Tahoe was still behind him, now gaining ground, likely supercharged for pursuit with a powerful engine and a bottle of nitrous oxide. No sirens or flashers—just patience, taxpayer-funded hardware, and a bigger fuel tank.

"They want you alive," Ghost said over the CB radio. "For now."

The radio clicked off.

Teddy didn't speak. Didn't breathe. He allowed the next turn to take him straight onto the overgrown driveway—half-frozen mud and shattered gravel crunching under the tires—as the warehouse loomed ahead like a memory ripped from a war photo. Its exterior was a patchwork of rusted corrugated steel with jagged edges, faded paint, and broken windows. The wide open door gaped like a mouth, revealing a dark interior filled with shadows and forgotten machinery. The scent of fabric and liquor had long since faded away.

He braked—hard—slamming both feet onto the brake pedal. Once he slowed down enough, he killed the engine and coasted the last fifty feet into the darkened interior. He grabbed the CB mic. "Ghost, Stone, get out of here. I'll be along shortly. See you in Mexico."

Inside, the world was dark, dry, and filled with the ghosts of the past. Dust swirled around him as he stepped out, pistol in hand, and his breath curled white in the freezing cold air. He left the car half-turned by the wall, pulled the rolling door shut behind him, and listened.

Engines roared outside, tires screeched, and boots crunched on the gravel.

The last chase was about to begin.

0735 Hours
January 15, 1984
Abandoned Warehouse
Spring Lake, NC

The freezing cold wind whipped grit across the cracked concrete parking lot as Colonel Vincent Cross stepped out of the unmarked olive drab U.S. Army sedan and adjusted his coat collar up to protect his neck.

The warehouse stood before him, a three-story monolith of rusted corrugated steel, pitted beams, broken windows covered with plastic sheeting, and flaking brick, perched on the edge of a forgotten industrial district outside Fayetteville, North Carolina. No markings on the building to identify what it once housed or the current owner. Abandoned to time and the elements. Just shadows and silence behind the few remaining soot-caked windows. The kind of place no one looked at twice—perfect for ghosts who'd made too many enemies in too many government corridors.

He stared at the entrance—an old loading dock overgrown with weeds and partially torn-down chain-link fencing. No footprints or tire tracks. Just stillness and the knowledge that the most dangerous man he'd ever chased was somewhere inside that hollow shell. Not dangerous because he ran. Dangerous because he didn't.

"Command wants him alive," the captain next to him said while checking his sidearm.

"They always want them alive—until they don't," Cross muttered.

He turned toward the parked MPs, two standard U.S. Army olive-drab Jeeps idling in the lot behind them, each carrying a fireteam. Too much for one man. Not enough for Colonel Roosevelt.

Cross had spent the better part of two years reading the classified files, followed by nearly another year realizing the extent of the redactions. Operation Shatterhorn. MACV-SOG extensions into Laos. That failed reconnaissance mission on the Bolaven Plateau was blamed on Roosevelt and his team with surgical precision. No survivors appeared in the official record, except for him.

And now they were trying to capture him with a net designed for criminals, not for Special Forces soldiers trained to kill with their bare hands, masters in the art of subterfuge.

He pulled a two-way radio from his coat pocket and keyed it once. "This is Iron Vince. Hold position. No breach of the warehouse without my order."

An electronic crackle followed, then confirmation of his order.

Cross knew Colonel Theodore Roosevelt IV, having served with him in Vietnam. He understood how his mind worked. If he were inside that warehouse, he wouldn't be panicked. He'd be waiting, thinking, and measuring every sound and shadow. Not for a fight—but for a window of opportunity.

"Don't run," Cross whispered, hoping the words might reach his quarry through the steel walls. "Just come out. Let me ask the damn question this time."

But no one emerged from the warehouse. Only the wind remained, carrying the weight of everything Cross hadn't seen soon enough.

A lieutenant approached him, nervously shifting his weight from foot to foot. "Perimeter's sealed shut, sir. We've got two squads covering the rear exit and north alley."

Cross ignored him. His eyes were fixed on the front roll-up bay door, slightly ajar at the bottom, with the darkness behind it thick and silent.

"He's in there," Cross said.

"Are you sure it's Colonel Roosevelt, sir?"

Cross nodded. "Yes. The highway patrol spotted him on a fire trail driving an old truck he swiped out by Route 50. Burned it in a field. Left nothing but the undercarriage and a pair of old dog tags."

"Tags?" the lieutenant asked, confused. "But, sir—why would he—"

"Because he wants us to know he's alive," Cross said. "And because 'Bull Moose' Roosevelt doesn't leave a trace unless he means to."

The lieutenant remained silent.

Cross stepped forward slowly, his boots crunching on the snow-dusted gravel. He narrowed his eyes as he surveyed the doorframe, its corners, and the swirl of dust in the faint beam of orange-red morning sun slicing through the sky.

He had spent five years trying to track down these men through records, whispers in the dark corners of the underground, mysterious sightings, intelligence briefings, and damage reports from other countries. Now, he could feel it—just as a bloodhound senses the edge of a scent.

Cross turned back to the officers and men gathered behind him. "Do any of you know who's in there?"

None of them answered his question, so he did it for them.

"Colonel Theodore Roosevelt IV. Call sign Bull, as in Bull Moose, for two reasons. First, he's built like one and charges into battle the same way. Second, that was President Roosevelt's political party. A West Point graduate, Special Forces operative, and fourth-generation soldier, he is also distantly related to his namesake, President Theodore Roosevelt. His

4

other nickname is Rough Rider. If you don't know what he looks like, he's a much taller, six-feet-two, blond-haired, muscular version of his great-uncle. He led an off-the-books reconnaissance team along the Ho Chi Minh Trail in Laos. To this day, he is the only man I've ever seen perform a full extraction under fire with half a radio and a broken leg."

He took another step toward the door. "Possibly with him—Captain Jack Stratton. Ghost. Grew up bouncing between different foster homes in Southern California. Intel officer turned infiltrator and a master at blending into a crowd. Speaks five languages. Trained with East German defectors in '69. If he's in there, we're already being watched by a consummate professional."

One of the men next to him fidgeted nervously, checking to see if his M16 was loaded.

"And Master Sergeant Eli Red Horse," Cross continued. "Member of the Lakota Sioux tribe. Demolitions and engineering expert. Excels in close-quarters combat. He spent two years at the Special Warfare School teaching hand-to-hand combat. Last seen hauling Colonel Roosevelt out of a failed CIA operation near the Bolaven Plateau in southern Laos. Stone. That's what they call him. Because once he plants his feet, you can't move him. Six feet four and all muscle. He'd have made one hell of an offensive tackle for the Dallas Cowboys."

Cross stopped and turned to face the group directly. "These men were ghosts long before Langley decided they were a threat. They didn't disappear because they failed. They disappeared because someone buried the truth."

He let the words hang there.

"You think we're here to arrest them? Wrong war."

The lieutenant swallowed hard. "Then why are we here, sir?"

Cross dropped his hand to the grip of his sidearm, an Army-issue M1911A1 Colt .45 caliber pistol, not to draw it—but to anchor himself. "Because they just surfaced after being off the radar for the last five years. And if they came back from the dead, it's for a reason, not to surrender."

A gust of wind blew sand and dust across their boots.

Cross looked back at the warehouse. "They're sending a message. Now it's our move."

1030 Hours
January 15, 1984
Abandoned Warehouse
Spring Lake, NC

The ambush was swift and unexpected, the kind of operation that came from good intel and bad luck. Teddy expected Colonel Vince Cross, a former friend from the Vietnam War, would head into town, not away from it. He'd seen the net closing in but couldn't move fast enough to avoid it.

Cornered with no escape route, Teddy had taken cover in a run-down warehouse on the outskirts of Spring Lake, NC, as a stalling measure, just long enough to weigh options that never materialized. Now he was boxed in as MPs surrounded the building with weapons drawn, prepared to wait him out. They had food, water, and heat in their vehicles. He had nothing. Not even the water worked in the unheated building. That meant no drinking water or even a functioning toilet. He'd have to piss in a corner among the rats and the spiders.

The next event was even more unexpected. Something Teddy would have done. A deuce and a half truck crashed through the rolled-down metal door, sliding to a stop on the concrete floor. A dozen MPs rushed through the opening.

Teddy dropped his pistol and raised his hands in a gesture of surrender, a wry smile playing on his lips. However, beneath his calm exterior, a gnawing discomfort had taken root in his abdomen—a dull ache in his right side that had been intensifying since last night, overriding the one in his left leg. It wasn't a pulled muscle but something deeper. The pressure was constant, grinding through his gut like a hot steel coil tightening with each breath.

Cross approached him, his face a mask of triumph—smug, like someone standing over a long-dug grave, ready to drop in his next victim. "Well, well, Roosevelt. Seems the great 'Bull Moose' luck has finally run out. You're not even going to make me work for it?"

Teddy shrugged. "Everyone gets lucky sometimes, Vince. Even you."

"Are you sick or just finally out of tricks?"

"Figured I'd let you win one for a change."

Cross waved his MPs forward. "Take him into custody."

The MPs surged forward, securing Teddy's wrists behind his back with handcuffs. He didn't resist. That would be foolish and a quick way to get beaten to a pulp. There was a reason Colonel Vincent Cross earned the nickname "Iron Vince," and it wasn't just because of his unyielding discipline in combat zones.

As they escorted him to the waiting transport van, each step sent a jolt of pain through his lower right side. He clenched his jaw, unwilling to show any sign of weakness. It wasn't the healed gunshot wound. Wrong spot. The discomfort had started as a vague sensation near his navel but had since migrated into a sharper pain on his right side. Nausea lurked in the distance, and he felt a slight fever setting in as sweat rolled down his back despite the freezing cold temperatures.

The transport's heavy suspension rattled after every pothole, and Teddy clenched his teeth to keep from flinching. He didn't want them to see that he was in pain. His back wasn't just sore anymore. It felt like something deep inside him was inflamed and angry. His right side, just below the ribs, had become the focal point. Every bump jarred it, sending hot, searing pain shooting up into his chest and down into his legs.

By the time they reached the Fort Bragg stockade, the nausea had struck with the full force of a volcanic explosion, burning in his gut. Fever chased closely behind. The guards at the intake desk stripped him of everything but his clothing, ignoring the mandatory medical check as if it were an inconvenience. They marched him through a dimly lit corridor that reeked of rancid water, bleach, and rusted metal, shoving him into a concrete cell with a dirty toilet, sink, and a single canvas cot bolted to the concrete wall like an afterthought.

"Here we are. Home sweet home. You'll get used to the smell...maybe," Cross said from outside the bars. "Not so cocky now, are you, Roosevelt?"

Teddy met his gaze. "Just pacing myself." The effort to maintain the illusion of indifference cost him dearly. The throbbing had transformed into something more persistent. He lowered himself onto the cot, keeping his expression neutral and resisting the urge to pull his knees up to his chest. He didn't want to give Cross the satisfaction.

"No wisecracks? No plan? Are you giving up, Roosevelt? The great 'Rough Rider' all alone in a cell?" Cross asked.

Teddy looked at him. "Ask me tomorrow." He might not survive the night.

Cross snorted. "Don't worry, I'll be back." He lingered a moment longer before leaving with his MPs. Only one guard remained at the door, looking bored and indifferent.

The clang of the cell door echoed long after Cross left, creating a lasting silence.

The room felt oppressively hot as sweat beaded on his forehead, soaked through his shirt, and trickled down his face. He glanced at the guard, who wasn't sweating. Maybe it was just him. He closed his eyes for a moment, bracing himself against another wave of pressure and trying to compartmentalize the sensation. It was no longer just his back. That had been the start of it, a kind of dull, muscular pull he'd blamed on sleeping on a cold concrete floor in a contorted position between two broken conveyor belts in another abandoned warehouse the previous night. Drawing his knees up to his chest and lying on his left side provided a modicum of relief, easing the relentless pressure in his abdomen.

Teddy raised his head and looked at the MP sitting at a desk near the wall. "My back's killing me. I need to see a medic."

The guard didn't even turn to look at him. "Yeah, sure. Save it, Colonel Roosevelt. You and every other guy locked up in here. Try harder. Find a better excuse."

"I'm not screwing around. I can't..." Teddy trailed off. Talking made the pain flare up sharper, and it was starting to radiate deeper now. "Just get someone."

"Forget about it. You'll live."

"Maybe not." Teddy let his head fall back onto the pillow, breathing slow and shallow. Talking made it worse. The pain was now rooted deep in his abdomen. A shiver ran down his spine. Something inside him felt very wrong. Fine. If no one was coming, then he would ride it out. That's what he did. That's what he always did.

CHAPTER 2

0005 Hours
January 16, 1984
Fort Bragg Stockade
Fort Bragg, NC

Teddy lost track of time. He couldn't sleep. That was impossible. Yet he drifted in and out of a dazed stupor. Hours passed, and the pain only intensified. He curled tighter on the cot, his arms wrapped around his midsection, desperately trying to hold something in place.

The pain had sharpened to a deep, stabbing burn, now centered low and to the right, with every twitch of muscle making it worse. He stopped moving altogether. Even swallowing sent the pain in his belly spiking into the stratosphere. He kept his knees drawn tight to his chest, breathing shallowly as nausea crashed over him in heavy, constant waves. At one point, he thought he might vomit, but nothing came up, only bile burning in his throat.

Teddy wasn't sweating anymore, even though he was soaked in sweat. His shirt clung to his skin like wet gauze. Despite this, he felt dry. His lips were cracked, and his tongue stuck to the roof of his mouth. His head spun when he tried to open his eyes.

The cramps kept coming. Tight, breath-stealing surges forced him to bite the inside of his cheek to stay quiet. He clutched his gut with both arms, curling around it in a futile effort to hold it in, keep it from unraveling. But there was nothing to hold, nothing to stop. Just pain, heat, and a gnawing wrongness he couldn't name.

And then they came.

Two MPs laughed as they entered the cell. One of them cracked his knuckles, treating the situation like a joke.

"You want a medic?" one asked, crouching beside him. "Maybe we should help you get comfortable first."

The other MP reached down and grabbed Teddy's arm. "Let's loosen you up a little, Colonel Roosevelt," the man said with mock sympathy. "You look really stiff."

Teddy didn't resist—he barely moved. Every breath was a controlled action, carefully measured to avoid worsening the pain in his gut.

His lack of response to their intimidation tactic seemed to irritate them more.

The blows weren't meant to be obvious. They knew what they were doing, targeting areas that wouldn't be visible under a cursory inspection while fully clothed, the ribs, lower back, stomach, and kidneys. Body shots only. A fist to the ribs, a knee to the side, a kick to the stomach—this was the worst of all.

They wanted to punish him, not to get written up. Each blow was agonizing, leaving him gasping for air.

He didn't cry out—couldn't. That seemed to bother them. One of them cursed and grabbed him by the collar, dragging him halfway off the cot before slamming him back down again. The jolt was worse than the fists. The sudden motion jarred everything loose inside him. A spike of pain flashed white behind his eyes, and he nearly retched from it. Still, he didn't scream.

He curled into a fetal position as instinct took over, protecting himself the only way he could—by not reacting at all.

When they finished, one man yanked him up by his collar and threw him onto the cot like a sack of dirty laundry. One of them muttered something about him being dead weight, then they walked out, leaving him there, curled up, shaking, sick, and alone.

Teddy had no idea how much time had passed after that. At some point, he vomited the meager contents of his stomach, mostly green bile and curdled blood clots. What little he'd managed to eat the day before was long gone. The bitter taste lingered in his mouth, acrid and burning in his throat. The heat inside him flared up again and then finally began to fade.

Not because he was feeling better.

Because he was running out of energy to feel it, becoming numb to the pain.

He lay there, unmoving, waiting for dawn to arrive—if it ever would.

0755 Hours
January 16, 1984
Fort Bragg Stockade
Fort Bragg, NC

The overhead lighting hadn't changed, but something in the air told him it was morning. Teddy hadn't slept. Not really. There was a windowless rhythm to confinement. Time still passed, even when his body was too wrecked to feel the movement. He lay where the guards had left him, curled in the fetal position on the cot, his shirt stiff from dried sweat. His arms protected the angry coil of agony rooted deep in his right side. Every small motion made it twist harder, like someone driving a railroad spike a little deeper between his ribs with each breath.

He tried to remain still. Moving was dangerous now. The slightest movement sent waves of nausea rising in his throat. His mouth felt like cotton and copper. The heat had baked into his bones.

Then came the sound of several pairs of boots. One pair moved slower than the others—measured and deliberate—Colonel Cross. Good old Iron Vince had arrived to gloat over his victory.

The cell door slammed open with a loud clang.

Teddy barely noticed the conversation until it unfolded right in front of him.

"I'm telling you, sir," the guard said, motioning at the cot, "he's been faking all night. Wouldn't stop moaning, curling up like he's dying, but he won't even stand up. Keeps lying there like a sick dog."

Cross strode confidently into the cell. "Move him."

The two MPs complied. One grabbed Teddy's shoulder while the other took hold of his arm. They hoisted him upright without warning, positioning themselves on either side of him.

"Get up," one of them ordered.

Teddy's body resisted for a moment. His vision blurred the instant his feet took his weight, then his legs buckled. He collapsed like a limp sack onto the concrete, slamming his left hip and shoulder hard into the ground. No sound escaped his lips. He was barely conscious enough to register the pain as separate from the fire already eating through his abdomen.

The world tilted. He didn't cry out. Couldn't. There wasn't enough air left in his chest to do anything but grunt. He caught a glimpse of Cross' boot heel in his peripheral vision then saw nothing but dirty white concrete and the sickening throb behind his eyes. He curled into a ball, clutching his stomach, even though the effort made the pain much worse.

"Jesus. What in the hell?" Cross exclaimed.

"He's been doing this all night," the guard said, shrugging. "Just wants attention."

Cross moved closer and crouched beside Teddy. He placed his hand on Teddy's forehead and then pulled it back. "He's burning up. Turn him over."

The MP followed orders, rolling Teddy onto his back. The effort sent another spike of pain through his belly and chest. He clenched his teeth, breathing through his nose, trying to keep the nausea at bay. His gut twisted beneath his ribs as though something alive were crawling underneath them.

"What's on the floor?" the MP asked, jumping back. "Jesus, he puked."

And the rest of him—his shirt clinging to his back, the fabric dark where it had once been white. But now it was dry. Dehydration. And something worse.

Cross stepped back, a tight line forming between his eyebrows. "Get someone from the infirmary down here. Now."

"But sir—"

"I said now!"

A guard spun around and sprinted from the room, leaving Cross standing in the cell with his arms crossed.

Teddy lay still, curled up on his left side, taking shallow, controlled breaths. It was the only position that didn't make the pain unbearable. He focused on conserving energy, keeping his limbs tight to his body, guarding the fire in his belly that worsened with each passing minute.

He heard two sets of footsteps. They weren't the casual, stomping strides of the MPs, but were smoother and more deliberate.

One of the men crouched beside him, placing a gentle hand on his shoulder. "I'm Dr. Rutledge, Colonel Roosevelt. I need you to stay as still as you can."

Teddy didn't respond. He wasn't going anywhere.

The doctor grasped Teddy's wrist to check his pulse. A second man—probably a medic—was setting up equipment out of Teddy's view.

The doctor carefully rolled Teddy onto his back and lifted his shirt. Cool air brushed against his skin, followed by the pressure of hands and fingers on his belly, probing gently at first. The contact started in the center and gradually moved to the right. When Rutledge located the inflamed area low on his right side, just below his ribs, Teddy jerked. A sharp, nauseating pain exploded inward as if someone had driven a red-hot knife into his pelvis and twisted it. He let out a deep, guttural groan.

"Severe guarding. Rebound tenderness. Rigid abdominal wall," the doctor said. "Localized to the lower right quadrant."

Teddy didn't understand what any of those words meant. All he knew was that it hurt more than ever before. His muscles had tensed up, instinctively trying to hold the pain in, hoping he could lock it away somewhere deep inside if only he didn't move again.

"How long has he been like this?" the doctor asked.

"He collapsed this morning," Cross said. "Before that...according to the guard, he was complaining about his back."

A moment later, the doctor lifted Teddy's right leg, bent it at the knee, and then drew it back toward his chest. Not far. Just enough to stretch something inside him.

The pain exploded. White heat tore through his abdomen, lighting up every nerve. He clawed weakly at the floor, unable to stop the motion or speak.

"Positive psoas. Classic presentation. We're done," the doctor said. "He's febrile, dehydrated, vitals are unstable, and showing early signs of shock. Tell the hospital to prep for abdominal imaging. Appendicitis is almost certain. He should've been in surgery hours ago. We need to move now."

Appendicitis? He knew the word, but the implication didn't fully register. He couldn't piece it together. His mind was too foggy, his thoughts slipping like oil on glass.

The medic stepped forward. "Stretcher's coming. IV's ready."

"He's been doing this all night, sir. I thought he was faking. He didn't say anything," the guard said.

Rutledge didn't even turn around. "He didn't need to. This isn't an act. You let it get this far. If his appendix ruptures, he dies in this room. That's on you, and I'll make sure you're charged for negligent homicide under the UCMJ."

The words hung in the air.

"How bad is it?" Cross asked.

"Bad. Appendicitis, possibly ruptured or close to it. He should've been in the OR hours ago. If he isn't septic already, he's close."

Teddy turned his head and saw Cross standing in the cell. There was no smugness on his face now, no hint of victory. Just a frown, suggesting he wasn't sure of what he was seeing anymore.

"You nearly let me die in here," Teddy whispered.

Cross didn't respond. He looked down at him, not as a man confronting a prisoner—but like someone facing something he couldn't accept.

The medic inserted the IV line into the vein at the bend of his elbow. Teddy felt the sting, but it was nothing compared to the fiery pain in his gut.

The medics surrounded him. One grasped Teddy's ankles while the other slid an arm behind his shoulders. "On three," one of them said.

He felt every adjustment as they lifted him. The angle changed. Gravity dragged the pain sideways, striking him like a live electric current traveling down his spine. He gritted his teeth, managed to ride it out, and didn't make a sound.

They carefully lowered him onto the stretcher. The thin pad was more forgiving than the cold concrete floor.

Cross was still there.

Teddy looked up at him. "You didn't ask what was wrong. You assumed. That's on you."

Cross averted his gaze, refusing to look Teddy in the eyes.

The medics wheeled the stretcher to the door. As they pushed him into the corridor, Teddy watched the hallway stretch out ahead of him. Same walls, same lights—but this time, he wasn't being thrown anywhere. He was being taken seriously.

0830 Hours
January 16, 1984
Womack Army Medical Center
Fort Bragg, NC

The lights in the ER were brighter than he expected. As they wheeled him into one of the curtained bays, Teddy tried to remain still. Movement meant more pain.

The temperature here was cooler than in the stockade, thanks to an efficient climate control system rather than an old-fashioned radiator heater turned to the highest setting.

Two young medics stood on either side of the bed, barely sparing him a glance now that the urgency was evident. Across from them, a nurse was already putting on surgical gloves and checking the saline bag hanging on a stand. Then a fourth figure entered, older, and wearing a white lab coat draped over OD-green fatigues. A stethoscope hung around his neck. The doctor from the stockade.

"Colonel Roosevelt," Dr. Rutledge said as he stopped beside the bed, "what I need now is for you to stay completely still."

Teddy swallowed. "No problem there."

"Push the saline," Rutledge said without looking up. "Full bolus. He's dehydrated and borderline shocky."

"Is it my appendix?" Teddy asked.

Rutledge met his eyes. "Most likely. If we caught it early, you'll be lucky. But based on those vitals and that rigidity, I'm not betting on early."

A nurse handed Rutledge a clipboard with an attached form. The doctor glanced at it, then turned to Teddy. "You're coherent. That's enough for consent," he said, handing him the pen. "Sign here."

Teddy took the offered pen, scrawled his name across the line, and handed it back.

"Get him scanned," the doctor ordered. "If the appendix is gone, take him straight to surgery. If it's not, we're going anyway. This man's septic, and I don't like his odds if we wait."

Teddy kept his head still, eyes forward, concentrating on a spot on the wall. The pain wasn't worse now—it just had form and direction. He had a name for it.

And maybe—finally—a timeline.

0900 Hours
January 16, 1984
Womack Army Medical Center
Fort Bragg, NC

Captain Ray Hollis had performed dozens of appendectomies during his fifteen years in the Army—some straightforward, some complicated, and a few memorable close calls. But this one hadn't even started, and already he felt it sinking deeper into the recesses of his memory.

The preoperative ultrasound told a story too ugly to ignore, a severely distended appendix, well over six millimeters wide, the lumen dark with fluid, and the surrounding tissues blurred by edema, shadowed by what was likely necrotic slough. More concerning still was the free fluid pooling in the lower right quadrant. The kind you never wanted to see. And the patient?

Barely conscious upon arrival. Blood pressure measured 84/50, inching up only modestly after aggressive fluid boluses. A fever registered at 103.4, with a heart rate exceeding 120. Diaphoretic, with a rigid abdomen and obvious guarding, suggesting possible borderline sepsis, potentially worse. The clock had already been ticking for far too long.

Now Hollis stood at the table, gloved and draped, with the sterile field laid out before him in surgical green. The OR was quiet except for the soft murmur of vital signs being called out by the anesthesiologist at the head of the operating table. BP was stabilizing, the pulse a little less frantic, and oxygenation was good. The man beneath the drapes—Colonel Theodore Roosevelt, per the chart—lay fully under now, his breathing regulated by the ventilator, and his color gradually returned from a ghostly pallor to what passed for normal.

"Scalpel," Hollis said.

The circulating nurse slapped it into his palm, handle first. He made a clean midline incision, cutting straight through the lower abdomen along the right side of the linea alba. The first layers of skin yielded easily—thin and dehydrated from fever. Fatty subcutaneous tissue was minimal, followed by the fascia, which he opened with long, practiced strokes. The surgical assistant carefully retracted, exposing the muscle wall, and Hollis moved deeper.

"Let's go slow here," he said, his voice steady but firm. "This thing's been stewing for a while."

The moment he opened the peritoneum, the smell hit him—sharp, sour, and unmistakably infected. It filled the OR, acrid even through his surgical mask. Hollis didn't flinch. He'd smelled it before—perforated bowels, necrotic bowel segments, gangrenous tissue—but it never failed to register.

"Suction."

The tube hissed to life as the first assistant positioned it inside the abdominal cavity. Pooled fluid, cloudy with pus and fibrin, was suctioned away to clear the view.

The appendix appeared—swollen, inflamed, and bulging against the cecum like a balloon stretched to its limit. The serosal surface was mottled, bluish-gray at the base, with necrotic streaks along the distal tip. It hadn't ruptured...yet, but it would within minutes. The mesoappendix was enlarged with edema, veins engorged and nearly black.

"Jesus," the assistant muttered. "It's huge."

"Biggest I've seen in years," Hollis replied without taking his eyes off it. "If we don't move fast, we're looking at full-blown peritonitis."

They worked quickly now but not carelessly. Hollis guided the retractors deeper, exposing the mesoappendix. He isolated the vessels, double-clamped them, and cut with precision. Hemostasis was maintained. No bleeders were present. The inflamed appendix was freed, its base tied off with a silk ligature, and he removed it in one smooth motion, placing it into the specimen tray.

It landed with a squishy thump, spewing gangrenous pus and serous fluid. No one spoke.

However, Hollis wasn't finished.

As he started the routine inspection of the surrounding bowel, he paused.

There, along the anterior abdominal wall—across the right flank and crest of the iliac—were deep, blossoming bruises. Bilateral contusions. Purplish-blue, some with red centers, shaped like long vertical ovals.

Others tracked closer to the obliques. They weren't surgical. They weren't from CPR. They were fresh. Finger-width. Focused.

Too precise to be accidental. Too deliberate to be ignored.

"Get the camera," Hollis ordered.

The scrub tech moved quickly, retrieving the sterile intraoperative photo device. The flash went off twice, capturing the discoloration under direct light. Hollis adjusted a retractor, exposing more of the contused muscle along the anterior wall.

"Timestamp both," he said. "Make sure they're filed under the operative report."

He continued the lavage, irrigating the peritoneal cavity to ensure no contaminated fluid remained. Every motion was methodical. His silence no longer stemmed from focus—it arose from what he wasn't saying yet. He placed a small Jackson-Pratt drain, verified there was no further bleeding, and began the layered closure—muscle, fascia, subcuticular. The final suture was tied with a sharp snap of his wrist.

Only then did he step back and strip off his gloves in a long-practiced motion. Next came the clear plastic face shield, his breath fogging the inside one last time before it cleared.

Hollis turned to the nurse. "Get legal. JAG. I want them down here now."

The nurse hesitated, surprised by his request. "Do you want to call, or—?"

"I want them in person," Hollis said, walking toward the scrub sink. "They'll want to see this for themselves. And someone tell Colonel Cross—if he wants to know what happened, he'd better start talking."

Behind him, the OR transitioned into cleanup mode. The patient was stable—unconscious and breathing under anesthesia, with numbers suggesting he would make it through the night. But Hollis had seen what he needed to see, and it wasn't just an infection.

He had operated on an appendix, yes—but he had also uncovered something else concealed beneath those layers of subcutaneous fat and skin.

Someone had attempted to allow this man to die. Not from neglect. Not from infection.

From a severe beating.

And now it was on the record.

CHAPTER 3

1020 Hours
January 16, 1984
Womack Army Medical Center
Fort Bragg, NC

Lieutenant Colonel Rachel Merrit, JAG Corps, usually didn't receive calls to report to the base hospital's surgical wing. This was a first for her. When her desk phone rang at 1000 hours, she was halfway through her first cup of coffee, expecting that day's crisis to involve a lost evidence form or an overeager lieutenant trying to avoid Article 15 proceedings. Instead, the voice on the other end was clipped, urgent, and unconcerned with legal formalities.

"We have a prisoner in surgery with injuries that don't match his intake report. Operating room two, Womack Army Medical Center. Surgeon's name is Hollis," the female voice said.

No rank or name. No preamble. Just facts.

She stood in the hospital parking lot twelve minutes later.

The hallway outside OR two was cold from recycled air, the white tiles gleaming under fluorescent lights and smelling of alcohol and floor polish. A lone gurney squeaked past, pushed by an orderly who didn't glance up from his duties. Merrit stood near the far end of the corridor, dressed in pressed OD-green fatigues and polished black leather combat boots with a stiff leather folio tucked under one arm. She scanned the printed surgical notes handed to her by the nurse on duty.

She didn't have to read far.

"Appendectomy?" she asked as a figure emerged from the scrub room.

Captain Ray Hollis still wore his surgical cap, his hair damp at the edges, and clean yet slightly sweat-soaked light blue scrubs. He looked like a man who had just come from a case he didn't want to repeat any time soon.

He gave her a brief nod. "Yes. A textbook case of advanced appendicitis. Inflamed, partially necrotic, and borderline rupture. He was septic going in, but we got ahead of it. That's not the part you're going to care about."

Merrit's eyes lingered on his face for a moment longer. "Then what is?"

Hollis accepted a small stack of glossy Polaroid prints from the nurse—still warm to the touch, with a faint chemical scent lingering in the air—and handed them to Merrit without any explanation. She repositioned the folder under her arm and took the photos, angling them to reduce the glare from the overhead lights.

What stared back at her were clean, clinical photographs—timestamped, high resolution, and cropped to focus—not of the incision or appendix, but of the bruising.

Oval-shaped and some elongated, concentrated along the lower right flank and hip. Others clustered near the obliques and lateral abdomen. None appeared on the face or forearms. Nothing you would notice if you merely glanced at a man in restraints.

These injuries were intentional and aimed.

Merrit's jaw tightened. "What's your medical opinion?"

"Blunt force trauma," Hollis said without hesitation. "Likely fists. Possibly knees. Or both. Not accidental or consistent with a fall. And considering this man was in so much pain from the appendicitis that he couldn't move, he didn't have a chance to defend himself, so no defensive injuries. By that same token, he sure couldn't attack anyone. Whoever did it knew exactly what they were doing—they avoided all visible, unclothed surfaces. And they did it recently. These bruises aren't more than twelve hours old, probably less."

Merrit looked up from the pictures. "So it happened while he was in custody."

"Without question. He came straight from the field to the stockade, never leaving the compound. There was no opportunity for contact with civilians or other detainees, and the chain of custody is tight."

She returned the photographs to the doctor. The internal wheels were already turning. "Did he request medical attention?"

"Yes. That's what I was told. At least once. Denied by the on-duty guard who thought he was faking." Hollis folded his arms across his chest. "By the time they brought him in, he couldn't stand. He collapsed in his cell this morning. If they'd waited another hour—maybe two—to contact the infirmary, he wouldn't have made it to the operating table."

Merrit exhaled through her nose to rein in her temper. She didn't swear, pace, or raise her voice. She closed the folder in her hand and looked him square in the eyes. "Documentation?"

"Complete. Photographs filed with the surgical report. I've signed and timestamped the operative notes. Tissue samples have been sent for pathology, and the appendix has been preserved. I also gave a verbal report to base legal before I called you."

Merrit nodded. Nothing dramatic. Just confirmation of the doctor's statement. Then she turned, reaching for the nearby wall phone. "Time to find Colonel Cross. He's going to have some explaining to do."

1030 Hours
January 16, 1984
519th Military Intelligence Battalion HQ
Fort Bragg, NC

Colonel Vince Cross had hardly made it halfway through his morning coffee when the knock came—two sharp raps, measured and intentional, not from any of his MPs.

"Enter," he said, not looking up from the file in his hand.

The door swung open, and Sergeant Maynard stepped inside—a junior clerk fresh from training at the base legal department. The kid looked unwell—too pale for someone who hadn't just worked an overnight shift, his eyes darting nervously, already second-guessing his presence in the room.

"Sir," Maynard said, standing at attention, "Lieutenant Colonel Merrit from JAG called. She asked to see you immediately at the base hospital."

Cross set the mug down, keeping one hand on the handle. "Did she say why?"

"No, sir. Just that it concerns Colonel Roosevelt. She didn't sound like it was optional."

Cross's jaw tightened. He wasn't used to taking orders from lower-ranking JAG officers. "Tell her I'm on my way. And while I'm gone, pull Colonel Roosevelt's entire intake report—the original processing sheet, the overnight logs, and the morning watch notes. I want everything from the last twenty-four hours on my desk when I return."

"Yes, sir."

He left without rushing, but his pace on the sidewalk was brisk. Womack Army Medical Center wasn't far, yet tension followed him the entire way. He hated being summoned and surprises alike. Whenever a JAG officer called before lunch regarding a prisoner already in surgery, it was never good news.

Especially not when that prisoner was Colonel Theodore "Bull Moose" Roosevelt IV.

Cross spotted Merrit outside the surgical ward—arms folded and posture rigid. A slim tan folder was tucked against her ribs, held under one elbow. Her boots were polished, and her uniform was immaculate with the silver oak leaf shining on her right collar and a gold JAG insignia—a pen and sword crossed over a laurel wreath—on the other. She was already watching him as he approached.

"Lieutenant Colonel Merrit," he said in a command tone. "I was told you needed to see me."

"Thank you for coming, sir," she replied without smiling. Her tone was respectful but clipped. "This concerns Colonel Roosevelt."

"So I heard." He nodded toward the folder. "Is that for me?"

She extended her hand. "Photographic documentation, surgical notes, and preliminary findings from the operating surgeon, Captain Hollis."

Cross opened the folder, flipping through the first set of glossy photographs. They were taken inside the OR—close-up shots under sterile light, timestamped in the corner. He first noticed the bruises. Deep ones. Clean oval marks across the lower abdomen and flank, some extending toward the hip. These were not the result of a scuffle or stumble. They indicated controlled force and focused placement.

He flipped further. Surgical notes confirmed advanced appendicitis with necrotic margins. The appendix was nearly ruptured. Vital signs on admission were critical—low blood pressure and a fever exceeding 103 degrees.

Cross held up the folder. "Where did these come from?"

"Captain Hollis took them intraoperatively. As you know, Colonel Roosevelt collapsed in his cell this morning and was brought in nearly unconscious. Hollis says the appendix was necrotic—on the edge of rupture. The bruising was discovered during the procedure."

Cross glanced back down at the images then shut the folder. "And?"

Merrit frowned. "None of that bruising was documented on the intake report. No medical request was filed. No altercations were reported. No one logged a refusal of care. Colonel Roosevelt asked for help and was ignored until he was no longer able to stand."

"You're saying someone assaulted him."

"I'm saying someone had hands on him between his arrest and this morning, and it wasn't in the report. The injuries are recent. Hours old. Blunt force, not impact trauma. No defensive bruising on his hands and arms. There was no bruising near his face or wrists. Whoever did it knew exactly how to avoid visible areas."

He stared at her for a long moment. "That's a serious allegation."

"It's not an allegation, sir. It's backed up by medical evidence. Hollis has signed the report. The file's already been copied to the Inspector General's office."

Cross stepped back and ran his hand across his mouth. "What are you doing with it?"

"I'm opening a formal inquiry," she said. "As of now, Colonel Roosevelt is under protective custody. No unauthorized personnel are to access his room. I'll be interviewing every person involved in his custody, beginning with the guards on duty at intake."

"And me."

"And you," Merrit said. "You were the ranking officer during that window. I don't believe you laid a hand on him, sir. But this happened under your command."

The words landed like a file drawer slamming shut. She didn't soften them. "If someone did something you didn't authorize, now is the time to say it. Because the moment this gets outside our immediate chain of command, we lose the ability to contain it. Any rumor of Army brutality after Vietnam becomes a feeding frenzy with comparisons to My Lai and the Fort Hood incident in the press. You will be the first casualty on the road to deniability by any and all superior officers."

Cross looked away for the first time, his jaw clenched. He didn't respond right away. Then he handed the folder back, crisp and controlled. "Where is he now?"

"Recovery room. Still under anesthesia. You'll be notified when the doctor clears him for visitors."

"I'll be back in an hour." He turned without another word, his boots echoing on the tile as he walked away, his back straight. Whatever this was, it had just escalated from uncomfortable to dangerous.

And for once, Colonel "Iron Vince" Cross wasn't holding the high ground.

CHAPTER 4

1130 Hours
January 16, 1984
Fort Bragg, NC

The walk back to the stockade felt longer than it ever had before today. Cross didn't speak to anyone on the way. He didn't bark orders or demand updates. He just walked, his jaw clenched and his arms swinging in time with his footsteps. The stockade had always been his domain—orderly, regulated, and efficient. A place where things were kept under control, but today, that familiar structure felt brittle, like something built too quickly, ready to collapse under the weight of a single truth.

It wasn't the bruises that haunted him. It was how easy it had been for someone to brutally assault Roosevelt inside the stockade.

Roosevelt hadn't run or fought against his capture. He hadn't even resembled the man Cross had pursued across three continents. And Cross, blinded by victory, had convinced himself it didn't matter. He told himself that maybe the great Teddy "Bull Moose" Roosevelt had finally decided to stop running after burning the candle at both ends for over a decade. But it hadn't been that.

Something was rotting inside him. His appendix was about to burst.

Now, JAG was involved. That could be a career killer.

Cross pushed through the steel door of the stockade and found Sergeant Greeley at the duty desk, still flipping through the logbook pages of the previous night's activities, treating it as though it really mattered.

"Sergeant," Cross said. "I want to see the cell block security footage. Yesterday through this morning. All of it."

Greeley blinked, his pen pausing mid-line in the logbook. "Sir?" he asked, uncertain whether he'd misheard.

"You heard me," Cross repeated. "Get me into the monitoring room. Now."

"Yes, sir."

Without saying another word, Greeley stood and led him to the back, past a scuffed steel door, into a room no larger than a storage closet. The walls were lined with metal shelves and half-stacked VHS tapes, each one labeled with a white grease pencil. A row of small black-and-white monitors hummed above the table where the playback deck sat, also humming.

The system wasn't perfect. Half the time, it recorded over itself. However, if luck was on his side for once, the relevant footage might still be available.

The sergeant reached for the logbook, thumbing back to the page from the previous day. "This should be it, sir. Camera Two had coverage of the hall and Colonel Roosevelt's cell."

Greeley inserted the first tape into the playback machine and queued it up. The recording began yesterday afternoon at 1517 hours. Roosevelt, in restraints, was escorted through the hallway into the cell under armed guard. The video had no sound, only grainy black-and-white frames. Still, it was clear enough to see the events as they unfolded.

Roosevelt looked...off. Pale. He was already unsteady on his feet, limping on his left leg, the one broken in Vietnam and implanted with an intramedullary nail. His posture was hunched, lacking the shoulders-drawn-back defiance that Cross had seen many times.

Cross watched his own boots in the corner of the frame and saw himself standing there smirking as Roosevelt moved stiffly, almost robotically, like a man walking with something broken inside him.

He hadn't realized how confident he'd looked. That smugness now sat bitterly in his stomach.

Greeley fast-forwarded the tape to the late evening.

Colonel Roosevelt lay on the cot, unmoving, curled in the fetal position, his knees drawn toward his chest. The camera captured him slowly shifting his weight, stopping every few inches, all the while hugging his stomach. At one point, he sat up and leaned toward the bars, mouth moving, clearly calling for the guard.

The guard didn't even look up, continuing to read his newspaper.

"Jesus," Cross muttered.

Then Greeley fast-forwarded to shortly after midnight.

Two figures entered the darkened cell. No uniforms were visible, but their erect posture gave them away—MPs. The way they moved, their familiarity with the layout of the cell, and the casual sense of ownership they projected over the small space made it obvious.

Cross leaned closer, placing his hand on the counter for balance. "Freeze that. Rewind. Play it again."

The MPs approached the cot. One of them reached down and grabbed the prisoner's arm. Roosevelt didn't resist or even seem fully awake. He didn't move at all.

Then the beating started.

One man drove his knee into Roosevelt's ribs then pounded the same spot with his fists. Next, a boot connected with his ribs. The blows kept coming—deliberate and practiced, targeting the abdomen, flanks, and kidneys. All strikes were aimed away from Roosevelt's head and face. The beating was systematic and calculated. They knew exactly what they were doing.

Greeley sat next to him, unsure of what to do.

Afterward, one of them lifted Roosevelt as though he weighed nothing, tossed him back onto the cot, and exited the cell with his partner, moving with the casualness of having just conducted a simple bed check.

The tape played for a few more seconds before Cross raised his hand. "Stop it."

Greeley hit pause.

For a long moment, the only sound in the room was the soft mechanical hum of the tape deck.

Cross stepped back, folding his arms over his chest. His mind wasn't racing—it was focused and singular. Cold. He'd witnessed men beaten in the field and seen discipline fail under pressure. But not here. Not under his command. And not like this.

"I want the names of everyone who entered that cell after 2000 hours yesterday," he said in a tone so cold it would freeze anything on contact. "I want the guard on duty in my office in ten minutes. Get that footage copied. Take it to JAG and confirm the chain of custody. I don't want anyone touching that tape except Merrit's people." He paused. "And, Sergeant—pull last month's footage while you're at it. All of it."

Greeley blinked. "Sir?"

"If they did it to Colonel Roosevelt, they've done it before."

Greeley scrambled to obey, but Cross was already out the door.

At this point, he no longer cared about what Merrit said or the repercussions. Something had happened here—on his watch. If someone under his command had taken justice into their own hands, then it wouldn't just be Roosevelt answering to the law.

It would be him.

1230 Hours
January 16, 1984
Womack Army Medical Center
Fort Bragg, NC

The first thing Teddy noticed was weight—not pressure on his chest, but a slow, dense heaviness that settled deep inside his gut, something stitched into him that pulled outward with each shallow breath. He inhaled carefully, and a tight, unfamiliar tug responded just below his navel. Pain flared immediately—dull but insistent—sending a warning twinge up through his ribs and forcing his last breath out in a quiet groan.

His eyes felt sealed shut, crusted, and heavy. But he forced them open anyway, feeling his eyelids resist the pull until they finally broke free from the seal.

The ceiling above him was white, not the cracked paint of a prison cell or the institutional yellow of the stockade. This room was polished and sterile, humming with bright white fluorescent lights. He blinked hard. The edges of his vision wavered for a moment before steadying.

Next to the bed stood an IV pole. Hanging from it was a clear bag dripping slowly into the tubing that snaked down to his forearm. A second bag dangled below it—a thicker label with red ink—Morphine Sulfate. That tracked. He could feel it. Not the numbness exactly—but a softness, like someone had stuffed cotton between him and the pain, telling it to wait its turn.

Teddy redirected his gaze. Green tubing ran from beneath his nose, the oxygen lightly pricking the back of his throat. Wires extended from his chest to a heart monitor just out of sight. The soft rhythm of beeping ticked in the background—steady and distant, like a metronome.

He licked his dry lips and swallowed, feeling the ache ripple down his throat, tugging at something deep inside. Stitches. Sutures. Maybe a drain. The pain was unmistakably surgical—controlled, localized, and clean, yet brutal in a way his body hadn't forgotten. They'd opened him up and cut out what was causing the pain. Appendix? It wasn't a theory anymore. It was fact.

The blanket felt heavy. He moved his hands, feeling neither cold metal handcuffs around his wrists nor restraints of any kind. Just the heavy stiffness of a man who'd been through too much and hadn't fully come back yet. The bed was a genuine hospital model, not an uncomfortable canvas cot, with clean sheets and metal rails. The kind of place they didn't send you unless they intended to keep you alive.

His memory drifted back in fragments.

The cell. The fever. The guard brushing him off. The fists. Cross' raised voice. A sudden wave of pain. Then motion. A bright light. An oxygen mask pressed over his nose and mouth. A voice shouting, "Let's move," as the ceiling streaked by overhead in a blur. Then nothing.

He blinked again.

Footsteps approached the bed—soft, not the heavy thud of combat boots, but the quiet tread of rubber-soled shoes. A nurse came into view, in her early thirties, with dark hair pulled back under her cap and a clipboard in her hand. She glanced up and locked eyes with him.

"Well," she said, her voice light, "look who's awake."

Teddy cleared his throat, but the words scraped against the soreness. "Unclear...if that's a good thing."

She smiled, both professional and practiced. "You're in the base hospital, Colonel Roosevelt. You came in early this morning for emergency surgery. Acute appendicitis. You were septic. But we got you into the OR in time. Dr. Hollis performed the procedure. You've been out for about two hours."

He turned his head—just enough to feel the tightness spreading across his belly. "Drain?"

She nodded. "Yes. Right lower quadrant. And internal sutures. You'll want to stay flat for now. If you try to sit up too fast, you'll regret it."

"No heroics," he murmured.

"That's right." She reached for a cup of water on the bedside table and tilted the straw toward his mouth. "Just sip it. Small amounts for now."

He took it slowly, the straw brushing his dry lips. The cool water touched his tongue like rain falling on cracked, parched earth. The first swallow tugged at his gut again as the water lodged in his throat, but he rode out the discomfort until it settled in his stomach.

"Where...am I?" he asked.

"ICU recovery ward," she said. "Critical observation, technically. You're stable now. Your fever broke about thirty minutes ago."

"And the meds?"

"Morphine. Five milligrams IV push post-op. You're on a regular drip for now—adjusted every hour. If you need more, we'll increase the frequency, but try not to chase pain with movement."

Teddy nodded. The edges of his world felt overly soft. He sensed the fog creeping in again—chemical, warm, and unwelcome. The morphine didn't eliminate the pain. It merely made it tolerable, which meant getting comfortable would be easy. Too easy.

He glanced at the door. "Colonel Cross?"

She hesitated. "I don't know. He hasn't come by since you came out of surgery. But—someone from the JAG office was here earlier. She was asking questions. Lieutenant Colonel Merrit. She seemed really sharp and on the ball."

Something had changed.

The nurse adjusted his blanket, checked the IV drip rate, and noted something on her clipboard. "You're stable," she said again. "Your vitals are strong. Just keep resting. The doctor will check in on you soon."

She turned and left with practiced efficiency.

Teddy once again stared at the ceiling, the warm hum of the morphine deepening as it coursed through the line into the vein in his forearm.

So they'd believed him—eventually. But not before it nearly killed him. And someone—maybe Merrit, maybe Cross—finally decided that letting Colonel Theodore "Bull Moose" Roosevelt die in a cell wasn't worth the fallout.

He was out of the stockade.

But the war hadn't ended. It had only gone quiet.

For now.

1550 Hours
January 16, 1984
Womack Army Medical Center
Fort Bragg, NC

The second time Teddy woke up, the light had changed. It wasn't brighter—just less direct, softer, and now filtered through a narrow slit of blinds that broke the fluorescent glare into bands across the ceiling. The heat that had gripped him earlier had eased. The worst of the fever had broken, leaving behind a low, sticky warmth that clung to his chest and collarbones beneath the white hospital sheet.

His abdomen throbbed with a deep, pulsing rhythm—not the sharp fire from earlier, but a steadier kind of pain. A dull punch delivered from within, each throb reminding him exactly where the scalpel had entered. He recognized that sensation. Sutures. Internal swelling. Muscle cut and reapproximated. The body remembered that kind of trauma long after the morphine faded.

But he wasn't alone.

The sound of footsteps approached—slow and deliberate. The soles were too smooth to belong to combat boots and too precise to be those of a nurse on rounds. Nurses moved with speed and compassion, but this gait was different. It was controlled and professional. He opened one eye.

The woman was already there, standing at the foot of the bed. Her class A dress uniform was pressed and immaculate, the gold JAG insignia on the collar catching a faint glint from the overhead lighting. Lieutenant Colonel Merrit, without a doubt. She stood with her hands clasped behind her back, her gaze calm and assessing. She didn't introduce herself or announce her presence, waiting for their eyes to meet.

"You're awake," she said. Her voice carried the steady cadence of an officer who never needed to raise it. "Good. I wasn't sure how long the anesthesia and morphine would keep you down."

Teddy blinked and reached for the plastic cup on the bedside table. Someone had moved it closer. The straw brushed between his lips, and he sucked a small mouthful of lukewarm water down his throat. Even that simple effort tugged at the incision along his lower right side, sending a flash of pain through the narcotic haze. He grunted and set the cup down with a trembling hand.

"Let me guess," he rasped, his voice as dry as sandpaper, "they decided to court-martial me while I was unconscious. Convenient timing."

A flicker of something crossed her face. Not quite amusement, but something similar. Irony, maybe? "No, Colonel Roosevelt. I'm not here to prosecute you. I'm here to find out who nearly let you die."

That brought him back to full awareness. He observed her more intently now, noticing how she remained perfectly still—not out of caution but by design. Her eyes never left his.

She stepped closer, pulling out a small leather-bound notebook from the inner pocket of her jacket. No microcassette tape recorder or legal pad—just a well-worn field notebook and a ballpoint pen. Very old school. "My name is Lieutenant Colonel Rachel Merrit. JAG Corps. I've been assigned to conduct a formal inquiry into the events leading to your hospitalization."

Teddy eased his head back onto the pillow, exhaled slowly, and let the pain settle. "An inquiry? That's the Army's polite way of admitting they screwed up."

"You requested medical care after being taken into custody?"

He nodded. "Told the guard my back hurt and requested a medic. Told him something was wrong. He told me I was bluffing and ignored my complaint."

"And after that?"

He closed his eyes for a moment. The timeline appeared in fragments. Pain didn't keep clear records. "It got worse. Couldn't straighten up. Started curling in on myself—classic guarding. Fever kicked up. Nausea. I tried again. Same response. Later that night, two of your MPs came in. They weren't there to check my vital signs but to tune me up a little."

Her pen paused on the paper, but her expression remained unchanged. "You're certain it was a physical assault?"

"They avoided my face," he said, bitterness filling his voice. "Went for the sides. Gut. Ribs. Kidneys. They knew what they were doing."

"I've seen the surgical photographs," she replied, her tone completely neutral. "The bruises on the abdominal wall. The condition of your appendix."

"Bet it made one hell of a first impression."

She turned to the next page in her notebook. "Captain Hollis described it as necrotic, distended, and on the verge of rupture. He estimated you were within hours of a full perforation."

He didn't respond to that. The intense pain was proof enough.

Merrit let the silence stretch for a moment before continuing. "The security camera in your corridor was operational. Colonel Cross reviewed the tape himself."

That grabbed his attention. He opened his eyes and fixed her with a more intense look. "'Iron Vince' Cross...did that for...me?"

She nodded. "Yes. He ordered the review this morning. The footage confirms two MPs entered your cell just after lights out. No med check was performed until he arrived the next morning."

"And the tape?"

"Sealed and logged into the property room under a restricted JAG chain of custody. The MPs are being brought in for individual questioning."

Teddy exhaled slowly, feeling tightness in his chest. "So the Army's finally paying attention."

"They're paying attention because you survived," she said. "You're the first man who came out of this with an OR full of witnesses and a folder full of medical documentation."

He studied her for a long moment, unsure whether that made him lucky or just harder to kill. "Not exactly the kind of legacy I was aiming for."

"No," she said. "But it might be the kind that keeps you alive."

The room settled into silence after that—quiet enough for the IV drip to become audible again. For the first time since the cell, Teddy felt something shift beneath the surface. It wasn't safety. It wasn't vindication.

But it was movement. The silence was no longer indifference. It was calculation.

Merrit stepped back, slid the notebook into her jacket pocket, and nodded at the monitors. "I'll be back tomorrow. Don't try to get up. We're not finished."

She turned away without waiting for acknowledgment and slipped through the door. The air behind her felt cooler somehow, and the silence was less suffocating.

He moved his left leg an inch to relieve a cramp, wincing as the drain tube tugged near his hip, and let his head sink deeper into the pillow. The ache remained, steady and raw, stitched into his core—but now something else lurked beneath it.

Someone believed him.

And for the first time in this whole damn decade-long mess, someone was taking notes.

CHAPTER 5

1730 Hours
January 16, 1984
519th Military Intelligence Battalion HQ
Fort Bragg, NC

The office door clicked shut with a decisive finality, one that resonated louder in the silence. Colonel Vince Cross didn't look up. He allowed the moment to stretch, thumbing through the pages in the open folder on his desk while the two MPs stood in front of him—Staff Sergeant Hollins on the left and Corporal Reese on the right.

Neither man stood at attention, nor did either feel at ease. They had noticed the change in tone across the base that morning—the sudden silence in the command hallway and the lack of backslaps over Colonel Roosevelt's arrest. Whatever they had hoped would go unnoticed clearly hadn't.

Cross didn't offer them chairs. He didn't look up until he was ready.

Laid out on the desk were the still images captured by the corridor security camera—black-and-white with timestamps. They provided a frame-by-frame account of who had entered the cell and when. Next to them were the color surgical photographs, more vivid in detail. Angry bruising marred the pale abdominal tissue. Internal notes from Captain Hollis were both clear and damning. Merrit's formal intake report and list of charges were clipped into the standard-issue JAG folder.

Cross raised his head. "You were on late watch last night," he said, his tone calm and precise. "Cell C-3. Prisoner Colonel Theodore Roosevelt IV."

"Yes, sir," Hollins replied.

Cross maintained a calm tone. He wasn't here to shout despite the urge to do so. "Did you enter the cell?"

"Yes, sir," Hollins reiterated.

Reese moved next to him, a half-step of tension that didn't go unnoticed.

"Why?"

"Welfare check, sir."

"You unlocked the door."

"Yes, sir."

"You administered a welfare check," Cross said, still not raising his voice, "by kneeing a prisoner in the ribs while he was curled up in a ball and visibly ill, then striking him multiple times with your fists."

The ensuing silence was absolute. Neither of them moved.

"I've seen the footage," Cross said. "Every second of it. You thought the camera in the hallway was broken?"

Reese turned pale and fidgeted with the button on his sleeve cuff.

Hollins cleared his throat. "No, sir—we didn't think it was broken. We didn't think it was recording."

Cross narrowed his eyes. "So you knew it existed. You knew you might be recorded. And you went in anyway."

Hollins swallowed hard. "Sir, we...we thought he was faking. We just meant to scare him. To let him know he couldn't bluff his way out of custody."

Cross stood, his movements smooth yet charged with energy. Six feet of command presence rising behind the desk, the storm no longer quiet. "He wasn't faking anything. His appendix was necrotic. His core temperature was over 103. He had free fluid in his abdominal cavity and visible signs of sepsis. If he hadn't gone into surgery when he did, he would have been dead before lunchtime."

Hollins opened his mouth to respond, but Cross didn't allow him to speak.

"Don't," he said, stepping around the desk and stopping just a single stride away from both men. "Don't make excuses. Don't insult your intelligence or mine. You're wearing a U.S. Army uniform. That means you're held to a higher standard."

The room had fallen silent except for the distant ticking of the wall clock and the faint hum of the building's ventilation system.

"You beat a prisoner who was visibly ill. You ignored a request for medical care. And you compounded that by using deliberate force against a nearly unconscious officer in a holding cell. This isn't a reprimand. This isn't 'extra duty for a month.' This is an assault on a superior officer under the color of authority."

"Sir...we didn't mean to—" Reese stammered.

"I said shut up!"

Both men stiffened, their backs ramrod straight, no longer defensive—just stunned. They looked cornered and hollow-eyed.

"This is going to JAG," Cross said. "And when they're done with you, the Inspector General is going to dig through every second of your time in uniform. You'd better start practicing your oath because you'll be reciting it a lot in the next six months."

He stepped back to the desk and pressed the intercom button. "Sergeant Greeley. Holding detail, two personnel. Confine to quarters pending formal charges. No communication, no contact with anyone until cleared by JAG."

"Understood, sir."

The door swung open, and Greeley entered with two MPs, professional and quiet. The two men didn't argue. Hollins looked like he'd bitten down on glass. Reese kept his eyes focused on the ground, his face pale.

Cross waited behind his desk as they were led out. Only when the door clicked shut did he move—sinking into his seat and dragging one hand across his mouth and chin, a fruitless move, as he couldn't wipe away the last fifteen minutes.

There was no satisfaction or vindication in it—only fury. Cold and rooted deep in his chest—not just at them, but at himself. For allowing this to happen right under his nose. For being so eager to claim a victory that he hadn't looked close enough at what was happening within his own command.

His eyes drifted back to the top photo in the folder. Roosevelt lay on the cot, curled inward. His face was pale, and his arms were tightly wrapped around his middle, holding something inside, afraid it might tear loose if he let go.

This was no longer just an incident. It had become a reckoning.

And Cross knew, as sure as ever, that Colonel Theodore "Bull Moose" Roosevelt wasn't going to disappear quietly.

Not this time.

CHAPTER 6

0830 Hours
January 17, 1984
Womack Army Medical Center
Fort Bragg, NC

The slow beep of the heart monitor became a rhythm he no longer noticed. It pulsed in the background like the ticking of a metronome—steady, persistent, and no longer threatening.

Teddy was still tired—deeply so. However, it was the kind of exhaustion that no longer clouded his mind. The morphine had worn off. He could feel it—the sharpness beginning to creep back in around the edges of his thoughts. Not fully, not yet, but enough to make him aware of the returning pain. The ache in his abdomen had changed again, from distant thunder to a low, steady burn. He could live with it.

He was alive, after all.

The nurse had come in earlier, changed his IV bag, and offered him the lukewarm beef broth he hadn't touched. She smiled, informed him that Lieutenant Colonel Merrit would return later, and reassured him that he was stable and improving.

Stable. That word again.

As if survival were the end of something. Teddy knew better. Survival was simply the doorway to the next game. He stared at the ceiling tiles, listening and contemplating the fates that had led him to this moment.

Outside the room, footsteps came and went. Most hurried past his door without slowing down. A few paused before moving on. Then came a knock—not one of the nurses' gentle courtesy taps. This was sharper. One decisive knock, and then the door swung open.

Teddy turned his head just enough to see a man enter and close the door behind him.

Captain Miles Braxton, the stockade administrator and Cross' adjutant, wore a clean, pressed uniform with two silver bars gleaming on his collar and a clipboard tucked under one arm. He was neither a medic nor a lawyer, and definitely not a friend.

"Mornin', Colonel Roosevelt," Braxton said, his eyes scanning the room before landing on him. "Didn't expect to find you awake."

"Lucky you," Teddy said. "Come to check if I'm still breathing?"

Braxton didn't smile. He approached the foot of the bed, gripping the clipboard with both hands. "I'm not here on orders, sir. Colonel Cross doesn't know I'm talking to you."

That statement grabbed Teddy's attention.

Braxton glanced at the closed door and leaned in—just enough to lower his voice to something intended only for the man in the bed. "I reviewed the videotapes. What those MPs did to you...it was deliberate and cruel. But that's not what I came to say."

Teddy waited, keeping his eyes fixed on the captain.

Braxton didn't flinch under the scrutiny. "There's something off in the paperwork. Your file. The chain of custody. Orders for your detainment were signed, but they were missing the field citation and transfer report."

"Sloppy," Teddy said.

"Too sloppy. Even for us." Braxton hesitated. For the first time, his rock-solid composure wavered. "I've only seen one other file like that in ten years. A black-bag case—foreign national, no formal charges, paperwork massaged to hide what wasn't supposed to be there."

Teddy didn't respond at first. He simply stared at him, observing the subtle cues—the tension in Braxton's shoulders and the deliberate cadence of his words. He wasn't bluffing.

"You're saying someone wanted me in that cell," Teddy said. "But didn't want a paper trail proving why."

Braxton nodded. "And whoever signed off knew it wouldn't hold up under scrutiny. Merrit's people are already hip deep in the files. If they keep going...they'll find it."

Teddy exhaled slowly, closing his eyes for a moment. Not from pain this time, but from the weight of something heavier—confirmation. This wasn't about an arrest. It was about disappearance. Silencing. And someone had hoped nature—or negligence—would take care of the dirty work before anyone asked questions.

He opened his eyes again. "Why are you telling me this?"

Braxton straightened. "Because I'm not sure who's going down when this thing unravels. But I've got no interest in being one of them." He turned to leave, pausing at the door. "You've got more people watching than you think, Colonel Roosevelt. Just...hang on."

Then he was gone.

The door clicked shut behind him, leaving Teddy surrounded by the quiet hum of machines and dim lighting. He lay motionless for a while, letting the weight of Braxton's words sink in deeply.

Teddy was no longer just a prisoner.

He was leverage.

And someone out there had a lot to lose.

```
1130 Hours
January 17, 1984
Womack Army Medical Center
Fort Bragg, NC
```

The room fell silent once more, broken only by the soft drone of machines, the slow rhythm of the IV drip, and the constant throb of pain beneath Teddy's ribs. It had been a long day—longer than he could measure. Amid the haze of medication and the steady, exhausting grind of recovery, time had merged into lengthy silences and fleeting moments of clarity.

So when the door opened—without a knock or warning—he knew who it was before the boots had even crossed the threshold.

Colonel "Iron Vince" Cross.

The man stepped inside like he owned the ground beneath him, his shoulders squared and his OD-green field uniform stiffly starched and immaculate. Yet there was something in his eyes—an edge dulled, a layer peeled back—that told Teddy this wasn't the same man who had strutted into his cell yesterday morning. This was a version of Colonel Vincent Cross who had watched a piece of his command unravel in real time and now stood in the middle of the fallout.

Teddy didn't speak or offer a greeting. He simply watched him, his head resting on the pillow.

Cross stopped at the foot of the bed, standing with his hands clasped behind his back. His jaw was tight. Not from anger—Teddy had seen Cross angry and had been the cause of it more than once—but from something else. Hesitation or restraint, maybe both.

"You're lucky you made it through the night," Cross said.

Teddy exhaled slowly, the motion tugging at the tight line of sutures beneath his ribs. "Wasn't luck but your camera system."

Cross didn't flinch at the sharp barb thrown his way, but he didn't look away either. "I reviewed everything. The footage. The medical file. The timeline. I should've caught it."

"That's the part I keep thinking about. You had me in that cell. No fight. No escape attempt. No smart remarks after the first five minutes. You had to know something wasn't right."

Cross's mouth formed a hard line. He didn't argue or defend himself. For once, there was no lecture or posture of authority to fall back on. "I didn't want to see it. Not then. I was too busy enjoying the win."

Teddy nodded. "And now?"

"Now?" Cross exhaled, folding his arms across his chest. "Two of my men are facing formal charges of assault and battery on a superior officer. Merrit's office is crawling through the detention logs. And your rotten-looking appendix the size of a damned baseball is sitting in a lab jar."

The room was still for a moment.

"You know this wasn't just your men. Someone gave the order. Someone didn't want me walking out of that cell," Teddy said.

Cross didn't answer right away. He stepped aside, now positioned to look down at him more directly. "I think you're right. And I think that's going to make a lot of people nervous."

"And you?"

"I'm not nervous. I'm pissed." Cross' tone darkened, edged with something sharper now—anger not directed at Teddy, but at the men who acted under his command without his knowledge, and those above them who might have wanted this buried.

"I thought you were the problem," Cross said. "For years, I told myself everything would make sense once I got you in custody. But that was too easy. You didn't run this time. You didn't even try."

"No point," Teddy said. "I couldn't stand, let alone climb a fence."

Cross flexed his jaw. "No. That's not what I mean. You gave up before you ever entered the cell. That should've told me everything." He looked away briefly, collecting his thoughts before they could turn into something else. Guilt. Regret. It wasn't an emotion Cross wore comfortably. "You should've had a medic the minute you said something was wrong."

"I did say something," Teddy reminded him. "Didn't matter."

"It does now," Cross said.

A long silence hung between them. No more accusations or posturing—just two men, one nursing fresh stitches in his side and the other grappling with the reality of what he had allowed to happen.

Finally, Cross took a half-step back. "You're not out of the woods yet. The charges against you haven't been dropped."

"I figured as much."

"The investigation is evolving. If it goes in the direction I suspect it will…things may appear different when you get out of that bed."

Teddy nodded. "I've heard that before."

Cross held his gaze a moment longer before turning to leave. Just before the door closed behind him, he glanced over his shoulder. "This time...it might actually be true."

1740 Hours
January 17, 1984
Womack Army Medical Center
Fort Bragg, NC

The afternoon drifted by in shadows. Teddy dozed, but never for long. The pain had settled into a manageable ache, yet his body remained stiff, heavy, and reluctant to move more than necessary. Every few hours, the nurses came in—checking vital signs, changing the IV bag, and noting his fluid intake. He answered their questions without sarcasm or evasion. There was no energy for games, nor any need for them.

He was no longer a prisoner in the cell. Not exactly.

But he wasn't free, either.

The door swung open once more just before sunset, and he didn't need to raise his head to know who it was. The rhythm of her footsteps was distinct, measured, purposeful, and unhurried. Merrit always walked with the confidence of someone who already knew where the evidence would lead.

She stood just inside the door for a moment, watching him. Then she stepped forward and placed a thick manila folder on the bedside table next to the untouched water cup. "You're looking better."

He turned his head enough to look at her. "Morphine and IV fluids do wonders for the complexion."

She didn't smile, but she didn't correct him either. "That's your transfer file. Or at least what's supposed to be your transfer file. The original version, pulled from the base archive, had two missing attachments and a forged timestamp. The authorization code on the detainment order came from a major in the Judge Advocate General's office—except that major retired six months ago."

Teddy remained silent. He simply watched her. She knew all the answers.

Merrit opened the folder, flipped through a few pages, and pulled out a single sheet created using carbon copy paper—the kind still used in lower administrative branches, outdated, easy to forge, but harder to track. "This copy was filed at Fort Belvoir, not here. But it references your transfer directly. It was never logged in the base's internal system. Which means someone wanted to make it look like you were being processed through legal channels…while bypassing every formal checkpoint."

She held the page up for him to see. "Someone tried to bury you, Colonel Roosevelt."

He stared at the page for a long moment before looking at her. "Why?"

"We don't know yet. But we will." There was no arrogance in her voice—only quiet certainty. She wasn't guessing anymore but tracking something and getting closer.

"Colonel Cross?" he asked.

"He's cooperating. More than I expected. He's the one who flagged the missing timestamp in the logbooks this morning. Whatever this is, he's not part of it. If anything, he's starting to realize he was used."

Teddy tried to find a more comfortable position in the bed, wincing at the pull in his gut, and released a slow breath. "So now what?"

Merrit closed the file. "Now I keep digging. And you stay alive." There was no softness to her tone, no false comfort. Yet something about the way she said it landed heavier than it should have. "I don't know who ordered the silence around your arrest. But someone went through a lot of trouble to make it clean. And quiet. If your appendix hadn't blown…this would've worked. You'd have been ruled noncompliant and found dead in your cell by morning. Internal injury. Unconfirmed illness. No autopsy. No accountability."

Teddy said nothing for a few seconds, using his command stare. It had always helped him get answers from lower-ranking officers. "And you? What happens to you if you keep going?"

Merrit's eyes didn't waver. "I don't care." She rose, tucked the folder under her arm, and turned toward the door. Before she left, she paused and glanced back at him. "You've made enemies, Colonel Roosevelt. Some of them wear stars now. If I were you, I'd rest while you can."

Then she was gone. The door clicked shut, and the light from the hallway disappeared.

And for the first time since waking, Teddy allowed himself to close his eyes—not to sleep, but to think. Organizing his thoughts, he began assembling the outlines of a new plan, piece by piece.

Someone had attempted to silence him.

Now he would discover why.

And then—he'd answer in kind.

CHAPTER 7

0610 Hours
January 18, 1984
Womack Army Medical Center
Fort Bragg, NC

The light streaming through the open blinds had changed once again. No longer golden or warm, it had transformed into a thin gray sliver cutting across the foot of the bed like a scalpel, cold and sharp against the bleached white sheets. Teddy blinked, his eyelids dry and lashes gritty. His mouth felt parched again—dry in a way that seemed chemical, not just dehydrated. Nevertheless, thirst no longer dominated his focus. Instead, his mind began to clear.

The pain in his abdomen had taken on a more specific quality—less like the wildfire of those first hours and more akin to a dull, heavy pressure. It wasn't constant, but impossible to ignore. It waited, coiled and alert, ready to punish him for any wrong move. Sutures tugged with every movement he made in bed. The internal repair site throbbed whenever he breathed too deeply or changed positions without bracing for it. It was the kind of pain he'd experienced before—honest, post-op pain. Not trauma. Not chaos. But controlled damage. The kind that came from a scalpel, not a boot or a fist.

His IV still hung at the side of the bed. The flow rate had been reduced overnight—he could tell without looking. The morphine drip had stopped. Now there were only fluids—saline, with some possible added potassium. They were weaning him off the strong medication, monitoring for rebound pain, and assessing how much he could tolerate without assistance.

Teddy glanced at the wall-mounted clock. It was just past 0600 hours, and there were still no footsteps in the corridor, indicating that no nurses were present. The shift change hadn't cycled through yet.

Golden silence.

He placed both hands on the rails—one slow, steady grip after the other—and inhaled shallowly through his nose. Then he moved. Not recklessly or to show off. Just to see how much he could tolerate.

The movement started with his arms, a subtle flex of his body on the mattress. Next, he rolled his shoulders forward, adjusting his center of gravity just enough to test the strain along his side. Gradually, he lifted his legs upward. The process was miserable. His core muscles responded with resistance and warning heat, every inch of movement triggering a reaction from the stitched tissue below his navel. His belly tightened beneath the bandages, and the surgical site flared, angry but intact.

Teddy pulled his knees up and let them rest for a moment, his muscles trembling from the effort. His stomach clenched involuntarily once, but the nausea persisted. No bile, just the dry burn of old acid in his throat and not enough food.

His pulse quickened, causing intense throbbing at the back of his jaw. Cold sweat dripped down from the base of his skull. Nevertheless, he pushed forward.

He changed positions again—slowly rotating, dragging his legs inch by inch until they slipped off the side of the bed. His bare feet touched the cold tile, and the shock of it was immediate, intense, and grounding. He paused there, breathing hard and leaning forward. Then he pulled himself upright, and the bandaged tissue around his lower abdomen responded with a sharp, warning stretch.

Teddy bit down hard as the pain radiated outward. It didn't just sting— it roared, sharp and punishing, slicing across his side in a diagonal wave. He saw darkness creeping in at the edges of his vision, feeling the backs of his knees buckle slightly.

But he didn't go down. He stayed upright. Barely.

A soft metallic click shattered the silence as the door handle turned.

A nurse. Shift change. He had only seconds to react.

He gripped the IV pole, wrapping his fingers so tight they turned white. He braced himself, pulling upward—not in a jump or a rush, but a simple maneuver, leaning up, using the pole like a second limb. The ache in his belly exploded as he rose—white-hot, stabbing, and immediate. Clenching his jaw, he endured it. His knees locked awkwardly, barely maintaining his balance. One more inch and he would have collapsed.

The door swung open.

"Jesus Christ—Colonel Roosevelt!" The nurse, tall and in her mid-forties, wore light blue scrubs, her long brown hair pulled back in a ponytail, and a stethoscope hanging around her neck. "What in the hell are you doing out of bed?"

She reached his side in two strides, one hand already moving to steady his elbow while the other caught the back of his shoulder. "You're three days out from surgery. You can't be on your feet without anyone in the room."

He didn't argue. His breathing grew ragged as his chest rose and fell rapidly. "I'm aware," he said between breaths.

"You have a drain in place, sutures in two layers, and an elevated heart rate indicating that you're minutes away from collapsing."

"I was trying to find out if I still worked."

"Well, congratulations," she snapped. "Everything works. Now sit your ass back down before I call the surgeon." She didn't wait for permission— just angled the IV pole to give him leverage and helped him back to the edge of the mattress. Each shift of his weight set his nerves on fire again. When he allowed himself to sink into the pillows, the sweat on his chest had turned cold.

"I'll notify Dr. Hollis you're awake," the nurse said while checking his vital signs. "And being reckless."

"Tell him I've been called worse."

"I'll write that down," she said, adjusting the oxygen line and checking the site for infection where the IV catheter entered the skin at the crook of his elbow. "Pain level?"

"Manageable."

"Good. You're on nothing but saline right now."

Teddy didn't respond. The ache persisted—pressing and unforgiving— but he embraced it. The pain outlined the boundaries of what had been done to him, defining his limits. It was information. He could work with that.

She scribbled something on the chart hanging on the wall. "If you tear a stitch doing that again," she said without looking at him, "I'll let Hollis close it without any anesthetic while you're awake."

"Noted."

She gave him one last glance—an experienced, unamused kind of look—then headed toward the door. "Someone from JAG may be back today. They were here again last night. The woman with a silver oak leaf on her collar. Merrit, I think."

That got his attention, but he didn't show it. "I'll be here."

She didn't respond. Just pulled the door closed behind her.

Teddy turned his head toward the light filtering through the half-open blinds. His body ached in places he hadn't noticed in years. His skin felt as though it had been sunburned from within. But now, his thoughts were clear. The haze had lifted. The pain was intense. And he was still here.

The question wasn't about how much damage had been done.

The question was who wanted him gone badly enough to leave him for dead?

And how much longer must he play the calm patient before he received his answers?

Teddy hadn't been back in bed for more than ten minutes when the door opened again—this time without hesitation or clipboard-bearing sympathy. It was Captain Hollis. The surgeon.

Hollis entered with brisk, clipped movements, the door swinging shut behind him with a heavy thud that signaled this wasn't a casual visit.

Teddy looked up from the bed. "Let me guess. She tattled."

"She did," Hollis said without missing a beat, "and good thing, too. Because if you'd taken one more step, Colonel, I'd be in there reopening your abdomen to reattach your fascia." His tone wasn't angry—but it wasn't gentle either. It was the voice of a man who'd spent the last forty-eight hours reading surgical notes about a near-fatal delay and wasn't about to let his patient undo all that hard work with stubbornness.

"You've got six inches of interrupted sutures holding your abdominal wall together. You strain them, you rupture. You rupture, you bleed. And let me be very clear, Colonel Roosevelt, the next time I see you on your feet without authorization, I won't ask if it hurts—I'll assume you've herniated and roll you straight back into the OR."

Teddy didn't respond. The pain lingered, clawing at his ribs, but he kept his jaw clenched against it. Maybe he just avoided a huge mistake.

Hollis exhaled, his frustration easing into something more clinical. "Look, I understand who you are. I've read the file. But you're not going to bluff your way through this recovery. You can't. The infection risk alone is still high, and if you want a bowel obstruction on top of what you've already got, keep testing your luck." He pulled out a small glass vial from his coat pocket and held it up. The clear liquid inside shimmered in the light.

"Morphine?" Teddy asked.

"Toradol," Hollis replied. "Non-opioid. It won't make you loopy or tank your breathing, but it'll take the edge off enough that your muscles stop bracing and give the incision a chance to stay closed."

The nurse returned with a saline flush and a new syringe. Hollis stepped aside to give her enough room to work.

"You'll sleep better, too," he added. "Which is the most important thing you can do right now. You need rest, not grit or gutting out the pain."

The nurse administered the injection through the IV port. Within minutes, the burning in Teddy's gut began to subside—not completely disappearing, but easing just enough for him to breathe without the muscles tensing against it. He changed his position in the bed, his eyes now half-closed.

"Thanks," he whispered, not out of gratitude, but because the man had told him the truth—and hadn't sugarcoated a word of it.

Hollis smiled, seeming appreciative of Teddy's stubbornness giving way to reason. "No more stunts. When it's time to move, we'll tell you. And you'll walk out of here under your own power." He turned toward the door, then paused. "Assuming you're not transferred to another location for medical treatment before that happens."

Teddy opened his eyes. "Meaning what?"

Hollis didn't turn back. "Just something to keep in mind. Headquarters has been unusually quiet since Merrit started her inquiry. That kind of silence usually means someone upstairs is buying time...or getting ready to pull the plug."

Then he left.

The door clicked shut, leaving Teddy alone once more—but this time, the pain felt more distant, like a dog finally leashed. He let himself sink into the mattress, his body slowly unwinding in the warmth of the injection. He didn't trust the thought of rest, but he could at least close his eyes for a while.

He would need the strength. Someone was still pulling the strings, and sooner or later, they would try to kill him again.

CHAPTER 8

0114 Hours
January 19, 1984
Womack Army Medical Center
Fort Bragg, NC

It was sometime after midnight when the hospital's rhythm changed again. By now, Teddy had learned to recognize it by sound alone—the muted squeak of a rolling cart, the soft-soled shuffle of overnight nurses exchanging brief greetings during the shift change. Somewhere down the hall, someone coughed, and another person laughed. Then the silence returned—thin and absolute, almost feeling like the building itself was holding its breath.

The morphine had been removed earlier in the day. He was on Toradol now—cleaner, sharper, and less forgiving. It dulled the pain, but that was all. The deep, leaden ache in his right side had returned, significantly more intense tonight. It lay like a stone beneath the dressing, a weight that pulsed whenever he inhaled deeply or changed positions on the mattress. Something felt wrong. Not new—but worse.

He blamed himself. He'd pushed too hard that morning, trying to test what his body could still do. Sat up when he shouldn't have. Stood for too long. He probably stretched or strained something but hadn't told the nurse, unwilling to invite another lecture or a higher dose of something to ease the pain. He needed his mind sharp now, not dulled.

The shadows crept across the ceiling. He lay still, his eyes half-closed, focused on the tile grid above, the IV stand in his peripheral vision, and the faint glow of the heart monitor casting a green reflection on the windowpane.

Then he heard it—the door. Soft. Precise. A practiced motion. Not the usual push and rattle of a nurse with a chart. The latch disengaged with a muted click, and the door opened with a hiss that didn't travel very far.

Teddy turned his head a few inches.

The figure who entered wasn't his usual nurse. It was a man wearing standard blue surgical scrubs, distinguished by his broader shoulders and slower pace. He didn't carry a clipboard or offer any greeting. The only sound was the door closing—quietly. The lock didn't catch.

A chill coursed down Teddy's spine.

The man moved closer. Teddy didn't speak, not yet. He watched. There was something unsettlingly steady about the way the man approached—no hesitation or sound. The figure came to a stop near the IV pole. Even in the dim light, Teddy could make out gloved hands and the faint metallic shimmer of something long and thin pulled from a pocket. A hypodermic syringe with no printed label. Not standard issue.

A jolt of adrenaline surged through his chest, but the pain and Toradol dulled the follow-through. His body wouldn't move fast enough. He tried to rise, but the pull in his abdomen screamed in protest, the bandages tight across still-healing tissue. "You're not supposed to be here," he rasped.

The man didn't flinch or hesitate. "Nothing personal, Colonel Roosevelt. Just finishing the job." He reached for the IV line.

Teddy reacted. He reached up, slow yet driven by pure instinct, and grabbed the man's forearm just as the needle moved. The syringe missed its target—the IV port—scraping against the metal bedrail. The attacker swore and adjusted his grip, but Teddy wasn't done. He twisted his torso just enough to drive his knee into the man's ribs.

Agony seared through his stomach as though someone had thrust a red-hot knife blade beneath the bandages.

However, his desperate move worked.

The attacker staggered back a step, just far enough to give him a few seconds.

Teddy sucked in a breath that burned like fire in his lungs. "Help! Nurse! Get in here!" The shout tore through his throat, raw and ragged, but loud enough to be heard in the hallway.

The door burst open five seconds later. A nurse appeared, followed by another. Their eyes widened in surprise. Alarms sounded—first one, then two. The heart monitor blared into overdrive as the attacker bolted, ducking toward the back hallway and disappearing before anyone could react.

But the damage was already done.

Teddy tried to sit up—but the movement brought something terrible with it. He felt it as it happened, a deep, tearing pull inside, sudden and hot—like something within him had come undone. He gasped as the nausea surged, bile rising in his throat. His vision blurred. Grasping his side, he attempted to brace himself, trying to stop what he already knew was happening.

Then came the pain. Real pain. Unfiltered. Deeper than ever. It radiated outward from his core like heat from a blast furnace. He could feel blood—

hot and spreading—beneath the bandage. The pressure built behind it, sharp and damp.

He let out a hoarse, involuntary cry of pain.

"Code Red! Get surgery prepped—we've got a rupture!" the nurse shouted behind him.

Another voice barked orders. Gloves snapped. The sheets were pulled back. Hands pressed against his abdomen, and he screamed again— nothing controlled now, no composure left.

"There's blood tracking across the lower flank," someone said. "Pulse is dropping—BP's tanking."

The oxygen mask was secured over his face a moment later. He tried to concentrate, to identify someone, anyone in the room, but the lights above merged into a single glow.

Pain. Cold. The scent of alcohol and iodine. A flurry of activity at his side.

"Get the gurney! We're not waiting!"

The words seemed to come from everywhere and nowhere. The room had descended into chaos. Someone grabbed his wrist, pulling his arm straight to administer medication. He felt a burning sensation rush through his arm, followed by a floating chill.

Then darkness came fast.

The last thing he heard—cutting clean through the haze—was a clipped sentence from a voice near his side, "Ruptured suture. Internal bleed. We're losing him."

0135 Hours
January 19, 1984
Womack Army Medical Center
Fort Bragg, NC

Captain Ray Hollis had been asleep for less than an hour when the call came through—ER Code Red, surgical standby. He didn't need to know the name. There was only one patient on his service involved with JAG, guarded by MPs, and surrounded by layers of political scrutiny. Colonel Roosevelt.

He was still buttoning his lab coat as he pushed through the trauma entrance doors. The sharp sound of his boots echoed on the sterile tiles, keeping pace with the trauma nurse jogging beside him. Her expression was grim, her voice low and clipped.

"Male, forty-nine, post-op day four from open appendectomy. Sudden-onset abdominal pain and drop in vitals. Blood pressure is in free fall. Found supine, sweating, and in acute distress. When the nurse turned back the sheets, she discovered active abdominal bleeding from the surgical site. Dark red. Pressure was applied en route."

"Pulse?"

"Thready. One-thirty-two and climbing. Oxygen saturation is at ninety-one on five liters. He's pale, disoriented, and showing signs of peritoneal pain. Guarding on exam."

"Get the OR prepped," Hollis said. "Page Kline. Tell anesthesia I want the same team we used on the primary. Notify the blood bank—type and cross for six units of packed red cells and two fresh frozen. Start a second wide-bore line and hang a liter of Lactated Ringer's now."

They entered Trauma Room Two.

Hollis didn't slow down. The bright overhead lights had a cold, clinical feel, and the scent of betadine and blood lingered in the air. Colonel Roosevelt lay motionless on the gurney, his face waxy with sweat, and his mouth open as he struggled to breathe under the oxygen mask. His skin had turned pale, with a gray tinge around his temples and jawline, resembling someone on the verge of circulatory collapse.

Two nurses worked by his side—one inserting a second 16-gauge IV into the left antecubital vein, while the other applied firm pressure with both gloved hands over the surgical site. Blood was already soaking through the bandage and pooling on the absorbent pad under his back.

"Let's see it," Hollis said as he stepped between the nurses.

The surgical nurse peeled back the soaked dressing. The gauze lifted with a wet sound, revealing a crimson bloom around the incision site that spread outward in a slow but steady tide. The lower right quadrant was distended, with the skin taut and warm to the touch, despite the overall chill of Roosevelt's clammy skin. The sutures were still intact—but there was subcutaneous give beneath them, a softness that had no place this far into healing.

Hollis applied gentle pressure as he pressed against the edge, sensing the tension in the tissue. "Peritoneal bleed. Suture failure or a mesenteric tear. We've got an intra-abdominal hemorrhage in progress."

The nurse at his side didn't wait. "OR two's ready. Anesthesia's standing by."

"Move him," Hollis said. "Now! I'll walk with you. Monitor vital signs and keep that pressure on the hemorrhage constant."

The orderly wheeled Colonel Roosevelt from the trauma bay with controlled haste, guiding the stretcher while a team of five assisted—two nurses flanking the IV poles, the respiratory tech at the head with an Ambu bag, and Hollis near the right flank, supporting his patient as the elevator doors opened to the surgical suite level.

As they rolled through the OR doors, the scrub nurse had already draped the Mayo stand, and the anesthesiologist was wearing a surgical mask, adjusting the bag valve as the ventilator engaged. The overhead lights were blinding, in stark contrast to the dim recovery wing. The blood pressure readout on the monitor showed 76/38, and his pulse was 138.

"Let's go," Hollis said, his voice low but urgent.

The team moved with mechanical precision. The scrub tech extended the scalpel in silence. Hollis took it and inhaled deeply through his surgical mask, centering himself before making the first cut.

He re-entered the abdomen through the original incision, working quickly but with surgical precision. The tissues beneath the skin peeled apart more easily than he liked—edematous, thinned by inflammation. He dissected with extreme caution, using blunt dissection to avoid deep vascular damage.

"Let's expose the field. Suction in. Retractor here. Extend another centimeter laterally to the midline."

The suction tube whined as the cavity opened. Blood poured out in a thick stream—dark and partially clotted—flooding the surgical field with alarming speed.

"Peritoneal rupture confirmed," Hollis said. "We've got an active arterial bleed. Find the origin."

He worked swiftly to isolate the bowel loops, retracting them with damp pads. The field gradually cleared under continuous suction. Hollis scanned for the source of the bleed, tracing the old suture line from the appendiceal stump across the mesenteric fan.

"There," Hollis said, his voice tightening. "Posterior mesentery—small vessel tear. One stitch ruptured. Surrounding tissue looks bruised."

Dr. Kline leaned in next to him. "Not from us. Do you see that pattern? That's focal. Compressive. Blunt force. That's trauma to the abdomen."

Hollis didn't acknowledge Kline's observation. He'd already seen it and placed two figure-eight sutures on the vessel wall, watching as the bleeding slowed and stopped. He reinforced the mesenteric edge with silk ties and began irrigating the cavity, flushing out pooled blood and clots.

"No other bleeders. Continue irrigation. Prep the surgical mesh—reinforced."

They worked for an additional twenty minutes, reapproximating the fascia with long, deliberate strokes and placing a protective mesh over the weakened area to prevent herniation. A new drain was positioned at the peritoneal edge, with the site marked and recorded. Closure was performed in three layers—fascia, subcutaneous, and skin—each carefully tensioned.

By the time Hollis applied the final dressing, the vital signs on the monitors started to stabilize.

"BP's coming up. 92 over 54. Pulse steadying at 116," Dr. Kline said.

Hollis stepped back from the table. Sweat clung to the back of his neck under the green scrub cap. He peeled off the gloves one by one, dropped them into the bin, then unhooked the surgical mask from behind his ears.

"Take him to the surgical ICU. I want full vital signs every fifteen minutes, continuous cardiac monitoring, and someone observing that drain for signs of rebound bleeding."

The room began to reset. Nurses started cleaning the operating room while the technicians prepared the patient for transport. Hollis turned to the wall phone and picked up the receiver.

He didn't waste time on introductions. The line clicked once before someone answered.

"Lieutenant Colonel Merrit," said the female voice on the other end of the line.

"There's been another attack," Hollis said.

Then he hung up.

And started writing his post-surgical report.

0300 Hours
January 19, 1984
519th Military Intelligence Battalion HQ
Fort Bragg, NC

Colonel Vincent Cross stood by the window in his office, staring into nothingness with his arms crossed over his chest. The light outside had changed, shifting from black to the slate gray of early morning, but he hadn't slept. Not since the nurse at the base hospital called him. Her message sent a shiver down his spine. "There's been a second incident, sir. Colonel Roosevelt's back in surgery. He's stable now, but the bleed was significant. The doctor believes it wasn't accidental."

The words hit him harder than he had expected.

He was already dressed by the time the call ended, halfway down the corridor before anyone could stop him. Now, standing outside the surgical recovery ward, he felt something he hadn't experienced in a long time.

Doubt.

Not only regarding his men or the chain of command, but also about the system he'd sworn to serve and how far someone would go to make a man like Colonel Theodore "Bull Moose" Roosevelt disappear.

Cross stepped into the corridor as Captain Hollis emerged from the OR suite, still in sweaty, bloodstained green scrubs, his scrub cap askew, and his hands freshly washed but steady. The look in his eyes wasn't one of anger or fatigue, but rather the unmistakable gaze of someone ready to go to war.

"You said it wasn't accidental," Cross said, walking to meet him. "Are you sure?"

Hollis didn't answer the question. Instead, he reached for the file tucked under his arm and opened it with practiced ease, flipping through the pages until he found the one he wanted. He turned it around without ceremony.

"There," he said. "Blunt trauma to the lower right quadrant. Not from coughing, sneezing, or trying to get out of bed. This was pressure applied with intent. The ruptured suture was clean, but the surrounding tissue shows bruising. It was a forceful strike. Likely a fist or an elbow."

Cross stared at the image—grainy and printed in monochrome, yet unmistakable. He didn't need a medical degree to understand its meaning. "How's he doing?"

"He's lucky," Hollis said. "Again. We stopped the bleeding and reinforced the fascia. But that luck's going to run out if someone else decides to finish what they started."

"Any sign of who it was?"

"We're checking the security cameras now. Colonel Roosevelt was stable at lights out. By 0120, he was hemorrhaging. A nurse heard him call out and got there in time. But whoever did it knew what they were doing. They got in and out without being seen by anyone, blending into the flurry of activity around Colonel Roosevelt. There was no forced entry into the room."

Cross nodded. That wasn't good. It meant someone in the hospital had tried to kill Colonel Roosevelt. The weight in his chest had grown heavier and harder to ignore. It was no longer just guilt—it was fury—quiet, focused, the sort that didn't shake hands or bark orders. The kind that made him dangerous.

He turned away from the photos and glanced down the hall toward the secured recovery room. Two MPs stood on either side of the door. This time, they were not his men but rather chosen by Merrit's office. Cross had insisted on that safety measure. After what happened in the cell—and now this—he wasn't going to trust a single face he hadn't personally vetted.

"I want a full list of every staff member who accessed the security wing after midnight," Cross said. "I don't care if they were sweeping floors or emptying trash. If they have a hospital ID or access badge, I want the name."

Hollis nodded. "Merrit has already put in the request for the same information. She's two steps ahead of all of us."

"I hope she's five," Cross said. He stood there a moment longer, hands now at his sides, the tight grip finally released, but the pressure still coiled inside him. He'd arrested Roosevelt with complete confidence in the system backing him up. But now that system had attempted—twice—to bury a man under a clean sheet and a file full of forged signatures. And Cross wasn't just caught in the middle anymore. He was the man who had delivered Roosevelt into it.

Cross turned to leave but paused halfway down the hall. "Who in the hell are we working for?" He directed it more at himself than anyone else, almost unwilling to believe that a superior officer might have hired a murderer.

There was no answer.

Only the silence of the recovery ward behind him.

CHAPTER 9

0610 Hours
January 19, 1984
Womack Army Medical Center
Fort Bragg, NC

Teddy emerged from sedation like a man pulled from the depths of a frozen lake—slowly, under pressure, weighed down, and through an aching stillness.

The pain arrived first. Not sharp or clean. It settled low and wide, a deep, gnawing ache stretched across his abdomen like someone had packed steel wool beneath his ribs and left it there to rust away. Every heartbeat nudged it. Every breath rubbed the edge of his nerves raw. It didn't surge or stab—but it was there, anchored deep in tissue that had already been carved open once before.

He didn't open his eyes right away. The world remained dark behind his eyelids, and he chose to keep it that way, recalling the shape of the room from memory. The stale hospital air filtered through the nasal cannula. The steady, muted beep of a heart monitor pulsed somewhere to his left. The IV in his arm felt colder now, less familiar than the morphine. The edge of his consciousness told him that the medical staff was weaning him off the narcotics—replacing them with cleaner, sharper medications. Toradol, maybe. Something they could use to monitor his pain tolerance. Something that didn't cloud the judgment they now needed him to maintain.

Everything beneath his skin felt worse than before—tighter and swollen. He didn't need to see the dressing to know they'd gone back in. The pressure in his abdomen not only hurt—it pushed, bloated with fluid, inflammation, or both. It felt like new trauma layered over something that had just begun to heal.

Teddy turned in the bed, trying to find a comfortable position, and his body protested the movement with a sharp reminder of his discomfort.

A pulse of pain flared white-hot across his right side, radiating through the drainage tubing and the newly reinforced sutures. He inhaled sharply but caught it halfway, turning it into a clenched exhale. An involuntary hiss escaped through his teeth.

It was enough.

A chair creaked to his left. Footsteps followed. Then came the sound of a page turning—or maybe a legal pad closing.

"Colonel Roosevelt?"

The voice was soft, feminine, and calm. Lt. Colonel Merrit.

Teddy opened his eyes. The bright white fluorescent lights overhead stung, but he forced his vision to adjust. The room felt quieter and larger than the previous one, offering a greater sense of privacy. Perhaps it was a new wing or at least a room farther from the main corridor. The heart monitor glowed in the corner. And there she was—Lieutenant Colonel Rachel Merrit, standing by the side of the bed in full uniform, arms crossed, her expression wary.

"You're awake," she said.

"For now," he whispered. His throat was dry. The words stuck on their way out.

"You're post-op again. Second surgery. Emergency laparotomy. You were bleeding into the peritoneal cavity."

He swallowed to soothe his dry throat, every muscle in his neck aching from the motion. "So I made it."

"Barely," she said. "They almost lost you on the table."

He exhaled. "Hell of a recovery rate. What happened? My memory is a bit fuzzy from the medication."

"There was an intruder," she said, her voice quiet now. "After midnight. He came in through a side corridor with a fake badge and tried to inject something into your IV line. You stopped him. Barely. The nurse responded to the heart monitor spike and found you struggling to stay upright."

Teddy rubbed the sleep out of his eyes. "Security?"

"He evaded them, but not without leaving a trace. We're currently reviewing the access logs. Someone on the inside helped him gain entry to the restricted wing. They knew about the blind spots in the security cameras and the shift change schedules. They were sent to finish the job, Colonel Roosevelt. That much is certain."

He closed his eyes—not in pain, not from defeat, but to concentrate. The pattern had emerged—the fake transfer, the ignored symptoms, the beating in the cell. And now, this.

Someone wanted him dead.

"How bad?" Teddy asked.

"Medically?" she asked for clarification.

He nodded. "Yes."

"You're stable now. But it was a serious bleed. Dr. Hollis found a ruptured mesenteric vessel. One of your sutures tore under pressure—possibly from the struggle or earlier strain. They reinforced the entire lower quadrant with mesh. You have a drain in place and internal tension sutures across the midline."

"Recovery time?"

"Slow," she said. "You're not going anywhere for a long time."

A faint smirk tugged at the corner of his mouth, though it never reached his eyes. "Wouldn't dream of it."

She gave him a long look. Then it softened—still professional, but with a gentler touch. "I've requested your room be transferred to a secure JAG-monitored ward. Colonel Cross signed off on it. Two MPs on rotation outside the door at all times, and nobody touches your chart without my clearance."

Teddy turned his head on the pillow. "So I've got a lawyer and a body count. That's new."

"This isn't a joke, sir," she said. "This is a conspiracy. Someone inside the system wants you dead. And if that's true, you're not the only one at risk."

He didn't respond right away but grasped the bedrail, wrapping his fingers around the cool metal. It steadied him—not just physically, but also mentally.

"They missed," he said. "They don't get a third shot."

A lengthy silence ensued.

Then, just as Merrit began to turn away, a single knock resonated at the door.

Not sharp or commanding. Just an ordinary knock.

The door opened a few inches at a time, as if someone was reluctant to enter, and Colonel Cross stepped through the opening. He wore starched OD-green fatigues, his sleeves rolled up to his elbows, holding his cap in his left hand. His posture wasn't rigid. He didn't stand erect. Cross looked like a man walking into a room he didn't want to enter but felt compelled to do so lest he appear a failure.

Merrit didn't say anything. She glanced at him before slipping out quietly, letting the door close behind her.

Teddy lay on the bed, remaining still and not offering a greeting.

Cross stepped closer, but not too close, clearly wanting to keep his distance. "I heard you pulled through."

Teddy nodded. "Despite someone else's plan."

"I know. Merrit told me." Cross hesitated then looked away, gripping the brim of his cap. "I came to say something I should've said a long time ago." He didn't wait for permission. "I was wrong. About all of it. About you. About what I thought I saw when we brought you in. You asked for a medic, and I didn't follow up. I thought you were bluffing, running one of your blasted con games. But you weren't. You were dying. And I let it happen under my command."

Teddy didn't respond, maintaining a neutral expression. However, something changed in his mind.

"I let two of my men rough you up and then failed to notice when someone tried to finish the job in a hospital bed. That's not just a mistake. That's a failure of command. My failure."

Another silence hung in the air. Teddy knew Cross wanted to unburden his conscience.

"I've already given Lieutenant Colonel Merrit access to everything I have—security logs, rosters, sign-ins. Whoever's behind this, we're going to find them."

Teddy stayed quiet. It wasn't the right moment to respond.

Cross's gaze fell to the ground again before he turned toward the door. "You didn't ask for an apology. But I needed to give one." He reached for the door handle.

"Vince," Teddy said, his voice rough.

The colonel turned to face him. "Yes."

"I wasn't faking," Teddy said. "Not in that cell. Not for a second."

Cross pointed at himself. "I know that now." Then he walked out, placing his hat on his head.

And Teddy closed his eyes, not in pain this time, but in reflection.

The war hadn't ended.

But now, at least, he knew which direction to aim.

1310 Hours
January 19, 1984
Womack Army Medical Center
Fort Bragg, NC

The afternoon sunlight cast long shadows across the floor, inching toward the far wall like a sundial no one bothered to reset. The secure room was quiet now, almost too quiet, and Teddy welcomed it. The pain had dulled into something familiar and manageable—he could breathe without wincing and move in the bed without drawing sweat to his forehead. The morphine had been reduced to half-dose drips, just enough to take the edge off.

They'd kept him alive. For now.

But someone still wanted him dead.

He lay still beneath the sheet, propped up on the incline of the bed with several comfortable pillows, his eyes half-open, watching dust float in the sunbeam near the window. A nurse had come in earlier to check his vital signs—polite yet quiet, clearly instructed to keep things efficient. Merrit hadn't returned yet, nor had Cross. While both had earned a sliver of his trust, Teddy wasn't the type of man to leave his fate in someone else's hands.

Not again, not after they nearly failed and luck saved him.

He had started cataloging items hours earlier, conducting a mental inventory. The layout of the new room featured one door and one window overlooking the motor pool below, outfitted with privacy glass but no blinds. The guards stationed outside now rotated every six hours instead of eight. He noted the name of the nurse who administered his IV push of dextrose, observing how she used her left hand to stabilize the port. Her name tag read *J. Linton*. She had a Southern accent and a steady gait.

Every detail mattered. It always had.

Even from a hospital bed, Teddy was able to read a system.

He spent years in the shadows studying people like Merrit and Cross, as well as the unknown bastard who tried to kill him. Systems break down when too many people start asking the wrong questions. The trick wasn't to expose the entire network in one dramatic move, but to find the weak link—the one loose thread that would unravel everything else.

And someone on this base had left those threads scattered all over the floor.

The forged transfer, the missing intake attachments, and the dead authorization code from a JAG officer who had retired six months earlier—none of it was sophisticated. That was the mistake. Whoever wanted him dead hadn't expected anyone to take a closer look. They had relied on bureaucracy to do what it does best—bury the truth under paperwork and plausible deniability.

But they hadn't anticipated his appendix becoming necrotic.

That failure brought him here—alive, injured, and now protected by the very system designed to erase him.

And now he was thinking.

The pain dulled his thoughts, yet they remained sharp. Every visit, name, clipboard, and sound in the corridor was recorded on his mental list.

Even though he couldn't walk yet, he made it a point to become familiar with every inch of this place. Sooner or later, someone would make a mistake. They always did.

His body would catch up in time.

But his mind was already out of the bed, crawling down the halls and mapping the escape route—not from the hospital, but from the trap that had tried to kill him.

They came very close to succeeding—closer than anyone ever had.

But they'd missed.

And Theodore "Bull Moose" Roosevelt IV never forgave a missed shot. When he fired back, he didn't miss.

CHAPTER 10

1750 Hours
January 19, 1984
Headquarters - Records Annex
Fort Bragg, NC

Lieutenant Colonel Rachel Merrit sat alone in the records annex, a slim manila folder open on the desk with a single lamp casting a pale circle of light on the far wall. The rest of the room remained dark. The air was thick with the scent of the Xerox machine, paper, and old, dusty HVAC ductwork. Outside, the base was winding down for the night. Inside, Merrit was just beginning her work.

She had requested the complete chain of documents regarding Colonel Theodore Roosevelt's detainment order, but she didn't trust the copies retrieved by the administration. She went herself—down into the base's physical archives where old carbon copy files were still sorted by hand, and where corrections left faint shadows of truth beneath layers of ink.

It took nearly two hours to trace the exact sequence of files—the detainment order, the custody transfer, the holding paperwork, and the authorization chain. Most of it was exactly what she expected—standard forms, stamped and signed by familiar officers whose names she recognized.

However, buried deep in the third section, where the approval chain should have concluded with the base legal officer, one more form remained in the packet.

One more name.

She held it up to the light and read it, furrowing her brow.

Lt. Colonel Andrew R. Dunning

No department was specified. No division, regiment, or battalion was mentioned in the assignment block. Only a signature, a date, and a typed line.

Authorization to detain Colonel Theodore Roosevelt IV under provisional hold authority, pending off-base transport.

Her fingers hovered just above the edge of the page. She flipped it again, angling it toward the yellowed copy underneath. Same name. Same ink. But the carbon transfer was...off—blurred where it shouldn't have been.

She reviewed the base personal roster.

There was no Andrew Dunning assigned to this installation. No one by that name existed in the JAG Corps. Regarding the authorization code next to the signature, it wasn't even a JAG reference number. A bit of digging revealed it was an internal designation from a non-standard clearance tier.

She reached for the phone in the far corner of the desk and dialed her office.

"Sergeant Delaney," she said when her junior legal clerk picked up. "I need you to pull up the secure base access logs for the last six months. I need a complete list. I'm looking for any temporary clearances or black-badge credentials issued to Lieutenant Colonel Andrew Dunning."

A pause.

"Ma'am...we don't have a Dunning listed in the personnel database."

"I didn't ask if he was listed. I asked if he had access."

Delaney hesitated then cleared his throat. "Yes, ma'am. Give me a minute."

While waiting, she turned the signature form toward the light again. It was real paper, genuine ink, and an authentic signature. However, it had no place in the official chain of custody. Someone had slipped it in, believing no one would examine it this closely.

She continued to stare at it, trying to find anything she might have overlooked, when the phone buzzed again.

"Ma'am? I found something. A clearance tier was issued two weeks ago, active for only seventy-two hours. Badge access was restricted to Level Four admin corridors and temporary file staging areas. No permanent assignment is listed. The credential was burned five days ago."

"Burned?" Merrit asked.

"Yes, ma'am. Marked for immediate deletion. Tagged *external liaison use only*."

"Was it the NSA?"

"No, ma'am."

"CIA? DIA?"

"No service branch or government agency was listed, ma'am."

Of course not. "Thank you," she said and hung up.

Merrit leaned back in the chair, gazing at the signature once more. Whoever Andrew R. Dunning was, he didn't belong on any personnel roster. Yet someone had granted him clearance—just long enough to forge a transfer order, slip it into the official file, and vanish without a trace.

Merrit closed the folder and rested her hand on it.

Someone had attempted to ghost Colonel Roosevelt from within—not through a court-martial or standard procedure, but by orchestrating a complete erasure from existence, crafted with just enough legality to mislead a system that wasn't paying attention.

But now, someone was watching. Merrit.

Merrit rose, tucked the folder under her arm, and left the annex without speaking to the guard at the exit. She didn't need speculation—only names. And if Dunning had passed through this base, someone must have seen him.

And she was going to find out who.

1050 Hours
January 20, 1984
Womack Army Medical Center
Fort Bragg, NC

Teddy heard Merrit before he saw her. The footsteps sounded different—measured, yes, but heavier than those of the nurses. Merrit never walked in a way that suggested she was simply a visitor. She moved like someone who carried consequences in her front pocket.

The door swung open, and her facial expression indicated that this wasn't a routine update. She didn't bother with pleasantries. Instead, she crossed the room, placed a folder on the rolling bedside table next to his bed, and stood there with one hand resting on it.

Merrit looked tired. Not from a lack of sleep—she seemed like the type who could run on adrenaline for days—but from the burden of what she was carrying.

Teddy pushed himself up higher in his bed, wincing as the sutures at the surgical site tugged. The pain had lessened but never completely disappeared. He gestured toward the file. "Good news?"

"Not the kind that makes you feel better."

He studied her for a moment longer. "But the kind that matters."

Merrit nodded and opened the folder but didn't hand it to him. She knew he couldn't sit up long enough to read it yet. Instead, she slid the top page free and placed it in his line of sight on the bedside table.

"Lieutenant Colonel Andrew R. Dunning," she said. "He signed your transfer authorization."

"Don't know the name," Teddy replied, his eyes fixed on the typed line at the bottom of the form. "But I know that signature doesn't belong on a JAG chain."

"Because he's not JAG. He's not even in the Army. There's no record of him anywhere."

That got his attention. "Then who is he?"

"I don't know yet. Temporary black-badge clearance. No assigned branch or personnel file in the Pentagon. Clearance was activated for only seventy-two hours—long enough to walk in, sign your paperwork, and disappear."

Teddy tapped the bedside table. "Which means someone gave him access. High-level. Off-the-books. And someone scrubbed the trail clean behind him."

Merrit nodded. "And not very well, which tells me something else. Whoever ordered this didn't expect you to survive. The paperwork wasn't designed to withstand questions. It was built to last just long enough to keep everyone in the dark."

He leaned back against the pillow, lost in thought. The light above him was too bright, yet he didn't close his eyes. He stared at the ceiling, hoping it might reveal more answers if he looked hard enough. "Any guesses?"

"Not yet," she said. "But I've got the security desk reviewing the base entry camera footage from the day the badge was used. If he set foot in this facility, someone saw him. And if I can't get a name, I'll settle for a face."

A moment of silence stretched between them.

"You were never supposed to get out of that cell alive," she said.

Teddy didn't respond. He didn't need to. The truth was just old news now.

"You're a high-value scapegoat, Colonel Roosevelt. Clean records don't get this kind of effort. Ghost orders. Doctored transfers. This wasn't about revenge. This was prevention. They don't want you walking into a courtroom to testify about what you know regarding these people and their organization."

"I've been in worse places," he said.

"I believe that." She paused before adding, "But I don't think you've ever been hunted from this close, with this many uniforms pretending not to see it."

That hit him harder than he expected—not because it shocked him, but because she was right. This wasn't a war zone. It was a hospital bed on a

U.S. military base. Yet someone had still come for him under the harsh glare of fluorescent lights and amidst official silence.

Teddy looked at her once more. She was watching him like a lawyer scrutinizes a man who still hadn't decided whether to fight or flee, the fight or flight response. "I'm not going to die in this bed."

"Good," Merrit replied. "Because if you're still alive in three days, I'll have a name. When I do, I'm going to burn whoever handed that man a security badge. I think you'll want to be awake for that. Rest while you can. You won't get many more nights like this."

She turned to leave, her steps as steady as when she arrived. However, the folder remained on the bedside table, easily within Teddy's reach.

He stared at it for a long time after she left, the name Dunning echoing in his mind like a shot that hadn't yet landed.

They'd come close.

But now it was his turn.

CHAPTER 11

1300 Hours
January 20, 1984
Fort Bragg Stockade
Fort Bragg, NC

The security room felt cold, not from the air itself but due to the fluorescent lights, cinderblock walls, the hum of the monitors, and the sterile atmosphere of a space designed to record events but not to protect those on the monitor screens.

Merrit stood behind the technician, arms crossed, her eyes fixed on the grainy black-and-white feed looping silently on the central screen. The timestamp in the corner read 0114 hours—six minutes before Colonel Roosevelt screamed for help. Moments later, the nurse found him doubled over in bed, bleeding out.

Cross stood a few feet behind her, his hands in the front pockets of his fatigues. He hadn't spoken since entering the room, only nodding when she briefed him and remaining silent since then. She appreciated that.

"Slow it here," she said, pointing at the screen.

The technician rewound the footage a few frames. In the far corner of the feed, one of the secondary hallways leading to the secure recovery wing showed movement. The resolution wasn't high enough for facial details, but it was adequate to see a figure moving along the wall—shoulders hunched, head down, and light jacket zipped up over the hospital surgical scrubs.

Merrit leaned closer to the monitor. "Freeze that image. Zoom in on the badge."

The image blurred for a second then cleared. There it was, a black clearance badge without a branch identifier or photo, just the barcode strip and a flash of white above it—a temporary credential issued to civilians.

She turned to face Cross. "That's your man."

Cross didn't argue. He stepped forward, studied the screen, then leaned down and placed his hands on the countertop. "He moves like he's done it before and knows the location of the cameras. Stays wide on the corners. Avoids facing any known checkpoints. Head down, minimal exposure. That's expert tradecraft."

"Not Army," Merrit stated. "Not one of yours. This wasn't an MP gone rogue."

"No," Cross agreed. "This man was brought in to do a job. A professional hitman. Maybe what the CIA calls a 'wet boy.'"

She straightened up, watching the rest of the footage unfold. The man paused outside Colonel Roosevelt's room, too far for the camera to capture what happened next. He appeared as a dark, hunched figure blocking the door for seven seconds before disappearing behind a closed door.

When the playback ended, she stepped back from the monitor and nodded to the tech. "Export that frame. I want the timestamp burned in and a full copy sent to my office and to base security. Quietly. Consider this classified."

The technician didn't ask why and left the room.

"You know what this means," Cross said.

"I do," Merrit said.

Colonel Cross turned to face her. For the first time since meeting him, his tone held no hardness—only quiet resolve. "We've got someone operating off the grid. CIA or contract hitman, maybe. Someone with enough clearance to sneak into a military hospital and walk out without a trace. That doesn't happen without a high-ranking officer or governmental entity signing off on it."

"Or a cover story," Merrit added. "I'm willing to bet this Dunning left a trail somewhere before that name was removed from the logs."

"When this reaches the division commander, there's going to be pressure from the Pentagon to sit on it. They'll want to push it up and kill it clean, especially if it involves anyone in the intelligence circles."

"I'm not in their chain of command," she replied. "And I don't sit easy."

Cross studied her for a long moment before nodding. "You really believe him, don't you?"

"Colonel Roosevelt?"

"Yeah."

"I don't think it matters whether I believe him or not. Someone tried to kill him. They forged an order to detain him, covered up the abuse, concealed the access logs, and falsified a JAG signature. That's not about belief anymore. That's about facts."

"He's not who I thought he was," Cross said.

"No," Merrit said. "He's something worse."

He glanced at her. "What do you mean by that?"

"Someone who knows how to survive. And now he understands what they did."

Cross exhaled through his nose and headed for the door. "I'm putting a second team on the hospital detail. People I trust. Nobody gets through that hallway without clearance from you or me."

"Good," she said. "Because the next time someone tries to kill him, I won't be writing a report."

He looked back at her and fully met her gaze. For the first time, she saw him not as a superior officer, not as a rival, and not as a man who had spent the last decade chasing shadows. He was someone ready to stand with her when this situation erupted, revealing all the pieces that no one wanted to see.

When he departed, the room fell silent once more.

On the monitor, the figure in the hallway appeared frozen mid-step—a blur, a shadow captured just before vanishing.

But Merrit knew one thing now.

Ghosts left tracks.

And this one had just made a mistake.

CHAPTER 12

0558 Hours
January 21, 1984
Womack Army Medical Center
Fort Bragg, NC

The pain in his abdomen had changed again. It no longer screamed when he moved. It didn't flare with every breath or roll under his ribs like a volcano waiting to erupt. Now it simmered—low, constant, and dull. A reminder more than a warning. It was still there, occupying space across his abdomen like a coiled spring—but it wasn't running the show anymore.

That told him he was healing. Slowly. Unevenly. But healing.

By the time the nurse entered at 0601 hours, Teddy was already awake. He sat propped upright against the head of the bed, surrounded by a mound of pillows. His legs were drawn up under the blanket for stability, and one arm casually draped over the bedrail. The IV line snaked up to the bag hanging on the pole. His face was freshly shaved, though not very well—he hadn't dared press hard enough for precision. The effort had left his jaw feeling raw and imperfect, but it achieved its purpose.

A cup of water sat half-full on the bedside table beside him, accompanied by a small stack of saltine crackers wrapped in crinkled plastic. An hour earlier, he had managed to eat most of one. It had settled—barely—but it was better than nothing.

The nurse, a calm middle-aged woman with crow's feet and zero tolerance for nonsense, paused in the doorway. "Well," she said, glancing at the monitor, "someone's feeling better."

"I've had worse mornings," Teddy replied, his voice rough but stronger than it had been for days.

She approached the machine and pressed a few buttons to check the IV infusion pump. He followed her movements—not out of suspicion but out of habit. She made a minor adjustment to the drip rate and checked his oxygen saturation.

"You're down to room air now," she said, more to herself than to him. "That's good. Pain level?"

"Manageable." It wasn't the truth, but close enough.

She studied his face, trying to read him. While she didn't challenge the answer, she also didn't accept it on faith. "Doctor Hollis will be by after rounds. I'll let him know you're up."

He nodded as she left without saying another word, the door clicking shut behind her.

Once she was out of sight, he tossed the blanket aside and swung his legs over the edge of the bed. This wasn't rebellion. It was reconnaissance.

His muscles responded in slow motion. Everything in his torso felt tight and foreign, as though the surgical mesh reinforcing his abdominal wall had altered his center of gravity. He could feel the pull of the sutures beneath his skin, the way the tissue gripped and resisted each movement. His balance felt unsteady, and his breathing was shallow. But he remained upright, gripping the bedframe with his hands until his legs could support his full weight.

One step followed by another.

Teddy walked over to the small wall-mounted sink, his balance tenuous, gripping the rolling IV stand for support, and noticed his reflection in the square mirror above the basin.

He looked...older. Not weaker or frail, just worn out in a new way. His graying hair was tousled. The bruises had begun to fade from purple to yellow at the edges, and the shadows beneath his eyes seemed deeper, while his skin still held the sallow tinge from blood loss and narcotics. But there was focus in the set of his mouth, purpose in the eyes looking back at him. This wasn't the same man who'd been dragged into a stockade cell with an appendix ready to rupture, having no idea why the world had just turned upside down.

This man had answers—not all of them, but enough to start drawing a line through the fog.

Teddy rinsed his face, feeling the cool water shock his skin. He ran it over his wrists until the chill reached his elbows. Bending forward created pressure that sent a pulse of discomfort through his lower abdomen, but it quickly passed.

He returned to bed one slow step at a time, each movement deliberate. He understood what his body could tolerate—and what it couldn't. Once seated, he reached for the bedside table and pulled it closer.

A plain government-issued notepad rested beside a glass of water with a sharpened HB pencil clipped across the spiral binding. Merrit's staff had left it the previous day without any fanfare—not as a gift or a nice gesture, but as a recognition—he was no longer an inmate. He was now something else—witness, asset, survivor. Possibly more.

Teddy opened the pad. The first page was already filled with names, observations, and timelines.

He provided additional details. First, the individuals he had encountered since the arrest—two MPs from the transport convoy, the guards from the cellblock—Hollins, Reese, and Davidson, and the infirmary doctor, Rutledge. Additionally, the three people closely involved in his life were Colonel Cross, Lieutenant Colonel Merrit, and Dr. Hollis.

Then there were the anomalies—the forged detainment order and the second set of forged transfer instructions that would have taken him off the base—if he hadn't collapsed and required emergency surgery.

He turned the page and wrote a name in the center—*Lt. Colonel Andrew R. Dunning.*

No branch assignment, file, or paper trail existed—only a name mentioned by Merrit during her last visit and a signature that didn't match any known personnel records.

He underlined it once, then drew a circle around it and wrote below the notation.

Ghost protocol. Civilian clearance. CIA? Internal CI?

Then, below that, he jotted down some questions.

How many people knew I was here? Who authorized the transfer? Why now?

He tapped the pencil on the edge of the pad, deep in thought, and then resumed writing.

This wasn't idle scribbling. It was reconnaissance in ink—the beginning of a map. Not yet a master plan, but something close to muscle memory. Just as he'd charted safe houses in Saigon and observed patterns in Laos, he understood the nature of operations like this. They began with silence, followed by erasure and bodies.

Someone expected him to be one of them.

A gentle, solitary knock shattered the silence.

He set the pencil aside. "Enter."

The young MP posted outside took a few steps into the room. "Sir, Colonel Cross asked me to inform you that Lieutenant Colonel Merrit will be here within the hour."

Teddy arched an eyebrow. "Is that all, corporal?"

"He said…" The MP hesitated, repeating the words verbatim, "He said you'd probably want to be sitting up when she tells you what she found."

"Did he?"

"Yes, sir."

"Dismissed."

The MP nodded and stepped back, closing the door behind him.

Teddy leaned back against the pillows, the edge of the notepad resting under his fingers. He folded the top closed and slid the notepad beneath the tray, placing his hand on it.

Something had changed. He could feel it. Somewhere, someone had crossed a line, left a trace, and spoken one word too many in the open. Big mistake. Secrets only remain secrets when kept in the shadows. In the light of day, they become evidence.

And Merrit—sharp, relentless, and purposeful—had found it.

They had attempted to kill him twice—once through negligence compounded by silence and once with a needle. While the first time was two stupid guards acting like jackbooted thugs, it still counted. At least for him.

And now the counterattack was beginning.

This time, he wouldn't wait to be dragged from his bed.

This time, he was already awake.

0705 Hours
January 21, 1984
Womack Army Medical Center
Fort Bragg, NC

The door opened with a soft, measured click. There was no announcement or hesitation—only Merrit, already moving with her usual determination and a plain manila folder tucked under her arm. She stepped inside, closed the door, and locked the deadbolt with a flick of her wrist. That signaled everything Teddy needed to know. This was a confidential meeting.

She walked to the bedside without speaking, placed the folder on the bedside table with deliberate care, and looked at him. "I told you I'd bring you a name. Turns out, I brought a face, too."

Teddy sat up straighter, ignoring the twinge deep in his abdomen. "Let's see it."

Merrit opened the folder and flipped it over. Inside was a glossy black-and-white surveillance photo, timestamped and grainy, yet still clear enough. A man in his late forties, clean-cut with a slender frame, wore a zipped-up windbreaker and kept his head down in the hospital corridor near the secure recovery wing. No insignia or ID card was visible, except for a clipped generic temporary clearance badge beneath the jacket lapel.

But Teddy's attention wasn't on the badge. It was on the man. Something about his posture—the tilt of the shoulders—wasn't exactly military—but it looked familiar.

"Do you know him?" Merrit asked.

Teddy studied the photo for a moment longer then shook his head. "No. But I've seen his type many times. Intel spook. CIA? DIA? Maybe a former field operative. He moves like someone who's used to walking out before questions get asked."

"He entered the base under the name Lieutenant Colonel Andrew R. Dunning. The same one used on the transfer orders. The temporary ID was real, issued by the headquarters unit—but the orders were not. Ghosted and burned the moment he left the base. The code he used was issued by an agency that doesn't officially exist."

"Langley?"

"Not directly, as far as I can tell. But close enough to smell like it."

"Why didn't headquarters tag him for additional security checks? Using the same alias twice should have raised a red flag."

"Unknown." She pulled another sheet from the folder and laid it beside the photo. "Base entry records show he was here for exactly three hours. One stop at legal records. One stop at the personnel office where he accessed the secure administration wing and signed another set of transfer orders my office flagged immediately. Then he went to the hospital."

Teddy examined the form—again that name, *Lt. Colonel Andrew R. Dunning*, typed beneath a line of legal jargon that no longer conveyed anything.

Merrit sat in the chair beside him. "There's something else. He didn't come in through the front gate."

"Really? Airfield?"

"Yes. He was flown in under civilian contractor credentials and landed at a restricted airstrip thirty miles to the north on an unmarked transport plane. His escort was waiting on the ground. He never touched base housing and didn't sign in through the security checkpoint."

Teddy exhaled slow and deep. "So whoever wanted me gone didn't just have a motive—they had access, a large budget, and a high enough clearance level to pull it off."

"And the confidence to think no one would dig." Merrit tapped her finger on the photo. "But they didn't count on your appendix. And they sure as hell didn't count on me."

He looked at her then—not as a lawyer, not as someone wearing a rank—but as someone he could finally trust. Not because she was kind, treated him with respect, or because she had spared him, but because she was stubborn enough to walk through fire with a clipboard in one hand and a warrant in the other.

Teddy pointed at the folder. "Are you still going through the records?"

"I'm just getting started," she said. "But this time, I'm not alone. Colonel Cross is backing the investigation now. Quietly. He's already flagged his own personnel files for review. We're building something that can't be ignored by the brass."

"And when it is?"

"Then we burn it down."

For the first time in days, Teddy allowed himself a genuine breath. Not relief—but focus and precision. It marked the beginning of something that resembled momentum.

"They aimed to erase me," he said. "Now they're leaving a trail of breadcrumbs right back to the people holding the match."

Merrit nodded. "And I plan to follow every damn one of them."

0001 Hours
January 22, 1984
Womack Army Medical Center
Fort Bragg, NC

The late shift had changed over two hours earlier. From his hospital bed, Teddy began mapping the rhythm of the night by sound alone—shoes sliding along the waxed tile, the low murmur of nurses exchanging updates outside the ICU doors, and the soft hum of the heart monitor echoing behind him. Even the occasional muted conversation between the MPs stationed in the hallway had developed a pattern by now. Yet, beneath it all, something felt off.

It wasn't just the ache pulsing behind the fresh surgical dressing stretched across his abdomen. It wasn't even the low, simmering fatigue that came from too many nights with little to no sleep. What had changed was the very air itself—something in the cadence of the hospital. A pattern he recognized from his time in hostile terrain. War never slept.

The smiles from the new nurses seemed overly polite and rehearsed. A hesitation lingered in their eyes—like they were reading from a script written by someone else. Earlier, a technician he didn't recognize entered the room, checked the IV infusion pump, and left again. He moved like he belonged but never made eye contact. His ID badge shimmered in the light as he turned, but Teddy hadn't seen a name, rank, or service branch—only plastic and glare.

That wasn't treatment but movement. And it had been practiced to blend in.

Teddy hadn't sounded the alarm. Not yet. His body was still healing, and any attempt to rise too quickly could cause something to tear loose. However, his mind remained sharp, and every instinct he had honed through decades of combat and covert operations urged him to wait, watch, and confirm his suspicions.

Ten minutes later, the same man returned. He moved with the same ease, entering the room with the confidence that it belonged to him. He didn't greet his patient or engage in polite conversation. Instead, he walked to the IV pole and examined the tubing. Teddy didn't move or blink, but he noticed the man's hand reaching into the lab coat pocket—not toward the cabinet at the foot of the bed where the locked medication was stored, but inside the jacket itself.

What emerged was a new bag of clear fluid—a standard 1000cc IV bag—labeled and sealed. However, Teddy had changed enough IVs in field clinics while helping the nurses in Vietnam to know what to look for. The label appeared genuine, but the plastic beneath it was wrinkled in an unusual way. The seal was loose at the top corner, and there was no barcode, scanning strip, or catalog number. This was not something that would be logged in the hospital's automated system.

The man clamped the IV line to stop the flow of fluids.

Teddy didn't speak. Not yet. The pain in his abdomen was rising again, connected to his breathing, but he remained still, pushing his hand under the blanket. The line was nearly switched now. He heard the subtle click of the clasp disengaging.

"That line's already been flushed," Teddy said.

The intruder froze, but only for a brief moment—long enough to confirm everything. Then he looked up, his face calm and composed. "Doctor Hollis adjusted your fluid rate. These are the new instructions on your chart, Colonel Roosevelt."

"Hollis went off shift two hours ago," Teddy said. "I watched him walk out."

The faintest twitch of tension pulsed along the man's jaw. His fingers tightened around the IV tubing. He didn't reach for a weapon—but Teddy knew it was inevitable.

Teddy found the nurse call button concealed beneath the blanket with his thumb. He pressed it once, then pressed it again.

The intruder didn't panic. Instead, he turned and slid his hand under his white lab coat.

Then the door swung open, slamming hard against the hinges.

Cross entered first, quickly scanning the room. Merrit followed closely behind, still in uniform and holding her pistol as she crossed the threshold.

The man reached into his coat again—but Cross was quicker. He crossed the room in three strides, wrapping one arm around the intruder's shoulders while slamming the other against his wrist, pinning it flat against the metal cabinet by the door.

A dull *crack* rang out, followed by the clatter of a metal object hitting the floor—a filled syringe with a bent needle. The safety cap must have dislodged on impact.

Merrit moved straight to the IV pole. She yanked the mysterious bag free, lifted it toward the light, and examined the label. "Get the guards. Secure him now."

Cross didn't let him go. "Who sent you?"

The man didn't respond or struggle. He stood there, breathing evenly, either highly trained to ignore everyone or believing the moment had already passed him by. His expression was blank, like someone who had come to realize that the consequences no longer mattered.

Teddy didn't try to sit up. He couldn't. The shock had sent a wave of heat through his chest, and the effort to remain conscious was already causing sweat to trickle down his neck. Nevertheless, he kept his eyes open and watched everything.

This hadn't been a genuine attempt, not entirely. It served as a test of reach, a probe to remind him that no matter how many guards were stationed outside the door or how many doctors stitched him back together again, they could still enter the room. Inside the system. Inside the chain of command.

He let his head sink back into the pillows, exhaling through clenched teeth. His stomach churned from the pain, the adrenaline rush, and the struggle to remain still while every muscle in his body screamed to act.

But he didn't flinch or look away because now he knew the truth.

This wasn't the kill shot. It was the warning.

And the next one wouldn't be quiet.

The door had barely shut behind the intruder when silence rushed in. It pressed against the walls like a weight. Not peace—just the absence of immediate danger. A kind of waiting stillness enveloped the space. Teddy remained exactly where he was, every muscle locked, his breathing shallow and uneven, and his heart still pounding like he had just sprinted across a battlefield. He wasn't cold, but his hands shook. Not from fear, but from the crash that always followed when the adrenaline stopped carrying the weight.

His fingers involuntarily curled into the sheet beneath him. He tried to straighten them, but they wouldn't budge. His legs trembled under the blanket. Each breath scraped against the tight band of pain across his midsection, and he could feel his pulse racing too fast in his throat. The edges of the room began to fade into a murky gray, the fluorescent lights unable to reach him.

The pressure in his chest tightened, not from panic—but rather from physiology—the fight or flight response. The familiar sensation of his body catching up to what his mind already knew—the cost had come due.

Teddy shifted his butt to reposition his weight in the bed, searching for a more comfortable position. The pain struck him so hard that it stole every ounce of air from his lungs. It wasn't the sharp tear of a suture giving way—at least not yet. But it felt close. Deep. Hot. No longer surface-level. Something internal had started to give.

A low moan escaped from the back of his throat before he could stop it. He squeezed his eyes shut. Then he heard Merrit's voice—low and urgent. "Get Hollis. Now."

She moved into his line of sight, one hand already resting on his shoulder to steady him. Not pushing him down. The pressure was firm and constant, and he realized only then how much he was leaning forward—how close he had come to curling up into a fetal position without even realizing it.

"Colonel Roosevelt. Stay still. Don't move," Merrit said.

He tried to answer, but nothing came out. His throat felt raw and dry, and his mouth had a thick, metallic taste. Sweat clung to his forehead, sliding down the curve of his jaw. Nausea followed—slow, crawling, and familiar. He gritted his teeth against it but failed. His stomach twisted into a hard knot, and his body seized in response as frothy vomit dribbled from his mouth.

Then, the door burst open again.

Hollis was by his side within seconds, his sleeves already rolled up. "What's his blood pressure?"

"Ninety over fifty. Pulse one-thirty and climbing," a nurse said, standing near the monitor.

"He's decompensating. Get the crash cart just in case. Run a line of normal saline wide open. I want fluids in him now."

Hollis pressed against the surgical site to confirm what Teddy had already suspected. The dressing was soaked, not with fresh blood, but with serosanguinous fluid—the type indicating internal strain, stress pulling on healing tissue. It was spreading quickly.

"No signs of rupture yet," Hollis said urgently, "but we're one wrong movement away from tearing something critical. His vitals are on the edge of a cliff."

A nurse arrived and replaced the IV with a saline bolus. Another nurse examined the drainage site and prepared an antiemetic as Teddy clenched his jaw to fight off a second wave of nausea.

"Hold off on any narcotics," Hollis said. "He needs clarity until we stabilize him. We'll sedate later if the pain spikes beyond tolerable levels."

Teddy forced his eyes open. Merrit hadn't moved. Her hand remained on his shoulder, her eyes fixed on him with that same unreadable tension she displayed in court—but now stripped down to its rawest form. This wasn't a formality. This was personal.

"The IV bag..." Teddy managed to say.

Merrit leaned in closer. "Did he connect it?"

He shook his head. "No. Tried. Didn't finish."

She nodded and stepped back, giving Hollis room to work.

Teddy could now hear the steady drone of the heart monitor—too fast. It sounded disjointed and erratic, and it was increasing again.

The cold from the saline bolus and the wide-open IV line rushed through his veins. It helped, but only enough to provide a little relief. His stomach still burned, and his chest continued to ache every time he inhaled more than a shallow breath. The effort of holding still was becoming as intense as the effort of moving.

"Easy," Hollis said. He was near his head now. "You're not dying, Colonel Roosevelt. But your body's redlining. We need to take control of your blood pressure before anything gives. You've pushed your body too far. That spike in your heart rate and pressure nearly blew out the sutures we reinforced after the last bleed. If you hadn't hit the call button when you did, and if we hadn't acted quickly..."

Teddy nodded. He could feel his blood pulsing behind his eyes now—throbbing at the edges of his vision.

Hollis gripped his shoulder. "I'm authorizing a low-dose beta blocker to bring your heart rate down. No opioids yet. Once you're stable, I'll give you something to sleep—but for now, I need you lucid."

Teddy didn't argue. He lacked the energy even though he wanted to respond, deflect, or maybe even smirk and say something clever. But all he could do was lie there, sweating, while his body recalibrated.

The nurse adjusted the second line—another clear fluid joining the first. Teddy felt the cold seeping deeper into his arm, helping to calm his mind. Not peace, but clarity. Or the beginnings of it.

His body was failing as it struggled to survive something it wasn't prepared for. The second attempt had not succeeded, but the cost it left behind kept growing beneath the surface.

And if he wasn't careful—if they weren't—there wouldn't need to be a third one.

He lay still, breathing shallowly, his eyes half-closed as the sedation began to take effect. Not the deep plunge into unconsciousness from before—just enough to dull the body's panic and stop the spiral. His breathing started to stabilize, each inhale no longer chased by fire. Warmth flowed through his veins, easing the tremors in his limbs and softening the sharp edges of pain in his gut.

Merrit stepped closer once again, watching the monitors. "We've got you."

Teddy nodded. His heart was slowing down. The tremors in his hands were subsiding, but his mind kept racing.

They hadn't killed him.

But they had nearly forced his body to finish the job. He could feel it—the weight of exhaustion, strain, and a body barely holding together.

"You're going to sleep," Hollis said, holding up a filled syringe. "And this time, you don't get to argue."

Teddy's last thought before he slipped into unconsciousness was not about the assassin, nor about Merrit or Cross, or even the war beyond the walls. It was about the bag—the unlabeled bag. And the realization that next time, they might not miss.

CHAPTER 13

0050 Hours
January 22, 1984
Womack Army Medical Center
Fort Bragg, NC

The hallway outside the secure recovery wing was dim and quiet, bathed in soft amber light. Just down the corridor, two MPs stood guard outside Colonel Roosevelt's door, their stances rigid and expressions unreadable. Neither Merrit nor Cross spoke until they were well out of earshot.

Merrit stopped next to a row of unused wheelchairs and leaned against the wall, still holding the plastic evidence bag. Inside was the IV bag—the one the impostor had tried to connect to Colonel Roosevelt's IV line. The label was clean, the tubing standard, but it lacked a barcode, inventory sticker, or any sign that it had originated from hospital pharmacy stock.

Cross faced her with his arms folded over his chest. He looked like a man who had been forced to confront the reality that the system he defended wasn't just compromised—it was now actively working against him.

"I had a lab tech run what's in this bag through an initial tox screen already," Merrit said. "It's not saline. It's Lactated Ringer's laced with potassium chloride. Enough to induce cardiac arrest if it were rapidly introduced into Colonel Roosevelt's central circulation."

Cross didn't respond right away. He stared down the hallway toward the door that led to the hospital wing they no longer trusted. "Would it have worked?"

"Yes," she said. "And it would've looked like a surgical complication. Like his heart just gave out. Stress, age, post-op trauma, elevated pain response—it would've gone unnoticed without an autopsy and an extensive tox panel."

"And the syringe? Did you check that as well?"

"Yes. It's standard Humulin insulin. Probably the backup plan. It's injected subcutaneously. If given in the amount in that syringe to someone who is not diabetic, it can be extremely dangerous and life-threatening by dropping the blood sugar levels. That would also show up as a post-surgical complication."

"Geez." Cross shook his head. "If you hadn't noticed that blinking call light above his door and gone in with me?"

"We would have discovered Colonel Roosevelt dead. I came back early because I had second thoughts about the surveillance footage. I thought maybe the infiltrator would double back to try again. And he did." She glanced down at the IV bag and slid it into a second evidence pouch before sealing it shut. "They're desperate now. This wasn't a professional cleanup. It was panic. He was still in the room when we arrived. That's not how these people work when they're in control of the situation."

Cross released a slow exhale, his eyes still fixed down the hall. "So, they're not in control anymore."

"No, and we never were," Merrit said. "And that makes them even more dangerous."

They stood in silence for a moment afterward. Just two officers illuminated by the dim light of a corridor, trapped in the narrowing space between duty and something more sinister. The weight of it lingered between them—not quite guilt, but an unsettling awareness that the war they were now part of was one their uniforms couldn't protect them from.

"I've got a list of personnel who've come on and off the base under temporary clearance in the last thirty days. No one's flagged it yet because most of those records are classified under contractor-level authority, not DoD. But I've got someone on the inside who still owes me a favor," Cross said.

"Pull the records," Merrit said. "Quietly. I want names, aliases, photos, and every piece of paper they left behind. I'll handle the legal firewall."

He nodded. "And the guards?"

"They stay. We rotate them every four hours. Background checks, no MP school rookies. I want only combat MOSs. People who've seen enough action to follow orders without second-guessing."

"Do you really think they'll try again?"

"I think they already know they've failed. What I don't know is whether they've decided to cut their losses…or just go louder."

Cross didn't flinch. "And if they go louder?"

"Then I take this investigation public," Merrit said. "Not quietly or carefully. I walk into a Pentagon briefing room with a complete lab analysis of what was in that IV bag, syringe, and a medical report from Hollis. I hand it to the first member of the civilian press corps I see."

Cross nodded, his mouth twitching—not quite a smile but close. "You're serious."

"I'm past serious," Merrit said. "They nearly killed a highly decorated command rank officer in a U.S. Army hospital. And they would have done it while I was sitting at a desk five hundred feet away writing affidavits. No more second chances."

1230 Hours
January 22, 1984
Womack Army Medical Center
Fort Bragg, NC

Waking came slower this time. Not like before—no sharp jolts of light, no choking pull into the present. Just the gradual rise of sensation from the dark—the faint weight of blankets over his chest, the distant hum of machinery, and the steady ache behind his ribs reminding him that his body was still repairing itself. The pain felt different now—deeper and duller. Not the raw stab of something fresh, but the slow, grinding soreness of trauma packed down beneath layers of gauze and stitches.

His mind surfaced first. Then he opened his eyes and blinked. The ceiling tiles came into focus. Teddy waited and turned his head, aware of the tug in his abdomen. The pain didn't surge like before. It remained steady—close and familiar.

He wasn't alone. Someone else was in the room. He sensed it before he saw it—a quiet, still presence resting at the edge of his awareness. Slowly, he turned his head and saw Colonel Cross sitting beside the bed.

Colonel Cross wasn't posturing. His arms were crossed over his chest, and one leg rested over the other. He didn't look like a watchdog or a jailer this time—just a man keeping watch for reasons he hadn't yet explained.

Cross must have noticed that Teddy was awake, sitting up a bit straighter, and giving him a subtle nod. It wasn't formal, nor was it forced either.

Teddy leaned his head back on the pillow and let the silence linger. He took a slow breath, feeling the bandages shift against his abdomen. There was still soreness there, but no tearing heat. That alone told him he'd made it through the worst—again.

"Second time in the hospital," he said, his voice a broken whisper.

Cross didn't pretend not to know what he meant. "Yeah, and the last one was clean and professional. Would've passed for a post-op complication."

Teddy didn't ask who or how. It didn't matter yet. "Did Merrit or your interrogators get anything from him?"

Cross shook his head. "No. Unfortunately. He vanished right under our noses. We had him cuffed and isolated in a high-security cell. Twenty minutes later, he was gone. The cameras stopped working for five minutes. There was no evidence of how he escaped or a paper trail of his release from custody."

Teddy allowed that information to settle in the back of his mind for a moment. His eyes drifted to the wall, tracing the pale streaks of afternoon light filtering through the blinds. He didn't need to vocalize his next question. Cross already had the answer ready.

"Merrit's still digging into everything. However, we're beyond the point where paper trails will save us."

Teddy exhaled slowly, letting the sound escape past his teeth. "Why are you here?"

Cross didn't flinch at the implication. "Because I put you in that cell. And because I should have seen this coming. You're not under guard anymore. Merrit made it official this morning. You're not being held under detainment protocol."

"No charges?"

"Not yet. The investigation is still active, but the focus is shifting. People are starting to ask the right questions."

A long pause hung between them. Not strained, just heavy.

"What happens next?" Teddy asked.

"If they try again," Cross said, "we'll see it coming. We've locked everything down. But if they don't—if they go quiet…"

"They're repositioning," Teddy said.

Cross nodded. "Exactly."

Silence enveloped the room. This time, it felt less like emptiness and more like a mutual understanding. No truce or handshake—just two men finally seeing the same battlefield.

Cross stood, brushing the wrinkles out of his pants. "I'm not leaving you alone again."

Teddy didn't reply. He didn't have to.

The room felt different now. Not safe. But watched.

For the first time since this started, that was something he could accept.

CHAPTER 14

1745 Hours
January 22, 1984
Womack Army Medical Center
Fort Bragg, NC

The light outside the window had changed again, softening into the deep amber that always appeared just before sunset. Teddy hadn't spoken for several minutes. Cross had moved to the window, standing in silence with his arms crossed, still absorbing the weight of what they'd both said. The hospital room was quiet—no monitors beeping, no nurse interrupting, no threat looming at the door.

"I need to make a call," Teddy said.

Cross turned around. "To whom? Merrit's already set up a secure channel to headquarters—if there's something you want moved through JAG—"

"Not JAG," Teddy said, cutting him off. "Not headquarters."

"Then who?"

Teddy reached for the notepad on the bedside table—still there from earlier, with the pages turned to the notes Merrit had left. He slid it closer, flipped to a blank sheet of paper, and wrote two important lines.

212-555-7483
Do not trace.

Cross moved closer to the bed and read the phone number aloud. "212-555-7483." He glanced at Teddy. "I don't recognize the number. Who is this?"

Teddy shook his head. "Someone who doesn't exist on your chain of command. Or Merrit's. Or Langley's, for that matter."

Cross didn't ask a follow-up question, probably because he knew Teddy would provide some sort of explanation.

"This isn't just about one forged order," Teddy said. "Or a ghost clearance. This was run through a dead loop with a live asset. That means someone used deep access to fake something clean enough to fool command-level authorizations—and they used it on me."

"You're saying this came from inside…but not inside any one branch of the government."

"I'm saying the people who tried to kill me aren't new at this. And they're not going to stop just because someone took their syringe away." Teddy looked Cross square in the eyes. "There's a different kind of war happening here, Vince. You and Merrit are on the edges of it. You can see the smoke, not the fire. I've lived in it. Operated in it. Buried people in it."

The room became as silent as a church at midnight.

Cross cocked his head. "If we let you make this call, what's going to happen?"

"That depends on who picks up," Teddy said. "But it won't be official. And it won't come through a desk."

Cross stared at him for a moment longer. Then he nodded and stepped back toward the door. "I'll get Merrit. You tell her. She'll decide how much rope to give you."

Teddy smiled. "She's smarter than you give her credit for."

"I'm starting to figure that out," Cross muttered as he walked out.

The door clicked as it shut behind him.

Teddy sighed and glanced down at the number again. His hand hovered above it for a moment before tapping it with his finger. He hadn't contacted this person in years.

But if anyone knew who was orchestrating events from the shadowy corners of the world—who was signing kill orders without documentation, trace, or even a whisper of jurisdiction—it would be the voice on the other end of that line.

And if not?

Then they were already in more trouble than he realized.

1830 Hours
January 22, 1984
Womack Army Medical Center
Fort Bragg, NC

The knock on the door was soft—a courtesy rather than a question. Teddy looked up from the notepad as the door opened and Merrit stepped inside first, Cross just behind her. She had changed since this morning. Her uniform was pressed, and she held a briefcase in one hand. The weight on her shoulders seemed heavier than before, and her expression remained focused and unreadable.

Cross moved to the wall and stayed there, silent.

Merrit approached the bedside and gazed down at the note. She didn't ask if the number was real, just looked at Teddy. "What's on the other end of that line?"

Teddy didn't hesitate to answer her question. "A man who only answers it if the world's about to tilt in the wrong direction."

"And if it tilts?"

"Then he does what he has always done. He tilts it back."

Merrit stood there for a moment longer, contemplating her answer. Then she set the briefcase on the bedside table, opened it, and pulled out a secure landline phone. She placed it beside him and plugged the cord into a wall jack behind the bed.

"I'll authorize the line," she said. "Once. You get five minutes."

Teddy nodded. "That's all I'll need. Maybe not even that much."

She didn't move away to give him any privacy. Neither did Cross.

Teddy reached for the handset slowly—he was still stiff and in pain. He closed his fingers around the handset, feeling it heavier than it should have felt, and brought it to his ear. With his other hand, he dialed the number from memory without even looking at the keypad.

The phone rang once, then again. After that, silence. No click. No voice.

Just the unmistakable sound of a line being connected without any fanfare.

Teddy waited five seconds as per protocol, a failsafe in case someone ever managed to obtain the number. "This is Theodore Roosevelt IV. Call sign Rough Rider. Authorization delta-one-niner-black. Condition—compromised. Confirm legacy protocol."

There was a pause—nothing but dead air.

Then a voice came through, old, smooth, and as dry as dust. "You're not dead."

"Not yet," Teddy replied.

Another pause.

"Who hit you?"

"Unknown assets," he said. "Dunning alias. Clearance forged. Attempted termination through medical infiltration."

The voice didn't respond for several seconds. "Is the asset secure?"

"I am," Teddy replied. "But not invisible and medically compromised."

"Understood," the voice said. "Message received."

And just like that, the line went dead. No goodbye. No promises. Just the silence of something ancient moving in the darkness.

Teddy placed the receiver back in its cradle, his hand lingering on the cool plastic for a moment longer than necessary. Then he looked up at Merrit.

"What now?" she asked.

"Now we wait."

"For what?" Cross asked.

Teddy smiled. "For the part they didn't plan for."

CHAPTER 15

1835 Hours
January 22, 1984
Black Site Unlisted Facility
Somewhere Outside Washington, D.C

The room was small, windowless, and cold enough to prevent paper from curling. On the far wall hung a single analog clock that ticked with nuclear precision. The only light came from a brass lamp over a wide oak desk, casting long shadows across the surface. There were no photographs or personal touches—only a black phone, a worn Rolodex, and a legal pad turned sideways without any writing on it.

When the phone rang, the man at the desk, call sign Zebra, remained still through the first and second rings. He waited until the third to answer, cradling it against his shoulder as he listened without speaking.

The voice came through clear and unmistakable. "This is Theodore Roosevelt IV. Call sign Rough Rider. Authorization delta-one-niner-black. Condition—compromised. Confirm legacy protocol."

The man didn't write it down. He didn't need to. He'd memorized the phrase years ago—back when it was created, back when Theodore Roosevelt IV was one of the few names they kept entirely off paper.

He didn't ask for details, just said, "You're not dead."

And when the voice confirmed what the world wasn't meant to know, he leaned back in his chair. It had been a long time since that protocol was invoked. Most of the people who created it were either dead, retired, or buried in Senate subcommittees. It was supposed to be obsolete—forgotten.

But Zebra always knew better. Some things never expire.

He hung up without saying a word, turned in his chair, and opened a drawer beneath the desk. Inside lay a phone without a keypad, only a keycard slot worn down from years of use. He inserted a card from his wallet, waited for the green light, and pressed a single button. It rang once.

Then he spoke. "Rough Rider is live. Legacy protocol activated. We're back in play."

He paused.

For the first time in a decade, he issued the order that only five men on the planet were authorized to say. "Initiate counter-separation."

1838 Hours
January 22, 1984
Womack Army Medical Center
Fort Bragg, NC

The silence after the call lingered for several seconds. Merrit stared at Teddy, her expression still locked in that courtroom focus. Cross had once again retreated to the corner of the room, arms crossed and now watching him with something deeper than mere curiosity. It was wariness, perhaps even a hint of fear.

"What is legacy protocol?" Merrit asked.

Teddy pushed himself up in the bed, trying to find a comfortable position, still aching but now calm. Steady. His body felt weak, but his mind had returned home. This was a language he hadn't spoken in years, yet one he hadn't forgotten. "It's a dead man's switch for black world cleanup. A call you make when everything else is compromised. Not for backup. Not for help."

"Then for what?" Cross asked.

"For recognition," Teddy said. "It tells them the asset is still alive and has been marked for termination from the inside."

Merrit's brow furrowed. "Them? Who exactly is *them*?"

"You don't want the real answer to that question," Teddy said. "You want the version that fits on a memo. But if you're asking who picked up that phone, I don't know. He's not listed anywhere. No office. No branch. No agency. Not anymore. No one knows the complete sequence or the location of the players to protect it."

Cross furrowed his brow and tightened his jaw, clearly ready to argue. His eyes narrowed, revealing a flicker of frustration, and he took a deep breath. "So what happens now?"

Teddy stared at the far wall, ignoring the ticking clock and the window. He focused on the empty space where something unseen had already begun to move. "Now they look at the board again. Now they ask themselves—what else did we miss?"

"And do they come to help?" Merrit asked.

"No," Teddy said. "They don't help. They only adjust the positions of all the pieces."

A beat passed. He looked at her, and this time, there was no mask—just the quiet clarity of a man who knew exactly what he'd invited back into the world. "They thought they were playing chess. But they left the wrong piece on the board."

1838 Hours
January 22, 1984
Black Site
Unknown Underground Location

The order had been received less than three minutes ago at Operation Subnet Echo. In a facility that did not officially exist, three stories underground in an abandoned nuclear missile silo, a sealed terminal unlocked itself with a code assigned to one phrase only—*delta-one-niner-black.*

The room was silent except for the blinking of electronic relays and the soft hum of filtered air. Fluorescent light illuminated the spines of inactive dossiers—names not spoken in decades and operations long erased from governmental budgets.

One file slid along its track and landed at the base of a terminal desk where a man known only as *Archivist* placed a hand over it. "Confirmed."

He turned to the woman beside him—*Oracle*, older and gray-haired, seated in front of a flickering CRT monitor, her eyes scanning a matrix of incoming subnets.

"Asset is active," he stated.

She didn't reply right away. The screen reflected in her glasses as the lines of data crawled upward like wisps of smoke.

"Then we're past the point of no return," Oracle said. "Everything buried is now exposed. Time since extraction?"

"Over twelve years."

"Then it's going to be messy."

Archivist gave her a dry half-smile. "It already is. There've been three attempts."

"From internal?"

"Unclear. Likely a hybrid. Private backend financed with an active high clearance level. Not standard Company wet boys or hired assassins."

Oracle turned and pushed her rolling chair away from the desk. "And they missed?"

"They underestimated him."

She studied the monitor screen where a list of names began to appear— partial hits, cross-referenced data across burn IDs, agency shells, and accounts believed to be decommissioned. One of the names near the top started blinking.

DUNNING, ANDREW R. (Alias)
Origin: Civilian Liaison Group D-7 – Sable Protocol
Inactive Since: 1979
Reactivation: Unauthorized – 48 hours ago

She tapped the screen. "There."

Archivist nodded. "Rebuilt credentials. The ones who sent him thought no one would dig into his true identity."

"They didn't expect Theodore Roosevelt IV to still be the Rough Rider." Oracle stood up, moved to the far wall, and pressed her palm against a concealed biometric plate. A sealed drawer opened revealing a simple black briefcase. She pulled it out. "You're going to need this," she said.

Archivist took it without asking what was inside. He didn't need to. He was no longer tracking the man they once thought was gone. Now he was running interference for him. It was time to invoke Directive Seven-Two—the last firewall between the truth and those who thought they'd buried it forever.

Unlike the Legacy Protocol which signaled an asset's survival and reactivation, Directive Seven-Two was unique. It dismantled the cover of any operation or individual threatening to eliminate critical assets to safeguard its own existence by releasing controlled intelligence leaks, executing targeted financial disruptions, and implementing asset-shielding countermeasures buried so deeply that they circumvented conventional oversight. Known to have been invoked only once prior to today.

CHAPTER 16

1747 Hours
January 23, 1984
Womack Army Medical Center
Fort Bragg, NC

In the quiet of the hospital room, Teddy lay still. The light was dim with the orange-red sunset filtering through the drawn blinds. The sedatives had long since faded from his bloodstream, but the fatigue lingered like smoke—low, deep, and familiar. The ache in his abdomen was sharper today but not unbearable, just enough to remind him of the last time he underestimated how far someone would go to silence him.

But this time he wasn't just sitting idle.

The notepad on the bedside table was no longer blank. Over the past hour, he'd been filling it with names. Not suspects—assets. Former contacts. People who owed him or those he had once protected from the same kind of machinery now grinding toward him.

He didn't write down any addresses. Each of them knew how to be found when the right signal came through the coded frequencies.

A few names had slashes next to them—slant marks he used solely for those who remained active, dangerous, and capable of moving through shadows without leaving a ripple. These deep-cover agents didn't need permission to act, only direction. These weren't favors—they were fire alarms, unspoken oaths from a time before politics transformed covert work into accounting exercises.

He still didn't have his full strength back—not even close. However, his instincts were sharp and alert to what would come next.

This wasn't the part where they sent in another man wearing a lab coat with a poisoned IV.

That strategy had already failed.

Now they would withdraw and reevaluate the situation. They would hide behind layers of proxy orders and compartmentalized deniability. The next contact wouldn't arrive with a weapon. Instead, it would come through a leak, a rumor, or a discreetly altered file designed to portray him as medically unstable. A history rewritten just enough to justify what came next.

He knew the pattern by heart, having used it a few times.

Discredit.
Isolate.
Disappear—just clean enough to bury the target.

If that didn't work, they would completely abandon the pretense. They would confront him with a great deal of noise. No witnesses and no survivors. Collateral damage would be authorized at the highest levels.

Merrit and Cross had bought him time—but time in this world was like air in a collapsing mine shaft. It didn't last long. The longer he breathed it in, the harder it became to distinguish between oxygen and smoke.

He flipped the page in the notebook and started writing again.

This time it wasn't a list of names but a message—short, encoded, block printing in stiff, even strokes—like a man filling out a customs form. Innocuous to the untrained eye, but to the right pair of eyes, it was a signal. A breach notice. A declaration that someone was in play who wasn't supposed to be.

The last line contained a phone number—not one that could be traced through base communications or any regional switchboard. It belonged to a long-dead operator from Ankara who had rerouted it through three nonexistent embassies and a relay station concealed under a front company in Zürich.

CODE: 113-ALPHA-RED
CONDITION: LEGACY BREACH
CONTACT: BX-17420-6QF
212-555-0851

Beneath it, Teddy wrote three words in all capital letters.

DO NOT TRACE

He capped the pen, tore the page free, and folded it twice—first lengthwise and then crosswise, creating clean, sharp creases. He slipped it under the corner of the empty food tray on his bedside table just as the door creaked and one of the night nurses walked by without entering the room.

No one would notice the paper unless they were meant to.

Teddy leaned back into the pillows, feeling the strain in his midsection tighten as he moved. His breathing slowed. He gazed out the window where the sky had darkened, and the stars were obscured by the glow of sodium lights on the tarmac.

They weren't going to kill him in a hospital bed.

They weren't going to drag him under while he slept.

If they wanted him gone, they needed to make it loud.

By the time they tried again, someone else would already be watching.

1910 Hours
January 23, 1984
JAG Operations Wing
Office of Lt. Colonel Merrit
Fort Bragg, NC

The message arrived through a secure channel on the computer in Merrit's office. It didn't originate from headquarters or anyone in the chain of command. Instead, it came through a routed line labeled "monitor only" connected to a communications filter that Merrit had installed herself to track unauthorized inquiries into Colonel Roosevelt's status.

The flag wasn't an urgent alert, just a ping, like a submarine measuring the distance to an enemy combatant.

She opened it out of habit, expecting yet another gentle inquiry from someone in Personnel or a curious junior officer probing the limits of their clearance.

It wasn't a name but a phrase.

Four words.

You are not alone.

No signature, source, or location—only those words blinking in green letters at the center of the dark screen like a shadow cast by something just out of frame.

She neither blinked nor spoke.

On the other side of the desk, Cross leaned forward in his chair. "What is it?"

She turned the monitor to face him.

"Do you recognize that?" Cross asked.

"No, I don't," Merrit said. "But it's not for me. It's a signal, simple and controlled. Planted in my computer to confirm they're listening."

"Who's *they*?"

She shrugged. "The legacy protocol, I guess. The ones who answered Colonel Roosevelt's call."

Cross rubbed his hand over his face. "So we're not running this anymore."

"I don't think we ever were." Merrit closed the screen, locked the terminal, and stood. "We stay the course. But from now on, assume nothing is private or safe. And no one who asks about Colonel Theodore Roosevelt IV is doing it casually."

Cross nodded. "Understood."

They didn't speak again as they left the room, but both felt it—the ground shifting beneath their feet like an earthquake ready to erupt. They were no longer just protecting a man.

They stood on the brink of a shadow war.

0300 Hours
January 24, 1984
A Safehouse with No Address.
South of Lisbon, Portugal

The man known only as Nero who received the coded signal, hadn't heard from Rough Rider in thirteen years—at least not directly.

But he kept an ear attuned to old ghosts, and when one whispered, he knew how to listen. The message had been embedded in a decommissioned broadcast from a defunct military radio relay—a signal woven into the final moments of a false weather report that aired for no one.

Except for him.

Nero turned down the radio, got up from his seat, and opened a narrow drawer concealed behind the shelving at the back of the room. Inside lay a small field case—military green with worn edges and taped hinges.

He unlocked it with the key he wore around his neck.

The case held a passport, three unregistered security tokens, and an envelope with a black line drawn across the front.

He hadn't needed the envelope for years, but he took it anyway.

Then he picked up the satellite phone, one of the few in the world outside of intelligence agencies and research labs, and dialed a number that no one was supposed to remember. He waited for two rings. "Rough Rider is active."

The voice on the other end didn't ask for clarification. It simply said in a staccato computerized tone, "Proceed to contingency."

0400 Hours
January 24, 1984
A Safehouse with No Address.
South of Lisbon, Portugal

Nero moved with quiet efficiency, each action practiced and each choice deliberate. The field case was already packed, and its contents had been checked twice—no electronics newer than ten years old. After one final wipe of the internal memory, he left the satellite phone behind, placed it in a steel container, and slid it into the fireplace where a layer of ash still lingered from last winter.

He turned on the gas, struck a match, and tossed it into the fireplace. It crackled as a brief flicker of orange flame appeared, followed by the smell of melted plastic.

Nero didn't burn the safehouse. It was too valuable for that. Instead, he left a single strand of wire behind the doorknob—tensioned so precisely that only someone trained would even notice the release. If anyone showed up before he returned, they'd either walk into it…or walk away quickly.

He drove a discreet Renault into Lisbon, blending in with the early market traffic. The forged passport he carried was under the name *Thomas Wakefield*, cleared through multiple diplomatic checks and tagged for limited security surveillance—just enough to render it unremarkable.

Nero arrived at the waterfront thirty minutes later, passed through a gate manned only by a man with a one-eyed mixed breed dog and a clipboard, and boarded a vessel registered out of Belize. The boat was already prepared, the crew paid in cash and informed only that their passenger was an American consultant heading for Casablanca. No questions asked.

He remained silent as they cast off. This wasn't a mission. It was a repayment of a past debt.

Theodore Roosevelt IV, call sign Rough Rider, had once led him out of a black-site holding cell in northern Sumatra, bleeding, concussed, and carrying the weight of three blown covers on his back. Roosevelt had never explained why. Now it was Nero's turn to return the favor.

2230 Hours
January 24, 1984
Womack Army Medical Center
Fort Bragg, NC

The lights in the room had been dimmed again, not from sedation this time but out of habit—an intentional quiet established by the night shift to help with what little rest the patient could manage.

Teddy wasn't asleep. The pillows behind his shoulders were propped at just the right angle to allow him to breathe without straining the stitches beneath the bandages, and he'd found a rhythm in it. Slow, shallow breaths—controlled—a kind of negotiated truce with the pain.

The IV infusion pump hissed and clicked at intervals, a mechanical breath out of sync with his own. Somewhere down the hall, boots clunked on the tile floor, the tread steady and low, part of the late-night watch rotation. Familiar sounds, and reassuring—maybe. But they didn't fool him. Not now.

He lay still, arms crossed over his chest, eyes half-open, muscles taut from the weight of fatigue. Not because he was guarding himself—but because he was remembering. Not the pain or the faces, but the structure of it all. The architecture of what had been done.

It was more than just an attack. The entire operation had been coordinated, timed, and layered.

The call. The forged orders. The silence from the brass at headquarters. The overly meticulous assassination attempts in the recovery wing. It was never about fear, but about complete erasure. Disappearance without resistance.

However, they had failed.

And now they were stalling for time, watching for his response and waiting to see what else he had to offer.

He allowed the stillness to stretch as he lay motionless until a soft knock at the door broke the silence.

Not loud or tentative. Just a single firm knock followed by a pause. The door eased open a moment later, and the young MP on night duty stepped inside. His expression was unreadable, and his posture was both professional and relaxed. No hand on his sidearm and no extra words. Just something folded in his hand.

"This came by courier, sir," the MP said. "Dropped at the west gate. No name, vehicle, or note on the log. Gone before the gate team could catch a license plate." He moved closer to the bed and held out the note.

Teddy reached out and took the piece of paper from the soldier's hand.

The MP nodded respectfully and stepped back, closing the door behind him.

For a long moment, Teddy held the note without opening it. He sat with it in his palm, tracing the subtle texture of the cheap cardstock with his finger—ordinary and unremarkable, with no markings or creases that seemed out of place. He unfolded it with the same care he might have once used to open a field map near an active line of contact.

Inside, there was a single word neatly printed in block letters.

PROCEEDING

No embellishments or flourishes. Not even a symbol.

He stared at it for a few moments, allowing the meaning to sink in.

This wasn't a reply or a question. It was a confirmation of a message received.

A node had been activated. One of the names he'd written—perhaps one of the old ghosts he hadn't dared to rely on—was moving. The signal had reached them. The words he'd recorded in the notebook and the number he'd sent had gone exactly where they needed to go.

Teddy folded the note in half again and set it on the blanket beside him. He didn't close his eyes as he leaned his head back against the pillow, exhaling through his nose.

The tension in his chest didn't fade. Instead, it transformed from a coiled spring ready to snap into a taut cable—something long buried starting to resurface.

They made the initial moves and dominated the board.

But not anymore. Not at this moment.

He was no longer alone in this. Anyone who thought the hospital bed would be the end of him had overlooked the most important rule of the black world. If you fail to finish the job, the job finishes you.

CHAPTER 17

0600 Hours
January 27, 1984
Casablanca, Morocco

The port shimmered in the late afternoon haze, heat rising in gentle waves off the concrete as trucks moved around the docks. The air was filled with the scents of diesel, sea brine, and old rope. It was loud—dockworkers shouted and gulls squawked overhead—but no one noticed the man who stepped off the Belize-flagged freighter with a small canvas bag slung over his shoulder and mirrored sunglasses hiding his eyes.

Nero wore an off-the-rack jacket in neutral tones and simple civilian shoes. Not a single item would raise a red flag with customs or security. Yet he moved like someone who had mastered navigating choke points with ease—his stride relaxed and his awareness sharp.

He didn't go to a hotel or call anyone. A prearranged car—a battered, rusty Peugeot with sand-encrusted wheel wells—waited for him at the exit gate. He drove inland until the city faded and the horizon flattened into scrubland. Two hours later, he arrived at a rundown gas station, the kind that had once been supplied by the Soviets. It hadn't pumped a gallon of gas in a decade.

However, it still had a working freezer in the back.

Nero stepped inside and nodded to the man leaning against the counter—old, blind in one eye, chewing something bitter—before accepting the offered plastic bag filled with ice and a small key wrapped in foil.

The key unlocked a hatch embedded in the floorboards of the old storeroom.

Inside, a long, narrow plastic case lay covered in dust.

Nero opened it, revealing a disassembled communication device and a pistol wrapped in vacuum-sealed plastic.

He didn't smile or speak, just nodded to himself and began assembling the rig.

The message he was preparing wasn't intended for broadcast.

It was meant to *override*.

1750 Hours
January 27, 1984
Womack Army Medical Center
Conference Room – Restricted Recovery Wing
Fort Bragg, NC

The conference room adjacent to the restricted recovery wing wasn't large, but it had been cleared and repurposed in the last twenty-four hours. The overhead fluorescent lights were dimmed, the windows covered with temporary blackout panels, and the table—originally intended for surgical scheduling—had been converted into an intelligence desk.

Glossy, high-contrast black-and-white satellite photographs covered the surface, each one marked with red grease-pencil notations. Their edges curled from the heat of the lightboard used for analysis. In the center of the largest photo was a container freighter docked at Pier 9 in the Port of Casablanca.

Lieutenant Colonel Rachel Merrit stood at the head of the table, one hand resting beside the image and the other holding a thick folder filled with field logs and intercept summaries. The photo had arrived by special courier less than two hours ago, marked with the clearance seals of both the DIA and Naval Intelligence. The ship had no listed arrival time, no customs stamp, and no crew declaration. This information came as an unexpected surprise. She hadn't ordered it, having no knowledge that this ship even existed or its connection to Colonel Roosevelt. Could it be the legacy protocol at work?

"That's the vessel," she said. "*Delilah 7*. Docked thirty-six hours ago. Came out of Lisbon under diplomatic charter and bypassed customs completely. It has no flagged country of origin. She slipped through a narrow window between monitored satellite passes. This shot came from the second pass—KH-1, codenamed Keyhole, out of Ramstein, run through Fort Belvoir's image enhancement suite before they couriered it over."

Cross sat across from her, elbows resting on the table, staring at the image without blinking. He had remained still for several minutes while his cup of coffee cooled beside his hand. The faint glare from the photos cast sharp shadows across his face.

"No arrival logs?" he asked.

"Nothing legitimate," Merrit said. "No port authority records, no crew declaration. Her hull ID number comes back as inactive—was supposedly scrapped in '78. But the superstructure matches an earlier ship under the same name which was used during a covert intercept near Benghazi in '76. That one vanished after the operation. This one is a clone."

Cross reached for the second photo, flipping it around for a better angle. "Hull markings match?"

"They appear to be reapplied by hand. The stenciling patterns are slightly different. The ship is flagged under a shell company that no longer exists, sailing a route that was never filed with any port authority. They used the same name on purpose, *Delilah 7*. Someone wanted us to notice it if we knew where to look."

He grunted and leaned back in his chair, his eyes still on the photo. "So this wasn't a random reflag. This was a signal, and whoever's aboard knows how to navigate legacy systems."

Merrit nodded. "Not just a signal. A response. They're using Cold War-era clearance overlays. Not forged or stolen. Access that was buried years ago. We're not dealing with contractors or rogue elements anymore. This is black-world infrastructure. Someone brought it out of the archives."

Cross leaned back, folding his arms across his chest. "Does that mean what I think it does?"

Merrit nodded. "Someone old-school is in play. Not CIA. Not officially. These are ex-field assets. Deeply entrenched in their aliases. No handlers. No oversight."

"And they're here," Cross said, "because of Teddy...ahh...I mean Colonel Roosevelt."

Merrit nearly laughed at his minor slip of the tongue. He cared more about Colonel Roosevelt than he let on in public. "Because of what Colonel Roosevelt survived. And because of what he still knows." She set the folder down and tapped a page with her finger—an extract from a communication log retrieved from a dormant DIA relay node in Ankara, cross-referenced through JAG's backchannel systems.

"What he knows," Cross repeated. "I wish he'd let us in on some of that information."

"I doubt he can due to secrecy oaths and signed NDAs. I can tell you that Colonel Roosevelt sent a coded message yesterday afternoon—he wrote it in block letters and had it quietly handed off by an MP who thought he was delivering a supply request. The number embedded in the message routes through a defunct switchboard in Zürich. It's black-world, disconnected from active networks. The only people who know how to access it are the ones who built it."

Cross cocked his head. "And one of them answered?"

"Within sixteen hours. This ship showed up in Casablanca with no crew and no paperwork. That's not a coincidence."

He leaned back, slowly crossing his arms. The room was quiet again except for the faint ticking of the wall clock and the distant sound of boots clicking in the hallway. "This just stopped being about guarding a man in a hospital bed."

"It was never just that," Merrit replied, closing the folder. "But now it's confirmed. Colonel Roosevelt didn't just survive the attempts on his life. He lit the fuse."

She approached the small window on the far side of the room, parting the blinds just enough to catch a glimpse of the blue light-ringed roofline of the secure wing across the courtyard where Colonel Roosevelt lay recovering under MP guard.

"They're moving," she said. "Whoever got that message. Maybe just one. Maybe a dozen. We don't know how many. We don't know how long they've been watching. But they're in play now. The legacy protocol just went live. Which means whoever's behind this doesn't control the board anymore. The kill orders failed. And now the cleanup's being interrupted. So what's our next move?"

Cross stood and joined her by the window. "We hold this ground until Roosevelt is ready to talk. Because whatever they wanted buried in '72 is about to resurface. We need to know what we're sitting on."

Merrit didn't turn away from the glass. "They're not waiting for orders. They already have them. This isn't about leverage. It never was."

"Then what are they doing?" Cross asked.

She turned her head to face him. "They're erasing the people who tried to erase him."

"And the next shot won't come in a hospital corridor."

"No, this time, it'll come wearing a suit. With high-level clearance. And a name that isn't real." She turned away from the window. "They're moving, and we're out of time."

CHAPTER 18

1830 Hours
January 27, 1984
Womack Army Medical Center
Fort Bragg, NC

The hospital room had settled into that early evening stillness—the kind that always came when the staff rotations thinned and the light outside turned golden along the blinds. Teddy lay half-upright, propped up on several pillows, arms folded across his chest with a blanket draped over his legs. His body still ached—no less than it had yesterday—but the edge of the pain felt different now. Familiar. Manageable.

There was a rhythm to pain, and he found it again.

The IV infusion pump clicked beside him, a slow metronome marking the seconds more distinctly than the clock above the door. Hours had passed since anyone entered except for the nurse who changed a saline bag and offered him a few careful sips of water. Even she didn't linger. No more small talk. Not since word had begun to spread.

Merrit hadn't said much after giving him the note earlier about the ship *Delilah 7*—just a glance, enough for him to know she understood the message.

Something had changed.

And she could feel it as well.

Teddy knew exactly what had happened. It was now beyond his control. The legacy protocol was active. They would never learn what had transpired. That occurred in the shadows where only those involved in the operation navigated in the dark. When it was over, if he survived, he would receive a final message indicating the operational success or failure.

He glanced at the empty chair by the window. Cross had sat there for a while, reading reports and watching the door. He'd left an hour ago to check the perimeter, although Teddy knew the real reason. "Iron Vince" Cross wasn't accustomed to being out of control. And this? This was far outside the comfort zone of rules, regulations, and chains of command.

Teddy had seen it before. Good men caught in deep water, learning to tread differently to keep themselves afloat.

He leaned his head back against the pillow and closed his eyes—not from exhaustion, but to focus inward. He pictured the map—not the literal kind, but the network of people he had once known. Those buried beneath operations that officially never occurred, who now led quiet lives under assumed names and false credentials. Some were watching. Some were waiting. One—he was certain—was already on the move. Nero.

It wouldn't take much. A line buried in an embassy brief. A ciphered phrase delivered through a dead drop that no one had opened in years. When the right people heard the right whisper, they didn't ask who issued the order. They asked how soon it needed to be done.

The legacy protocol, once activated, was not a fail-safe. It was a ticking time bomb.

And now that the timer had been triggered, Teddy couldn't take it back. The wheels were in motion. The men and women he had once called allies—those who owed him a favor, feared him, or trusted him—were now in play after years spent in the dark.

Not because he was in danger, but because one of their own had been marked for deletion.

He opened his eyes again and stared at the ceiling, listening—not for footsteps or gunfire.

Just for the quiet space between.

The moment right before the consequences arrived.

0729 Hours
January 28, 1984
Womack Army Medical Center
Fort Bragg, NC

The sun had barely crested the treetops when they entered the room. Cross led the way, his jaw clenched, his fatigues crisply starched, and his combat boots spit-polished to a mirror shine. Merrit followed him in with a folder tucked under her arm, but she didn't open it. This wasn't about evidence. Not yet.

Teddy lay awake, propped up on several pillows, a fresh dressing covering his lower abdomen and a neatly folded blanket draped across his waist. He looked up when they entered, already interpreting their body language before either of them spoke.

They weren't here to provide him with an update, but rather in search of the truth. From him.

Cross didn't waste any time. He moved to the end of the bed and crossed his arms. "You were a decorated Special Forces officer. Two DSCs, Silver Star, Legion of Merit, Soldier's Medal, four Bronze Stars with Valor device, four Purple Hearts, an Air Medal, and numerous Army Commendations on your nonredacted service record. I'm sure there are more. Three combat tours. Then you disappeared off every official grid for almost two years before reappearing in country with a team that didn't exist, codenamed *Shadow Lance*, assigned to a mission no one signed off on."

Teddy remained silent, simply watching him and waiting for the right moment.

Merrit stepped closer, lowering her voice to sharpen the weight of her words. "You want us to protect you from whatever's coming next, Colonel Roosevelt? Then we need more than a list of names whispered in the dark. We need to understand why someone with access to executive-level clearance just tried to assassinate you in a military hospital. And we need to know why, after more than a decade, they're still covering up Operation Firelight."

That name hung in the air for a long moment—sharp and heavy.

Cross leaned over the bed. "You were the ODA commander. But Operation Firelight didn't come from MACV-SOG, did it?"

Teddy didn't answer right away. His gaze lingered for a moment on an indistinct spot on the ceiling, his eyes distant, memories clouded by something he'd long kept buried. When he spoke again, his voice was low, each word chosen with deliberate weight. "No…it didn't."

"So where did it come from?" Merrit asked.

"Then who exactly ordered it?" Cross asked, almost talking over her.

For a moment, silence filled the hospital room, broken only by the faint hum of monitors and the gentle, rhythmic drip of the IV at Teddy's bedside.

Merrit watched him closely, her expression unreadable.

Cross straightened and tapped his foot impatiently, waiting for an answer.

"Have either of you ever heard of the Mongoose List?" Teddy asked, his voice low and filled with a bitter understanding of the consequences.

Cross cocked his head, a flicker of recognition flashing in his eyes.

Merrit raised an eyebrow, waiting for him to elaborate.

Teddy took a slow breath, his gaze fixed on the foot of the bed. "It started back in 1961—a CIA and DIA joint venture. A precursor to the Phoenix Program. Officially, it was created to track and disrupt enemy banking networks that were laundering money throughout Southeast Asia. But the original targets weren't just enemy fronts or guerrilla strongholds. They were politically protected and untouchable."

Cross narrowed his eyes. "The Mongoose List was officially dissolved after the Bay of Pigs. President Kennedy shut it down himself."

"Officially, yes. That's what the files say," Teddy agreed, looking up at him. "But unofficially, it was never dismantled. It evolved into much more. The people in charge changed the name of the operation and its scope. By 1972, the list wasn't about banks or money trails anymore. It became something darker—a ledger of inconvenient people—informants, contractors, diplomats, even our own allies—anyone who knew too much, moved too freely, or asked uncomfortable or wrong questions."

Merrit broke her silence. "So Operation Firelight wasn't really about monitoring the Chinese arms smuggling routes through Laotian villages on the Ho Chi Minh trail to the Khmer Rouge in Cambodia?"

"No," Teddy said, turning his head to face her. "That was the cover story. Our real orders came from Langley through a CIA liaison named Christopher Armstrong. Firelight was never about reconnaissance or intelligence gathering. It was an off-the-books mission aimed at creating conditions on the ground—a false flag operation that would justify future U.S. intervention in Laos to wipe out the Pathet Lao after Nixon's disastrous invasion of Cambodia. Villages were burned, and massacres carried out by covert CIA strike teams using paid mercenaries. All under the guise of enemy aggression."

Cross's jaw tightened as the implications settled heavily between them. "And your team was sent to light the fuse."

Teddy's voice grew colder, and the bitterness was sharper now. "No! My team was sent because Langley knew that if the truth ever got out, we'd be the perfect scapegoats—deniable and expendable. But they didn't count on me figuring out the real objective, the one we weren't cleared to know—planting evidence of Chinese atrocities, enough to trigger direct U.S. intervention in Laos. Instead of planting the evidence, the CIA did it for real once I figured out the original plan."

"Jesus, Teddy," Cross said, anger evident in his voice.

"Oh, it gets better. When I confronted Armstrong and refused to complete the last phase of the mission, they cut us loose and left us stranded in hostile territory, hoping we'd never make it back. We humped out of Laos the hard way—just boots on the ground, bruises, no food, and the original orders tucked in my shirt. We made it back after a week, hungry, dirty, and tired, only to be slapped in cuffs before the blood even dried and falsely accused of war crimes associated with the massacres."

Merrit leaned forward, her voice low but clear. "Why frame your team specifically?"

Teddy exhaled slowly, meeting her hardened gaze. "Because I was the one officer with a clear enough conscience who'd seen enough behind the black curtain to connect Langley's covert funding streams directly to the highest levels of U.S. Army Intelligence. They didn't just want a scapegoat. They wanted to erase the evidence—and the witnesses— permanently."

He paused for a long moment, his determination hardening with quiet resolve. "That's why all this has resurfaced now. Firelight never truly ended. It's still burning. And this time, someone wants to finish what Langley started back in '72."

"Finish how?" Cross asked, his expression cautious as he processed the revelations.

Teddy stared at him, his voice even but heavy with a decade of painful memories. "By removing the last piece of evidence that ever mattered— me. I was pulled out of the 5th Group under a falsified operational reassignment. No record or chain of command. The orders were verbal. My CO thought I'd been rotated stateside. I spent the next nineteen months running asset retrieval and termination missions that didn't exist. Not under MACV or the CIA. And definitely not under Congressional approval."

"What about Sergeant Red Horse? Captain Stratton?" Merrit asked. "They were in country then."

"They joined my unit later," Teddy said. "Eli was assigned to a transport unit. Jack was a MACV liaison officer. I brought them in after my first team got wiped out in Cambodia during the failed invasion. I never told them where the missions originated. Only that we were taking on targets that high-ranking brass in the Pentagon wouldn't touch."

"So they don't know," Merrit said.

"Not all of it. They know what they need to."

Cross stepped back from the bed, his hands curling into fists, clearly angry at the implication. "Then you let them take the fall for something they never understood or agreed to participate in."

"No," Teddy said, calm but firm. "I kept them alive. If they'd known what we were part of—if they'd known who gave the real order for Operation Firelight—they wouldn't have just been court-martialed. They would've been silenced."

Merrit looked at him, something cold and quiet settling behind her eyes. "And you?"

"I was supposed to disappear with the records. Armstrong and his bosses thought I wouldn't survive the extraction. They were wrong." He leaned back against the pillows, the strain of speaking beginning to show in his voice. "I deviated from standard black protocol. I didn't burn the last document and kept a copy. Not because I wanted leverage. But because someday, someone was going to come asking the right questions."

Cross regarded him with a soldier's gaze, assessing every detail.

"Do you still have it?" Merrit asked.

"I know where it is," Teddy said.

She nodded. "Why now? Why bring it out after all this time?"

"Because someone's laundering black-world money again. And they're afraid the last man who saw it the first time is still breathing."

Cross stood motionless at the window.

Merrit stayed at Teddy's bedside, arms folded, waiting for more information.

And Teddy knew they deserved it. "You want to know why I wasn't killed in '72? Why I was arrested instead of erased and dropped into a deep, unmarked hole in the Vietnamese jungle?"

Merrit nodded. "Yes. You survived a black-world kill order? We need to know why you're still alive. You're too dangerous to hold. But too public now to disappear. So why the halfway measure?"

"Because I ran." He met her gaze directly. "The plan was never to put us in the stockade."

"Then what was it?" Cross asked.

"I wasn't supposed to be taken alive at all," Teddy said. "Not then, and certainly not now. Getting arrested was never part of the plan. Halfway back across the Bolaven Plateau, I realized that our extraction route was compromised—radio silence hit earlier than planned, and promised air cover never appeared. But the final proof came when we reached our designated fallback safehouse outside Pakse—it was completely stripped of everything. No handler or extraction gear. Just a one-line burn notice shoved under the door."

Cross turned away from the window. "The op was sanctioned?"

"Yes. But buried inside a ghost protocol. No paper trail. Verbal orders passed through three cutouts. It was designed to vanish—target, funds, team, all gone."

"And Red Horse and Stratton?" Merrit asked. "They were part of it?"

"Like I already told you, they were members of my team," Teddy said. "But they didn't know the source. I never told them who gave the order or what was really behind it. I suspected the double-cross by Armstrong. But by the time we reached the final checkpoint, I knew."

"You were being set up for removal."

He nodded again, slower this time. "Yes. And I knew what came next."

"So what did you do?"

"I made a choice," Teddy said. "I didn't wait for the hammer to fall. I pulled Eli and Jack, changed the extraction plan, and ghosted us into the shadows before they could finish the job."

"You vanished," Cross said.

"We escaped," he corrected, looking directly at Cross. "And when they couldn't finish the job in the jungle, they rewrote the narrative. Painted us as rogue mercenaries, war criminals who massacred civilians and ran for the border. No one questioned or wanted to address the obvious problems with that story when we arrived at Firebase Buttons after escaping Laos through Cambodia."

"That's when the Army charged all three of you and scheduled a court-martial."

"You mean they buried us in lies," Teddy said, his voice tightening. "No one wanted the real op made public. So they fabricated the court-martial proceedings, all the paperwork, then sealed it under a classified and compartmentalized designation. And locked us in a stockade, believing that would solve the problem."

"They were going to kill you inside the stockade," Merritt said.

"They had to," Teddy said. "Operation Firelight was a political disaster if ever made public. If that happened, the whole house of cards would have come down since the next target on that list for intervention was Cambodia." He adjusted the pillow behind his head, suppressing a wince. "But when the MPs at Firebase Buttons actually followed protocol—made the arrest, filled out all the appropriate forms, and brought us in alive—they had to improvise."

"They didn't want a prisoner," Merrit said. "They wanted a body."

"And once I was in a holding cell back in the States, they had to find another way. That's why there were delays in the official paperwork, the Article 32, and confinement hearings. No assignment of a JAG lawyer. They were scrambling."

Cross raised an eyebrow. "But you slipped the net."

"We had a five-minute window arranged by a contact at the stockade, and I took advantage of it," Teddy said. "I burned the IDs left for us at a dead drop near Bragg, fell off the radar, and made sure the three of us remained loud, unpredictable, and hard to control."

"And that's why they didn't come after you again?"

"We were fugitives, Cross. But we were visible. Television, newspapers, sightings, chatter, all that stuff in the underground networks across the world made us legendary as conscientious mercenaries willing to put everything on the line for a good cause and part of urban myth, thanks to the press. Too many eyes were watching, including the U.S. Army. Killing me then would've drawn fire from every direction. I became more dangerous as a story than as a body."

"So what changed now?" Merrit asked.

"You caught me," Teddy said simply.

"And by doing it clean and following the regulations, Cross gave them a window."

Cross stepped forward now. "You're saying the attempt in the hospital…wasn't the first plan. It was the backup."

Teddy nodded. "For the first time in years, I was in a box. No press watching, no way to escape, and no witnesses. Just four concrete walls, a hospital bed, and a red file waiting for the right trigger."

"And they moved," Cross muttered. "Too fast."

"They always do," Teddy said. "The longer I stayed in custody, the greater the risk they carried. Someone like you was bound to start asking questions. Merrit would dig into every detail before scheduling a hearing. Dr. Hollis would document my injuries. Every extra minute I stayed breathing made their original lie harder to maintain. They thought they could fix it quietly. Drug me. Stage a medical event. Problem solved. But every hour I stayed alive inside that system made it riskier for them. And now they've exposed themselves."

Merrit sat in the chair next to his bed. "And if they had succeeded? If you had died from a complication?"

"No one would've asked questions. The case against me would have been sealed again. The file closed. The press would have moved on. And somewhere in a basement file room, the last witness to a forty-year black-world money laundering operation would've gone silent."

The weight of that truth hung heavily between them.

"So what now?" Cross asked. "You survived Operation Firelight because you saw what was coming. But what about now? Are you saying they're back? That someone's picking up the pieces of that old network?"

"I'm saying they never stopped. Just went quiet and found new funding streams. New flags to fly under. But it's the same engine underneath. And if they're this desperate to erase me now…it means someone else is getting close." Teddy looked at him. "Now you understand that this was never about Operation Firelight. Never about breaking out of Fort Bragg. That was the smoke. But this…" He paused, pointing at himself. "This is the fire."

Merrit unfolded her arms. "So why now? You've been out there for years being loud, public, and impossible to ignore within the intelligence circles. Why wait until now to try and erase you?"

For the first time since they entered, there was something darker behind Teddy's voice. Not bitterness or fear, but certainty. "Because the things we exposed during Operation Firelight never really stopped. The people behind it just got smarter…and I think someone's resurrecting it. Quietly. Carefully. The same channels, money, and laundering infrastructure, maybe even the same names. They didn't care about me as long as I stayed loud and unpredictable—too public to kill, too chaotic to control."

"But you got too close again," Cross said, his expression hardening like stone.

"No," Teddy said. "I didn't. Someone else did."

That statement landed like a shot between them.

"Who?" Merrit asked

"I don't know. But someone started pulling on the same thread we did, and they weren't supposed to. That's when my name started circulating again. Not because I was a threat, but because I'm a loose end in a play they never closed."

"What does that mean?"

"It's simple. They don't need me silenced because of what I'm doing. They need me gone in case someone else finds out what we already saw, because if I'm alive, I can confirm it. I can prove Operation Firelight was never a rogue operation. That it was sanctioned by the U.S. Army and the CIA. Funded at the highest levels of the U.S. government and buried by the same people who are resurrecting it now."

Merrit stood in shocked silence. "What about Sergeant Red Horse and Captain Stratton?"

"They don't know this part. They never did. I kept them out of it. And if I have my way…" Teddy let the sentence trail off, but they understood. If he had his way, they still wouldn't. Because this world wasn't theirs. It was his. And the cost of knowing about it was too high.

"And the black world contact you called? The one who answered legacy protocol?" Merrit asked. "Is he moving on this?"

"Yes, he knows what's coming," Teddy said. "And that changes the equation. Because now it's not just about me. The people who tried to erase me have a new problem."

Cross arched a single eyebrow. "What's that?"

"It's about whoever's rebuilding the old machine…and what they're going to do when they realize I still remember how it works." Teddy let a ghost of a smile tug at the corners of his mouth. "And I'm not the only one they forgot to kill."

CHAPTER 19

1300 Hours
January 28, 1984
Womack Army Medical Center
Conference Room – Restricted Recovery Wing
Fort Bragg, NC

The lights in the conference room hummed overhead, but the air felt somewhat stagnant. Merrit stood at the whiteboard with a grease pencil in her hand, a list of names written in front of her—some real, some aliases, and a few crossed out. Cross stood off to the side, thumbing through a printout of clearance requests related to the old Mongoose protocols. None of them matched anything in the U.S. Army's computerized records system.

Merrit circled a name near the bottom, *Thomas Daniels.* "This one came up in the '72 intercept logs. He's dead now. Died in a car crash in Langley six months after Operation Firelight."

Cross looked over at her. "Is it confirmed?"

"Yes. Too clean to be a coincidence." She stepped back and drew a thick ring around the center of the diagram. "The funding structure used for Operation Firelight was funneled through a shell company called Carroway Consulting. The company was dissolved in '75, but its assets were absorbed by a private logistics firm—Orion Five."

Cross raised an eyebrow. "I've seen that name. It came up on a few Department of Defense contracting bids last year. It's supposed to be a civilian organization."

"Until you pull the paperwork. Their executive director once held a non-official cover through Sable Protocol."

"What's Sable Protocol?" Cross asked.

Merrit didn't answer right away. She glanced at him, then reached into the folder and pulled out a page marked with a five-digit clearance code—731-X5—and a red diagonal slash cutting across the page like a wound.

TOP SECRET – EYES ONLY
OPERATIONAL CONTAINMENT DIRECTIVE
SABLE PROTOCOL
Clearance Code: 731-X5
Handler: DUNNING / OCN-7017
Issued via: Task Group D-7 // SAD-L

SUBJECT: FIRELIGHT ASSET CONTAINMENT
In accordance with the contingency clause outlined in Directive
SABLE/731-X5, all field assets related to Operation Firelight will be
classified as non-acknowledged and designated as externally exfiltrated in
the event of premature exposure, failure to achieve the objective, or
deviation from the narrative script.

Primary asset: Colonel Theodore Roosevelt IV (USASF)
Support assets: Captain J. Stratton (INT), MSGT E. Red Horse (ENG),
multiple

Containment Tier: Full — Class 4 (denial and discreditation)

Recommended actions:

1. Cease routing of mission files before the post-operation debrief.
2. Blacklist all attached signals and disavow all field activities under code
   714.
3. Construct an alternative explanation for the incident: unsanctioned raid,
   loss of command integrity, or hostile crossfire casualty event.
4. Create fictitious communication logs for JPRC/MACV-SOG to
   simulate miscommunication.
5. Burn the safehouse cache. Remove the handler presence prior to asset
   return.

This directive is effective as of 4 June 1972. Activate if operational drift
exceeds an 8-hour window or if the asset attempts post-field verification.

Authorization: D-7/OV-77-C

Seal: [REDACTED]

"It's not in any official manual," she said. "Not unless you've worked inside Task Group D-7." She slid the page across the table toward him. "Sable Protocol was designed to erase black-world operations from the inside out. Not by hiding them, but by eliminating the individuals who carried them out. Field teams. Commanders. Witnesses. Anyone who knew too much once the mission went sideways."

Cross frowned. "It mentions the JPRC. So it's a clean-up and body retrieval directive."

"No! The JPRC's mission was to recover the bodies of U.S. and allied personnel listed as Prisoners of War or Missing in Action during the Vietnam War. This is a containment directive dressed up as essential to national security. You carry out a sanctioned mission, and if it becomes politically inconvenient or the money gets dirty, your orders vanish. Your chain of command disavows you. And if you're lucky—very lucky—you just end up in a courtroom."

Cross glanced down at the paper again. "And Dunning used this?"

Merrit nodded. "He wrote half of it."

"Jesus." Cross shook his head. "How did Teddy get involved in this black world? He's got too much of a conscience to do this kind of work."

"They probably recruited him because he's one of the best, and being an idealist and a patriot, he said *yes*. Chances are, given what we know, he didn't realize what he was getting into until it was too late. But in the world of covert operations, the only way he could leave was in a body bag. A star on the wall." A grim testament to the price of loyalty in a game where the rules were written in blood. Merrit turned to face him. "Whoever revived this isn't just cleaning up old work. They're rebuilding it. Not as a government program—but as a private, heavily funded enterprise. They're taking what was left in the wreckage and building something they can control."

Cross closed the file. "So what do we do?"

"We keep Colonel Roosevelt alive and follow every thread they thought they cut."

1330 Hours
January 28, 1984
Abandoned Airstrip
Baja Peninsula

The late afternoon sun hung low over the dunes, casting long shadows across the rusted tin walls of the toolshed. Heat shimmered above the sand-packed road, and the scent of oil and rusted steel lingered in the still, 100-plus-degree air.

Eli Red Horse crouched beside the truck, tightening the last bolt on the rear axle. The frame had seen better days—patched together from three countries and two escapes—but it ran smoothly, and that was all that mattered.

Jack Stratton stood a few paces away scanning the scrubland beyond the fence line. His mirrored aviator sunglasses hid the squint in his eyes but his posture remained tense. He didn't like staying in one place for this long. Not even in Baja where supposedly no one was looking for them in a country not known for honoring U.S. extradition orders.

The rumble of an engine caught his attention. A beat-up green Jeep crested the ridge and rolled toward them, kicking up a cloud of dust behind it. It didn't come in fast, didn't swerve, just glided in, indicating that the driver knew exactly where he was headed.

Jack tucked his hand under his khaki photographer's vest, gripping his .357 Magnum revolver in a shoulder holster as the vehicle came to a stop.

The old man behind the wheel didn't turn off the engine. He sat there, letting the engine idle in the heat, one hand on the stick shift. He didn't speak or make eye contact. Instead, he reached across the dashboard, grabbed something, and tossed it out the open window. It landed in the dirt near Jack's boots.

Without saying a word, he pulled away. The Jeep turned back down the road and disappeared into the haze as though it had never existed at all.

Jack crouched down and picked up a matchbook. Faded and curled at the edges, the logo was nearly illegible—until he flipped it over. The name sprang out like a ghost—*The Half Moon Club*. Saigon. 1972. A place that had not existed for a very long time.

Inside, handwritten in red ink, was a single line.

Roosevelt. Silence Order. Watch your six.

He straightened, his jaw tightening.

Eli stepped out of the toolshed behind him, wiping his hands on a rag. "Is that who I think it was?"

"Who knows?" Jack handed him the matchbook.

Eli took it and opened the cover. "'Roosevelt. Silence Order. Watch your six.' Is this some kind of joke?"

Jack shook his head. "You know damn well it's not. And if someone's sending us ghosts from Saigon in a matchbook, it's not a prank."

"That bar burned down in '72. No one's used this signal since the Laos mission." Eli turned the matchbook in his hand. "Only one kind of message shows up like this."

Jack nodded. "Someone's gone to ground. And if they're sending this through a back channel..." He trailed off, watching the swirling dust trail the Jeep had left behind. "Then Teddy's not just in trouble. He's being hunted."

Eli twisted the rag tighter in his hand. "Why now?"

"I don't know. But if it's a silence order?" Jack looked him straight in the eye. "Then someone's already made a play."

Eli didn't ask what kind and tossed the rag aside. "I'll load the truck."

"Get the commo box too. If there's anything left on the old channels, we'll need it." Jack grabbed a duffel bag from the open garage door and tossed it into the truck bed. "Get the portable radios and the old ID case. We don't know where Teddy is yet, but if he's still breathing...he's going to need backup."

In just a few minutes, they loaded the truck with every item from their inventory. As Eli secured the final strap over the duffel bags in the truck bed, Jack stood nearby with the matchbook in his hand, flipping it over, convinced the message might change if he blinked.

It didn't say where Teddy was or who sent it. But it said enough.

Jack tucked it into his shirt pocket and walked over to the truck. "Do you still have that old telephone line test set from when we burned out of Arizona last month?"

Eli nodded. "The box is in the foot locker next to the cab."

"Good. Did you prep the backup IDs?"

"Of course. Do you think we're gonna need to disappear again?" Eli asked

Jack met his gaze. "If this is what I think it is? No. We're not going to disappear." He opened the passenger door, climbed in, and stared straight ahead as Eli settled into the driver's seat. "We're going to get Teddy out, then we're going to find out who wants him dead bad enough to leave ghost messages in the middle of the Mexican desert."

Eli turned the key, and the truck rumbled to life with a low growl. They were on the move...again.

Neither man said another word.

But the silence between them didn't signify hesitation. It was war.

Teddy was in trouble. That much was clear. No matter how deep the sand or how far the distance, they weren't going to let him face it alone.

CHAPTER 20

1530 Hours
January 28, 1984
JAG Operations Wing
Office of Lt. Colonel Merrit
Fort Bragg, NC

Merrit stared at her office terminal, her fingers hovering above the keyboard. The blinking cursor remained frozen next to an encrypted access log she hadn't requested.

"What is it?" Colonel Cross asked from the doorway.

She didn't turn around. "This file. I had it locked behind Tier Four security protocol. One-time key, known only to me. It's the surveillance archive from Colonel Roosevelt's first twelve hours in custody."

Cross stepped closer. "Do you think it was accessed?"

"No." Merrit clicked the enter key twice, and the cursor disappeared. "I think someone remotely hacked into the system with credentials that don't exist on this base." She turned to face him. "And someone's still inside the system."

Cross clenched his jaw. "Watching us?"

"Worse. Planning around us. I don't know if it has to do with Colonel Roosevelt or this legacy protocol business." Merrit pushed her rolling chair back and scanned the small wall map pinned over the duty roster. It was a tactical overlay of deployment stations and command pathways. But now, she wasn't focused on personnel. She was searching for routes.

"Do we move him again?" Cross asked.

"No. That's what they're waiting for. They need him in motion. In transition. If we keep him here, under our control, at least we know the terrain."

"And if they make a move anyway?"

She looked him in the eye. "Then they'll have to do it out in the open. And if they do…I'll burn down the program they built to hide it."

1805 Hours
January 28, 1984
Rooftop Bar
Tijuana, Mexico

Jack leaned against the railing of a rooftop bar in Tijuana, Mexico, watching the city blur into gold and violet as the sun dipped below the horizon. Below, traffic crawled, and blaring horns mixed with the rhythm of salsa music from a radio someone had left on. Eli sat at a back table, scanning a black notebook filled with names they hadn't used in a decade.

"I got a ping off that old signal relay in San Diego," Jack said without turning. "Our friend in the telecom racket logged a ghost pulse an hour before that matchbook hit my boots."

Eli didn't look up. "East Coast? DC?"

Jack shook his head. "No. Military. Fort Bragg, or near it."

"Then that's where they took him."

"Are you sure?"

Eli flipped to the next page in his notebook. "I know Teddy. They wouldn't risk civilian containment. Not if 'Iron Vince' Cross is involved. That man sticks to the damn Army manual like it's glued to his ass."

Jack turned and walked back to the table. "Then we get moving."

"We don't have papers."

"We haven't had official papers since Vietnam," Jack said with a faint smile. He tapped the side of the notebook. "But we've got names. We burn two of these IDs and passports, and we're back in the United States by morning."

Eli closed the notebook. "Do you think they'll see us coming?"

Jack slid into the seat across from him and picked up his beer. "They won't. But they'll feel us when we hit them."

2300 Hours
January 28, 1984
Womack Army Medical Center
Restricted Recovery Wing
Fort Bragg, NC

The lights in the hallway were dimmed for the night shift, but Merrit didn't leave. She stood at the nurse's station, reviewing a new security manifest while Cross checked the weapon clearances for the guards on the current shift.

"Three of the names on this new list were cross-pulled from a logistics battalion out of Norfolk," Merrit said. "One of them—Sergeant Dwyer—has a clearance tag that predates his enlistment."

"Pull him. Quietly. Replace him with one of mine," Cross replied.

"We need to assume the hospital is compromised. Until we identify the source of the breach, no one goes near Colonel Roosevelt unless it's one of us."

Cross looked through the glass window where Colonel Roosevelt slept or appeared to under half-light, pale and still. "They'll come again."

Merrit nodded. "They have to. This isn't about punishment anymore. This is about erasure."

"Then we control the field and initiate full lockdown in the hospital." Cross closed the file. "We strip the personnel schedules to hourly shifts and arm the guards."

She looked over at him. "You're expecting a firefight?"

"No," Cross said. "I'm expecting an armed ghost."

CHAPTER 21

0230 Hours
January 29, 1984
Womack Army Medical Center
Restricted Recovery Wing
Fort Bragg, NC

The overhead lights were dimmed to their lowest setting. Outside the room only a single MP was visible through the narrow window, his silhouette cutting through the semi-darkness in the dull red glow of the hallway. Inside, Teddy lay awake, unable to sleep.

His body was exhausted—his stitches pulling, skin still raw from healing—but his mind refused to rest. The pain felt deeper tonight. Not the surgical kind, but the echo of impact. The bruises from the first beating were now surfacing, embedded in muscle and layered with the ache of being hunted from bed to bed. His breath hitched at times when he turned, and even the slightest movement drew sweat to his temples.

But none of that mattered as much as the silence. It was too quiet.

He felt it again—the stillness that seemed out of place. The kind of quiet born not from peace, but from anticipation.

The door swung open wide enough for one person. Cross entered, closed the door behind him, and paused just beyond the shadows, watching Teddy in the dim light. "You're still awake."

Teddy looked at him. "Figured sleep might be dangerous to my health."

Cross nodded. "True."

Teddy noticed that Cross looked exhausted. His uniform was wrinkled from hours spent sitting upright in a chair. He clearly hadn't slept either. As Cross approached the bed, Teddy spotted a bulge beneath the colonel's jacket. "Do you have something for me?"

Cross reached inside his coat and pulled out a bundle wrapped in sterile gauze, resembling a surgical tool. He placed it on the bedside table and unwrapped a small Smith & Wesson .38 caliber snub-nosed revolver. It wasn't military-issue but a police model, small enough to hide under a pillow.

Teddy looked at it for a long moment. "Thanks."

"It's loaded with hollow points. I shouldn't be doing this. Technically, you're still a prisoner," Cross said.

Teddy offered him a weak smile. "Technically, you've been chasing me for five years without any luck until a few days ago. Let's not pretend we're still on page one."

Cross didn't smile back. "I'm down three guards in as many days. One went missing. One is under review for falsifying log entries. The third is dead. Fell down a stairwell at his apartment. And all of them had access to this floor."

No wonder he hasn't slept. "So someone's still inside."

Cross nodded. "And if they come again, it won't be with a poison IV bag or a pillow over your face like in the spy movies. They'll finish it up close and messy. The kind that doesn't leave anyone alive to testify."

Teddy picked up the revolver. It felt heavier than it should have. His hand trembled from the strain, but he held it steady and flipped open the cylinder to check the rounds. Sure enough, 158-grain jacketed hollow points. "You know I can't sit up fast. I can't walk. I can barely reach the damn call button."

"That's why I brought it. You won't get more than one shot. Maybe two. But it's better than none." Cross stepped back, shoved the gauze into his pocket, and looked down at Teddy. "I'm not asking you to trust me. Just to live long enough that all this matters."

Teddy slid the revolver under the blanket, just beneath the edge of the pillow. "Thanks, Vince."

Cross paused at the mention of his first name, then gave a single nod. "I'll be outside."

With that, he stepped into the hallway and closed the door behind him, leaving Teddy alone once more—but no longer defenseless.

0310 Hours
January 29, 1984
Security Camera Room
Womack Army Medical Center
Fort Bragg, NC

The breach was no longer theoretical, a hunch, a flag, or a ghost in the logs. It appeared on-screen in live footage—night vision, one hallway, two figures. One wore standard MP gear while the other was dressed in surgical scrubs, their badges turned just out of frame. However, Merrit recognized the uniforms—and she understood the movement. The man in scrubs wasn't a medic. He moved like a killer.

The video feed suddenly cut out and turned to static on the monitors just before the intruder reached the junction of the ICU hallway.

The timestamp at the bottom of the screen froze at 03:11:04.

Merrit slammed her hand on the intercom button. "Lockdown! Secure the restricted recovery wing! Now!"

0313 Hours
January 29, 1984
Womack Army Medical Center
Restricted Recovery Wing
Fort Bragg, NC

Teddy heard it first—well, he felt it in his gut as the hinges didn't creak and there were no footsteps—just an absence of sound. A silence too clean to be accidental. He didn't move or reach for anything, knowing that would give away his advantage.

Slowly, he inched his fingers beneath the blanket, moving upward until they found the wood-handled grip of the revolver Cross had given him. He wasn't strong enough to hold it properly—not without pain tearing through his abdomen—but he didn't have to. If the assailant came in close, all he needed was one good shot.

The door opened with deliberate care. A figure slipped inside, broad-shouldered and gloved, without a uniform, insignia, or visible plastic ID badge, wearing only plain blue surgical scrubs and sneakers. A cloth-wrapped straight-blade knife glinted in the low light—definitely not a firearm, which would be too loud for this mission. This was a job that called for restraint.

The intruder glided across the room with surgical precision, approaching the bed in silence. He understood the layout, knew where Teddy was, and that he would be unable to defend himself.

But Teddy moved first. He twisted with a breath-stealing lurch and pulled the pistol from under the pillow. The gunshot cracked loudly in the small room. The round struck low, hitting the assailant in the hip. The man staggered but didn't go down.

Teddy fired the second shot as fatigue set in. It grazed the man's shoulder, then the pistol slipped from Teddy's grip, now too heavy to hold.

The man lunged forward with the blade raised high. Teddy attempted to block the attack by raising his arms, but he was too slow. The sharp edge sliced deep into his upper left bicep, igniting a searing pain that coursed through his nerves. They crashed sideways, the man's full weight pinning him down as blood soaked into the sheets.

The man wrapped his hands around Teddy's throat, squeezing tightly and leaving him gasping for air.

Teddy couldn't fight him off, but he could think even though he had only a few seconds before passing out from a lack of oxygen to his brain. With the little strength he had left, he shoved the IV pole with his right hand. It crashed to the floor with a loud metallic clang that echoed down the hallway.

The door flew open.

Two sharp cracks echoed through the room. The man above him collapsed, falling heavily onto Teddy's chest. Blood dripped off the mattress and pooled on the tile beneath the bed.

Cross stood just inside the doorway, his Colt .45 caliber pistol still raised, breathing hard, his expression unreadable. He crossed the room in three strides, yanked the dying man off the bed, and kicked the knife away before leaning over to check on Teddy.

Merrit followed moments later with her identical pistol drawn. She took a quick glance and spun toward the hallway. "Trauma team, now! We've got arterial bleeding!"

The pain surged back—not the dull ache of healing or the sharp pressure of old bruises, but something entirely new. Something worse. It bloomed hot and fast under his arm, searing deep into his ribs and coiling around them like unyielding wire. His vision faded to gray, every nerve screaming in protest. He tried to move his left arm but discovered he couldn't. The cut was deep.

"He wasn't alone," Teddy whispered, his throat tight with pain.

Merrit glanced down at him. "What?"

"This isn't just cleanup. They're done pretending."

A nurse arrived, followed by another. One of them pressed her hands against the wound in his arm to control the bleeding.

"Get...Hollis," Teddy whispered.

Merrit leaned over him. "He's on his way. You're going to be all right."

Teddy coughed, the movement sending a jolt of pain through his side. "No. Listen—Merrit—this isn't...this isn't just about me." He grabbed her wrist to get her attention. "They're escalating. This wasn't a cleanup job. This was a declaration of war."

The lights above him began to blur and sway. Not dimmer—just drifting away.

"Dr. Hollis!" the nurse exclaimed. "We need him now."

Teddy fought to catch his breath, closing his eyes. His vision narrowed into a tunnel, fading to gray, then edging toward black. It was hard to breathe. "They've gone operational—"

0325 Hours
January 29, 1984
Womack Army Medical Center
Restricted Recovery Wing
Fort Bragg, NC

The corridor outside Teddy's room was cordoned off with mobile partitions, two MPs standing tense at either end. The attacker's body lay on a gurney inside a partially zipped black plastic body bag. Medics had taken Teddy to the trauma room a few minutes earlier. Now Cross stood in silence, blood spattered on his uniform, his jaw clenched so tightly that the muscles along his cheek twitched.

Merrit walked up to him, the sleeves of her white blouse stained dark red past the elbow. She met his gaze and answered the question before he could ask. "He's alive. Barely. Lacerated brachial artery and the sutures around his peritoneal closure line ruptured again. He lost a lot of blood. Hollis had to take him back into surgery," she said.

Cross exhaled through his nose, but it wasn't relief. It was the release of pressure following a life-or-death decision.

Merrit approached the gurney where the attacker's body lay. "No real ID on his body. Just a fake clearance badge with his picture. Fingerprints are still being examined. Whoever he was, let's hope we get a hit in either our database, Interpol, or Langley's."

"He came through an access corridor that wasn't even mapped on last week's security report," Cross said. "That section was rerouted during electrical maintenance."

She nodded. "Signed off by a civilian contractor with dual clearance. We traced the badge. It doesn't exist within base records."

"They didn't just send a cleaner. Someone with clearance escorted him through this place directly to Colonel Roosevelt's room."

Merrit crossed her arms. "I agree. This wasn't a breach by an outsider. It was engineered by someone embedded in the hospital. An officer above us cleared that corridor. They gave the attacker maintenance access and cleared internal hallways. They knew the rotation schedule and timed this down to the minute."

Cross punched the wall, using the pain in his knuckles to focus his anger. "They deployed a kill team inside a military hospital on U.S. soil during a JAG investigation, and they almost got away with it."

"Because someone within the system supplied them with everything they needed to do it."

They remained silent for a long moment.

Cross glanced toward the hallway where Teddy lay behind closed doors, fighting for his life after the third assassination attempt on him in two weeks. "They want him dead. Dead, silent, and forgotten."

Merrit placed her hand on his arm. "Then we raise hell until they can't hide behind the wall of silence anymore."

CHAPTER 22

0325 Hours
January 29, 1984
Operating Room
Womack Army Medical Center
Fort Bragg, NC

As soon as they rolled him in, Dr. Hollis realized they were already behind the eight ball. He caught only a glimpse of Colonel Roosevelt's face as they rushed past—his pallor was striking, his skin waxy, with a faint bluish tinge around his lips. The attending nurse pressed a blood-soaked compress to his shoulder, her fingers already stained crimson, while calling out vital signs over her shoulder that were dropping too quickly.

"Systolic in the sixties. Pulse rapid, thready. He's hypovolemic—"

"Get two large-bore IVs in him now," Hollis ordered as he donned his gloves and secured his gown. "Type and cross for four units. Start him on O-neg. He doesn't have ten minutes to wait for a cross-match."

The monitors activated as they moved the patient to the table. Blood pressure was dropping rapidly, and the pulse was irregular. The incision line from the previous surgery appeared distorted—not due to infection or simple dehiscence, but from blunt force trauma. The abdomen was swelling again, and the bruising pattern across his ribs looked fresh and severe. And if that wasn't enough trauma, the surgical staples had come loose.

The attacker hadn't just reopened the wound. He tried to destroy it.

"Prep a laparotomy tray," Hollis said. "And I need suction ready. We're going in fast."

Even as the anesthesia took effect and Colonel Roosevelt's eyes closed behind the mask, Hollis could see signs of a struggle—dried blood at the corner of his mouth, a bruise high on his jaw, and bloody defensive wounds on his knuckles. He had fought back. Somehow. From a hospital bed, with torn sutures and a half-shattered body.

And he was still breathing. More than anything else, that kept Hollis going.

Once the sea-green surgical drapes were in place and the sterile field was prepared, Dr. Ray Hollis lowered his gaze into the wound and realized they were in trouble.

The shoulder wound wasn't the priority, but it was bleeding more than anticipated. The laceration had cut deep through the deltoid muscle, shredding the anterior fibers and grazing the brachial artery with a ragged puncture rather than a clean slice. It had torn jaggedly, like a screwdriver forced through canvas. Hollis packed the site to stem the bleeding before turning his attention lower.

The condition of the abdomen was worse.

"Let's re-enter through the original incision," he said, already taking the scalpel from the scrub nurse. "Midline—scalpel. Bovie on standby."

The electrocautery tool hummed in the background as he reopened the surgical incision from the previous appendectomy, carefully navigating through layers of scarred fascia and inflamed peritoneum.

The abdominal cavity resembled a battlefield. Blood had pooled in the lower left quadrant, partially clotted yet threatening to compromise the bowel. The internal stitch line had ruptured, likely due to torsion and pressure.

The tissue had barely begun to heal from the last procedure, and now it looked like someone had ripped it apart by brute force. Half the sutures were gone. Others hung in long threads, surrounded by fresh hemorrhage and tissue sloughing. Blood pooled in the recess near the right lower quadrant—dark, slow-moving, but a steady flow.

"Suction."

The nurse moved in, clearing the area as Hollis deepened his view. The cavity was mottled with new ecchymosis—purple and green patches across bowel loops and omental fat. Fluid was present everywhere— blood, plasma, and thin strands of fibrin where inflammation had spiked. He probed gently toward the mesoappendix. The previous resection stump had held, but the surrounding tissue had not.

"Intestinal wall's intact," he said aloud. "No bowel perforation. But the internal bleeding's coming from torn adhesions near the peritoneal edge. It looks like the internal mesh pulled loose—probably from a fall or sudden torsion."

He didn't need to ask what caused it. The bruises along Colonel Roosevelt's right flank told him everything he needed to know.

"Let's get a cross-clamp on that arterial feeder," he said. "Clamp...now."

The assistant passed it over with steady hands. Hollis applied it just as another monitor alarm chirped behind him.

"BP's eighty systolic and falling," the anesthesiologist called out. "He's tachy, pulse one-forty and thready. Pupils are slow to react. Pale and near hypoxic."

"Push another unit of blood," Hollis said. "Add four units, type-specific. Platelets too—start the transfusion now. And get him on Zosyn and Flagyl—broad-spectrum coverage. I want no septic window after this."

"Already running Cefazolin," the nurse stated.

"Keep it. Add the combo anyway. We're not gambling on coverage."

He worked quickly, his hands moving with clean efficiency. Not frantic—never that—but fast. Purposeful. The bleeding wasn't massive, but it was diffuse and persistent. The kind that crept instead of poured. Silent hemorrhage was always more dangerous. It didn't alert you until the patient was halfway gone.

"Retract here—good. Okay, we're visualizing the source. Clamp the omental artery at this junction—there. That's it. Hold tension."

The team moved as one unit. Suction cleared the remaining fluid. The peritoneum remained raw, still irritated from the previous surgery, and Hollis hated the idea of going back into it so soon, but the alternative was worse.

He closed the bleeding sites one by one, carefully suturing along the delicate edges. Every knot needed to count.

And yet—he didn't relax. Because this wasn't a post-op complication. This damage was intentional.

The man on the table had been opened up twice, and now someone had tried to use that fact as a permanent kill switch.

"Pressure's coming back," the anesthesiologist said. "BP stabilizing at ninety-five over sixty. Pulse is slowing. Now down to one-twenty."

Hollis nodded. "Sponge count?"

"Eleven in, eleven out," the scrub nurse replied.

"Good."

When the arterial bleed in the shoulder burst open due to pressure, Hollis didn't flinch. He adjusted the lighting, widened the incision, and fully exposed the damaged vessel. The attacker hadn't used a blade designed for precision—it was a punch knife—thick and jagged. It had torn more than it sliced.

Someone had come to finish the job.

"We're closing. I want Vicryl on the deep layer. Use running PDS for the fascia. Irrigate everything before we seal."

He didn't take his eyes off the field until the final suture was tied and the last sterile dressing was applied. Only then did he peel off his gloves, one at a time, and step away from the table.

He stared down at his patient's face—still unconscious beneath the drape. Although his skin had regained some color, it was still far from healthy. He breathed shallowly, still on oxygen and pallid, a man teetering perilously close to the edge.

"Move him to the ICU, surgical side," Hollis said. "I want vitals on the hour. The Foley catheter stays. Keep him on half-rate fluids. Call me if his pressure drops more than ten systolic." He turned to the circulating nurse. "And tell JAG. They need to know this wasn't a surgical failure. This was an engineered murder attempt."

She didn't ask any questions, just nodded, went to the wall phone, and made the call.

Hollis removed his gown and walked to the scrub sink. As the water flowed over his hands, he closed his eyes for a moment.

Whoever wanted this man dead hadn't made a mistake. This wasn't just a trauma case or war zone medicine. This was a political execution gone wrong—a ghost bleeding out on his table who was never supposed to survive the first time, let alone a second, and now a third attempt.

Yet, here they were, and he had no doubt they would attempt a fourth.

He left the OR, wondering how many more times this man would survive before the system he was entangled in finally collapsed around them all.

0455 Hours
January 29, 1984
Recovery Room
Womack Army Medical Center
Fort Bragg, NC

Waking up was even worse this time. The world returned in fragmented pieces. At first, there was only a weight on Teddy's chest, in his arms, and even on his eyelids. Everything felt heavy, as though the air itself had thickened around him like a dense fog. A low hum resonated near his ear—not a voice or a machine, just a presence.

He took a moment to recall where he was and even longer trying to figure out why.

Teddy tried to swallow, but his throat was dry and burning. His tongue felt thick and heavy. He moved his lips but couldn't quite form a word.

Beneath his nose was the soft hiss of oxygen from the cannula and the gentle tug of an IV in the back of his right hand. His body ached, not just on the surface but more deeply now, more completely. It was the kind of pain that suggested they'd cut into him again.

His memory returned next, both blunt and sharp at the same time.

The attacker. The gun. The fight. The flash of "Iron Vince" Cross behind the doorway. The fist striking his ribs. The heat radiating from his side as the world bled sideways into shadow.

Teddy struggled to open his eyes, making two attempts before he succeeded.

The ceiling above him looked different now—he noticed that first. Not the ICU—a more restricted wing, quieter and colder. A monitor to his right clicked in rhythmic low tones. Nothing urgent. A nurse's silhouette passed the edge of the room but didn't come closer. She was giving him space or had been instructed not to hover. Either way, he appreciated it.

He turned his head toward the window. Every muscle protested. The new sutures in his side felt tight and raw. Something must have torn—probably during the struggle. His left arm was wrapped high on the bicep with thick layers of bandages covering the knife wound. It throbbed with each beat of his heart.

However, he was alive.

Again.

And they had tried harder this time.

He stared at the glass, allowing his eyes to focus on the faint reflection—sunrise bleeding pale orange against the eastern sky, light just beginning to break through the clouds. He wasn't restrained. That was the first surprise. He'd expected shackles. Something symbolic. But instead, the room was simply...quiet.

That conveyed more than a thousand words.

Teddy pushed his good hand under the blanket, moving slowly, aware of the tightness in his abdomen. The sidearm Cross had given him was gone. Of course, it was. But someone had replaced it with something else—a slip of paper, folded once.

He pulled it out with trembling fingers and opened it.

It contained a single handwritten line.

You're not alone anymore. – M

It bore no rank, name, or signature, other than a single letter to designate the writer—M. Yet he recognized the author by the slant of the handwriting. Merrit had good instincts. More importantly, she was adapting. That mattered now.

He let the paper rest on his chest and closed his eyes again.

There would be more attempts. That much was certain. However, the silence around him no longer felt like isolation. It felt like the calm before the counterstrike.

And somewhere beyond that window—whether through an official chain of command or backdoor favors—Jack and Eli were on the move. He could feel it, like distant thunder.

It wouldn't take long.

They'd come.

And when they did, the balance between life and death tipped precariously, giving no one an advantage.

He only needed to hold on long enough to tip the balance.

CHAPTER 23

0500 Hours
January 29, 1984
Parking Deck, Level Three
Fort Bragg, NC

Merrit stood next to her green Army-issue SUV, her Motorola "brick" phone pressed to her ear. Cross stood beside her, hand on his sidearm, as he scanned the parking deck for any watchers. The background chatter of the base had faded away. This section of the structure was unmonitored since it wasn't located in a high-security area and allowed full public access. There were no cameras or sign-in logs at either entry or exit. There was no reason for two senior officers to meet here at 0500 hours.

However, the signal had come through—a coded relay via the base switchboard requesting a meeting. It wasn't military or authorized, and it originated from two men who weren't supposed to be in the country.

The vehicle that pulled in two minutes later didn't look like much—a dust-covered, nondescript white pickup truck with civilian tags and a front grille held together by duct tape. It wasn't the white conversion van reported to be in their possession, possibly out of caution or because it had been impounded somewhere again. Rumors had been circulating among U.S. Army intel units for over a month about their daring escape from a jail in Arizona, executed during a derecho that knocked out all the security cameras and electronic locks.

Captain Jack "Ghost" Stratton was the first to exit, wearing tan slacks and a denim button-up shirt. Clean-shaven with a brown crew cut, he appeared far too calm for such an early hour. Following him, Master Sergeant Eli "Stone" Red Horse moved more slower, scanning the lot with the awareness of a man who anticipated violence around every corner.

Cross stiffened, shaking his head. "You've got to be kidding me."

Stratton smirked. "Nice to see you too, Colonel Cross."

Merrit raised her hand. "Stand down. All of you. We're here for the same reason."

Red Horse didn't move, but his eyes softened when he looked at her. "Is he alive?"

Merrit nodded. "Barely."

Stratton stepped forward, jabbing his finger at Cross. "Then let's skip the pleasantries. You don't like us, and we don't like you." He reached into his jacket and handed Merrit the matchbook.

She lifted the cover with *Half Moon Club* printed on it and looked at the message. *Roosevelt. Silence Order. Watch your six.* "This is how you knew to come here?"

"Yes. That club was in Saigon. It burned down in 1972 under, shall we say, suspicious circumstances. You want to stop this?" Jack asked. "Then we need to talk about what happened in 1972."

Merrit nodded and glanced at Cross.

No one spoke for a long time.

She opened the door to her SUV. "Follow us. I'll get you through the checkpoint."

0615 Hours
January 29, 1984
Exterior Holding Corridor
Womack Army Medical Center
Fort Bragg, NC

The hallway outside the recovery suite exuded a cold sterility, reminiscent of a space longing to be forgotten, characterized by blank white walls and smooth tiles. The scent of antiseptic made the environment feel too clean to be trustworthy. It was the kind of place where events unfolded in silence—where men in uniform moved through without leaving a trace behind.

Merrit stood at the end of the corridor, arms folded, her sweatsuit jacket unzipped and hanging open over a gray U.S. Army t-shirt as she waited for Colonel Roosevelt's men to catch up. While she escorted them through the checkpoint, they still needed to register with the hospital for visitation rights.

Busy completing reports, she hadn't slept since Colonel Roosevelt's last surgery. Ever since the attacker had bled out on the colonel's bed, her world had narrowed to a single task—keeping him alive, breathing, and talking while preventing the walls from closing in around them.

She heard the men before she saw them. Two sets of boots echoed down the hall. One was deliberate and measured, almost casual in its rhythm. The other was heavy and forceful, demanding the ground's attention. She didn't look up until they reached the corner—until Jack Stratton came into view, his coat collar turned up and sunglasses tucked into the front pocket of his shirt, trying to blend in, even though they both knew it was too late for subtlety.

Eli Red Horse followed, broader and bigger than she remembered from an hour ago, maybe because she was exhausted. His posture was coiled, ready to spring into action at a moment's notice, but restrained in the hospital setting. The tension in his shoulders wasn't just caution—it was concern. The kind that didn't wear off, built over the years of living life on the run.

Colonel Cross met them first, standing halfway between them and the recovery room, bowed up, almost challenging them to get past him by force. He didn't reach for a weapon, but he didn't need to. His eyes carried enough weight.

Jack didn't slow down. He stopped two feet away from the older man, his hands hanging loosely at his sides. "We're not here to start anything."

"No," Cross said. "You're here because something has already started, and we're all in the middle of it."

Merrit stepped forward to prevent the standoff from devolving into old habits and turning into a shouting match…or worse. "Let them in."

Cross stood his ground for a moment before stepping aside. "Go on."

Jack nodded, the tension in his jaw easing enough to convey his appreciation. "Thank you." He glanced toward the closed door at the end of the corridor. "He's in there?"

Merrit nodded. "Post-op. He lost a lot of blood. They had to reopen the original incision from the appendectomy. He was seconds from coding due to blood loss."

Eli glanced at the door, then back at her. "Is he conscious?"

"He was. Briefly. Long enough to warn me that this wasn't over." She looked at Cross. "We agree."

Jack looked from Merrit to Cross then back again. "So what are we walking into?"

"Something old, unfinished, and something no one wants above ground in the light of day and Congressional scrutiny."

Jack seemed poised to say more but held back. Instead, he ran a hand through his hair, the weight of everything all bearing down on his shoulders. "This wasn't supposed to happen."

"No," Merrit agreed. "But it's happening anyway."

For a moment, none of them moved. The lives of four people revolved around a man fighting to stay alive behind a barrier of surgical steel and IV lines. They weren't exactly friends, but the lines had blurred. The past didn't matter right now—only what came next mattered.

Jack was the first to break the silence. "I want to see him."

Merrit nodded and gestured down the hall. "He's got a .38 caliber revolver hidden under the blanket. Don't startle him."

Eli raised his eyebrows, clearly shocked. "'Iron Vince' Cross gave him a gun?"

"Cross saved his life."

There was a moment of stillness. Then Stratton chuckled. "Well. I guess hell really did freeze over." He began walking toward the room.

Eli followed behind him, dragging his feet, looking almost fearful of what he was about to see.

Merrit and Cross stayed quiet as the door opened.

For the first time in years, all four of them were together in the same place for the same reason.

Not to finish a mission.

But to stop a war.

0630 Hours
January 29, 1984
Recovery Room
Womack Army Medical Center
Fort Bragg, NC

The room was darker than expected. They had dimmed the overhead lights and left only the bedside lamp on, angled toward the far wall, its light filtering through a sheer curtain. The air carried a faint scent of antiseptic and plastic tubing. A heart monitor beeped from the left side of the bed, but it was far too slow for comfort.

Eli entered the room, stopping after two steps.

Jack followed, almost hesitant, his eyes adjusting not only to the dim lighting but also to what awaited them in the bed.

Teddy lay still. His chest rose and fell shallowly beneath a clean white sheet, with the thin hospital gown awkwardly tied around him to avoid disturbing the surgical site. His left arm rested elevated on a pillow, encased in a sling, with thick dressings wrapped from bicep to elbow. The tape along his side looked fresh. IV lines extended from both arms. He hadn't shaved. His skin appeared pale, his jaw shadowed by stubble, and his lips were dry and cracked.

The meeting occurred in silence, not because anyone mandated it that way, but because no one knew how to begin. The hospital room wasn't meant for this—four people standing around a man half-strapped to machines, bruised and stitched from shoulder to gut—but it was the only place left where the war hadn't overtaken them.

Eli inched closer to the bed, hesitant and unsure if it was real. His shoulders remained tense, anticipating that Teddy might sit up at any moment and give him hell for looking so worried. But he didn't.

Jack stood at the foot of the bed with his arms crossed. His expression didn't change, but the tightness around his mouth revealed his true feelings. He swallowed hard. "I've seen him shot. Seen him bleeding in places a man shouldn't walk away from. But this…"

Eli remained silent. He stared at the bruises on Teddy's forearm—deep, yellowing beneath the bandages. Not from surgery or an accident, but rather the result of fists.

"This isn't right," Eli said, his voice rough like gravel.

"No," Jack replied. "It's not."

Merrit locked the door after using her authority to clear the hallway and post her own handpicked guards outside.

Cross stood by the far wall with his arms crossed, his eyes scanning the corners of the ceiling, acting like he didn't trust the wiring. A convenient façade to conceal his emotions or guilt.

The heart monitor beeped in a slow, steady rhythm.

Then Teddy stirred, his breathing quickened, and the muscles around his closed eyes tightened.

Jack took a tentative step forward. "Colonel? Bull?"

Teddy opened his eyes, barely more than a squint, and even that effort cost him something. But when he focused and saw their faces, something changed. He didn't smile. Not yet. But the tension in his shoulders eased a tiny fraction.

Jack moved to the side of the bed, crouching down to Teddy's eye level. "We're here. You're not alone."

Teddy struggled to speak. "Took you long enough," he whispered.

Eli huffed—a mix of laughter and exhale—but his eyes stayed locked on Teddy's, still searching for signs of life. "You look like shit, Colonel."

Teddy blinked once. "Feel worse."

Jack nodded. "They came close."

"I noticed," Teddy whispered, trying to push himself up in the bed, a faint wince showing the effort it cost him. He moved his hand toward the edge of the blanket, but Jack stopped him with a gentle touch on his arm.

"Don't. You're held together with more staples and stitches than skin," Jack said.

Teddy let his arm drop. He looked between them, his eyes clearer now despite the exhaustion weighing down each breath. "They don't stop now. They'll double down."

"Then so do we."

"They trust you?" Teddy jutted his chin toward Merrit and Cross.

"Not yet," Jack said. "But Merrit opened the door. And Cross—he's the one who pulled the trigger and saved your life."

That acknowledgment of the truth elicited the slightest hint of a smirk from Teddy. "About time."

Eli moved closer now. "We got you, sir. No one's taking you out while we're still on our feet."

Teddy didn't respond right away. His eyes seemed unfocused for a moment. "Good. Because it's not just me they're after anymore."

Jack leaned against the windowsill, one hand resting on his thigh and the other tucked under his coat near the wooden grip of his .357 Magnum, something he wasn't technically supposed to carry in a military hospital.

Eli chose the chair closest to the bed—not because it was offered, but because he didn't want to tower over Teddy while he was down.

Teddy lay half-upright in bed, propped up by several pillows, pale yet alert, with one hand curled over the edge of the blanket. His eyes darted between Jack and Eli, clearly assessing how much longer they would continue to dance around what needed to be said.

"You said it wasn't just about you anymore," Merrit said. "Why is that?"

"Because it hasn't been for a long time. I'm just a pawn on the board, and they're done playing defense. Just like in chess, sometimes pawns are sacrificed to gain a strategic advantage. I was set up to take the fall while they make their next move. Now, they're consolidating, maybe even reactivating the network that buried Operation Firelight," Teddy said, his voice rough from exhaustion and the constant pull of pain.

Eli stared at him intently. "You mean the people who tried to kill you after that mission in Laos…they never stopped?"

"They stopped watching," Teddy said. "Or they thought they could. For a while, it was easier to let us be fugitives. We were too loud, too unpredictable, too public to kill clean. But something changed."

"Because Colonel Cross caught you?" Jack asked.

Cross remained silent, though his jaw visibly tightened.

Teddy glanced over at him. "It's not your fault, Vince. You did it right and followed procedure. You gave them a window they didn't expect. They had to improvise and failed. But they'll try again."

Merrit edged closer to the bed with her arms crossed over her chest. "We've confirmed at least three breaches—access logs rewritten, guards shuffled without proper routing paperwork, hallway surveillance tapes scrubbed clean."

"They're inside," Cross said. "Or above it, planted inside headquarters."

Jack snorted. "Same difference."

No one disagreed.

Teddy adjusted the pillow behind his head, and the pain must have flared, tightening the muscles around his eyes. He didn't show it otherwise. "They're trying to finish what they started in '72. Not just covering a trail. This isn't about justice or optics. It's about removing me from the board before I can name names."

"And if you do?" Merrit asked.

"Then it burns. The whole damn fucking thing. The operation, the funding chain, and the surviving architects of the system. A few of them are still embedded within the federal government in places no one would ever suspect. Most have gone private, doing contract work, logistics firms, and serving as embedded advisers in so-called demilitarized zones. It's not part of the government anymore. It's a multi-billion dollar business."

Jack shook his head. "Jesus, Teddy! I hate these assholes."

"Me too. I knew it would come back eventually," Teddy whispered. "But I thought I'd be gone before it did."

Eli leaned forward, resting his elbows on his knees, his gaze locked on Teddy's. "So what do we do now? Sit here until they make another run at you?"

"No," Merrit said. "We build an impenetrable firewall. First, around Colonel Roosevelt. Then around the story. We lock down this hospital, take control of the communication flow, and cut the chain of command above us out of the loop."

"That's against the regulations, Merrit," Teddy said. She had made significant progress in understanding how the system truly worked in just a few short days. So had Cross.

"Screw the regulations."

Cross nodded. "Agreed. Anyone who asks for transfer orders, medical records, or visitation rights goes on a list to be vetted and cleared. No exceptions."

"And after that?" Jack asked.

"We dig into every piece of information available," Merrit said. "We use what Colonel Roosevelt gives us and find the cracks. The people funding this can't hide if we rip the floorboards up and expose the truth."

"It's not enough to find them. We have to make it public. We need to expose them where the black world system can't be hidden behind a wall of paperwork and lies," Teddy said.

Merrit turned toward him. "And can you do that? Do you still have the documents?"

"Not here. But I know where they are. And I know who I trust to get them." He looked at Eli and Jack. The message was clear.

Eli nodded. "Then we'll get it done."

Cross pushed off the wall, moving closer to the bed. "You've been hunted for years. Betrayed by the brass, blamed for a war crime, written off as a rogue officer and a traitor. Are you sure you still want to fight this? Why not ride off into the sunset and live a quiet life in the shadows under another name with no one trying to kill you?"

Teddy didn't smile, but there was something sharp in his eyes—older than anger, deeper than pride. "Because I want to end this. That's why I never stopped fighting."

The silence that followed was not hesitation. It was an agreement.

And the war had just become theirs.

CHAPTER 24

1200 Hours
January 29, 1984
Rural Back Roads
Spring Lake, NC

The dirt road curved east through long, desolate stretches of pine trees and scrub brush—the kind of nowhere that wouldn't show up on a map unless you already knew it was there. Eli gripped the wheel like he was driving a combat rig in a war zone, using both hands while continuously scanning the road. The old white Dodge Ram didn't look like much, but it was geared correctly, stripped of anything traceable, and armored where it mattered.

Jack sat next to him, his boots resting on the dashboard and mirrored aviator sunglasses concealing the tension that had settled into his jaw hours earlier. He hadn't said much since they left the hospital, and neither had Eli. They didn't need words to understand the gravity of this situation.

If they were followed, there wouldn't be a second chance to get what they came for.

They veered off the main road onto a narrow gravel track, barely wide enough for the truck, overgrown with two-foot-tall weeds and hidden behind an abandoned, dilapidated barn. No signs pointed them in the right direction, only old tire ruts in the dirt and a gate rusted through at the hinges. Jack reached under the seat and pulled out the map again—hand-sketched by Teddy weeks before Operation Firelight, the kind of thing you drew if you never expected to live long enough to return.

Eli grunted as the suspension snagged on an upraised root. "He really buried this?"

"Wouldn't be Teddy if he didn't," Jack said, adjusting the map to match the terrain.

They parked half a mile off the nearly non-existent road and walked the rest of the way as the forest quickly closed in around them. It was thick here—dense with underbrush, and roots curled up from the ground like ribs. Jack carried a U.S. military surplus folding shovel while Eli had a crowbar and an AR-15 rifle slung across his back. They had no radio. If anything went wrong, it would happen out here in silence, without any backup available.

The site was marked by three stones arranged in a crooked triangle beneath an old pine tree. Teddy had chosen it for the tree, not the clearing. That tree had been struck by lightning twice. It now leaned, scarred black, having endured every punishment the world could throw at it while refusing to fall.

"Figures," Eli muttered.

Jack knelt and removed the grass, rocks, and debris from the soil. The earth felt looser than it should have—disturbed long ago then left to seal itself with time and weather. Five minutes into digging, the shovel struck metal.

Not a box or a crate, but a 155mm shell casing. Jack dug faster, clearing the outline of the old munitions tube—Cold War era, sealed and watertight, buried six feet below the ground, and wrapped in layers of rubber and plastic sheeting. Eli pried it loose with the crowbar, then reached in and pulled the cylinder out of the hole.

It was heavier than expected.

After they broke the seal, three things were inside.

A bound stack of carbon-copy orders lacking an official header with names redacted but not erased.

A microfilm reel stored in a clear plastic, waterproof sleeve.

A sealed, yellowed standard mailing envelope addressed to Jack.

Jack didn't open it. Not yet. That should be done in a secure area, not in a wooded clearing.

Instead, he reviewed the paperwork while Eli scanned the woods, remaining vigilant for anyone who might have followed them.

"This is it," Jack said, more to himself than to anyone else. "Everything he said. Everything they tried to erase is here."

Eli glanced back at him. "Then let's get out of here before someone else comes looking for us."

Jack placed the items into a reinforced leather satchel, slung it over his shoulder, and took one last look at the grave. The hiding place had served its purpose well.

Now it was up to them to make sure the truth saw the light of day.

They moved fast on the way out.

The trees watched them go.

```
1430 Hours
January 29, 1984
Secure Conference Room
Womack Army Medical Center
Fort Bragg, NC
```

The hospital had been under a controlled lockdown since Jack and Eli left to find Colonel Roosevelt's evidence. Not a full martial law type security—Merrit knew better than to attract that kind of attention—but every hallway was now staffed by people she trusted. Handpicked MPs, internal sweep teams, and even a communications scrambler were masking external transmissions from the west wing. They couldn't stop what was coming, not entirely, but they could delay it. That mattered now.

The conference room, located just off the restricted recovery ward, had been repurposed. The windows were covered, and the door was secured with triple locks. Cross stood near the far wall with his arms folded over his chest while Merrit operated the flatbed microfiche reader that hummed on the corner table. The screen glowed, and the glass reflected the light.

Jack set the satchel on the table. His face was pale from fatigue, and dust still clung to the collar of his coat.

Eli stood behind him like a silent wall, watchful as always.

Merrit unzipped the bag and removed its contents—the carbon copies of the orders—on faded, yellowed paper that still carried the faint smell of dirt—followed by a black plastic canister containing the microfilm. There was also an unopened envelope with Jack's name on it, resting untouched in the center of the table.

She picked up the orders first.

The top sheet was a deployment routing issued under a false operations header—Project VESTIGE. There was no official record of such a designation. The dates matched those of Operation Firelight, and the coordinates were identical.

The authorizing signature had been redacted—chemically burned out, not inked—yet the protocol string that followed remained legible.

Cross pointed at the papers. "That string shouldn't exist."

"It doesn't," Merrit said. "Except in compartmented networks."

"Legacy black-world clearance," Jack said. "The kind you can't pull with a subpoena."

Merrit flipped to the second page of the carbon-copy orders. The paper was old and brittle at the corners, yet the imprint of typewriter keys remained crisp and legible. She paused when she found a string of characters typed at the bottom of the authorization block, a cluster of letters and numbers that didn't belong to any formal military routing chain.

OP/SEG-9 — VST-714-AZ9/OR5

Jack leaned over her shoulder, reading it upside down. "Is that a routing number or a unit designation?"

"No," Merrit said, pulling her reading glasses from her breast pocket and placing them on her nose. "It's not an official chain. It's a protocol string. An internal compartment code. I've seen this kind of classification code before—only in post-war audit files, buried under three layers of red tape. Compartmentalized projects tied to long-retired operations that never went fully public. Not even JCS has access to these operations."

"Do you recognize it?" Cross asked.

"I've seen this format before. A similar format, in a classified review I was assigned to back in '78—an oversight file from a failed DIA asset extraction. The mission file was sealed, redacted so deeply it barely made sense. But there was a string at the bottom. Just like this one. No names or unit assignments. Just alphanumeric like a call sign nobody wanted traced. These strings don't go through standard command levels. They're embedded identifiers for black compartmented operations. Legacy projects. Ones so far outside doctrine that even top brass don't get briefed unless they're directly involved." She tapped the edge of the string with one fingernail. "This one—VST—probably shorthand for Vestige. That was a codename buried in some of the older MACV-SOG archives. Cold storage stuff. No one's admitted it existed. It matches a suppressed field reference that came up once in a war crimes oversight report I reviewed in '77. No source. Just a string—no names or origin. These strings are only used on chain-of-command documents for black-compartmented ops."

Cross glanced at her. "You're telling me this is a ghost program."

"I'm telling you, this code has always been linked to black-world funding, used only when someone wanted total deniability from the chain of command, even stretching as far as the President."

Jack straightened, the tension settling behind his eyes. "So it's real. If this string links to Operation Firelight…the mission…was authorized. And buried before we ever made it out."

Merrit nodded. "And now we have the evidence. The orders, the financial trail, and a protocol string that ties it to programs that were never supposed to exist."

Eli moved closer. "Are you sure about this?"

"I spent ten years reading the footprints of these people. Trust me—I've never seen a clearer trail."

"If it's not traceable—how do you even prove it's real?" Jack asked.

"You don't," Cross said, already knowing the answer. "That's the point."

"But if you recognize the structure, and it shows up on a document tied to a real-world op...it's enough to break the silence," Merrit said.

"So this is proof we didn't act alone?" Eli asked. "It was sanctioned, and they meant for us to die in Laos."

Merrit didn't look away from the document. "This is proof someone gave you the order and designed the mission to vanish after you died completing it. And since these orders survived, it means Colonel Roosevelt kept the only surviving link to whoever gave the kill order."

Eli crossed his arms. "And they've been trying to erase him ever since."

She turned the next page, detailing the funding chain funneled through offshore banks and connected to shell corporations with names that hadn't been in use since the early '70s—Orion Five, Redleaf Export, Dynstar Solutions. These companies were established not to evade foreign enemies—but to stay off the radar of Congress and the oversight committees.

Eli shook his head, his brow furrowed in disgust. "So it was real. All of it. They sent us in, then tried to bury the mission and us along with it."

Merrit nodded. "This wasn't instigated by a rogue agent. This was planned, authorized, and deliberately erased after the fact. They killed the paper trail—except Colonel Roosevelt kept a copy."

Cross narrowed his eyes. "The moment we make this public..."

"They'll try to kill him again," Jack said. "And maybe the rest of us too."

Merrit reached for the microfilm. She loaded it into the reader, adjusted the focus, and brought the image into view. A scanned report appeared on the screen. It was a mission debrief—typewritten and smudged near the staples. The author wasn't from Colonel Roosevelt's team, but from the operative who had signed off on the final security bypass of the Senate Armed Services Committee—a man believed to be dead.

"Lieutenant Commander Nathan Kaufman," Merrit read aloud. "Attached to Naval Intelligence, loaned to Joint Task Force Phoenix. No official unit designation. No return routing. This guy wasn't part of any official Naval personnel roster."

Cross stepped forward. "Kaufman disappeared in '73 on a top-secret classified mission. He was declared MIA in Laos."

"He wasn't missing," Merrit said. "He was black-bagged, and someone scrubbed the records. Probably due to fallout from Operation Firelight."

The next frame on the reel displayed a hand-drawn organizational chart—lines sketched in pencil and scanned for duplication. Kaufman's report had been smuggled out of the records section. The names were incomplete, but two of them were clearly marked in ink beneath a shared directive line connecting to the protocol string at the top of the chart.

Major Gen. Franklin A. Dorsey – Strategic Planning, DIA
Colonel Martin Kohrs – Operations Liaison, CIA Task Group D-7

Jack leaned over her shoulder. "They ordered it?"

"They engineered and funded it," Merrit said. "Dorsey's still alive and active, consulting, private defense contracts, and high security clearance advisory roles. He's in the private sector now. Kohrs disappeared in '76. That's no coincidence."

Cross glanced at the names again, his jaw tightening. "These aren't ghosts. These are architects. And if Dorsey's still walking around free, moving within the national defense circles, then he's part of whatever's being rebuilt."

Merrit turned away from the screen. "We need to take this to Colonel Roosevelt. Because he's the only one who can explain all of it, and he made damn sure these orders survived the purge."

Jack nodded. "I agree. We need to do this now. But before we go…" He picked up the envelope addressed to him from the table, slicing open the top with his pocket knife. Inside was a handwritten letter on yellowed typing paper. He placed it on the table for everyone to see. The instruction at the top was irrelevant at this point in time.

To: Captain Jack Stratton
Private – Eyes Only

Jack,

If you're reading this, it means something went wrong. Maybe I didn't make it. Maybe I had to disappear for good. Either way, I'm trusting you with the one thing I never trusted anyone else to carry—the truth.

You always had a knack for getting into places the rest of us couldn't. Now I need you to do the same with this evidence, with what we were a part of. Don't let them bury us or the truth again.

I kept the files. The orders. The money trail. Not for revenge, but so one day someone could put the pieces together and understand the reasons why we were sacrificed.

Use what's here. And if Stone's still alive, bring him in.

I don't need a legacy, Jack. I just need you to make sure they don't rewrite ours.

Keep the faith, my friend.

Teddy

Jack shook his head. "This letter. The evidence. Everything is so Teddy and his blasted honesty. And his twelve-year-old prediction almost came true…now we go see Teddy and find out what in the hell is going on."

CHAPTER 25

1545 Hours
January 29, 1984
Private Room 512
Womack Army Medical Center
Fort Bragg, NC

The air in the room was still when they entered. The afternoon light filtered through the blinds in dull streaks, casting soft shadows on the linoleum floor. The machines by the bed hummed steadily. The oxygen line remained silent, and the cardiac monitor ticked in a rhythm that hadn't changed since his last sedation dose. At first glance, Teddy appeared to be asleep—still and pale, his face slack beneath the shadow of an unshaven cheek.

But his eyes opened before anyone spoke. He saw them immediately—Jack, Eli, Merrit, and Cross—all gathered next to the bed. Then he noticed what Jack held in his hands—the microfilm, the now opened letter, the file, the weight of everything he had buried in that field so long ago.

He didn't attempt to sit up but gestured with two fingers to indicate they should place it on the bedside table beside him. Merrit pushed the bedside table closer, and Jack laid the folder next to a half-full plastic cup of water and a coiled line of IV tubing.

No one spoke as Teddy opened it.

The papers crackled beneath his fingers. He moved slowly—not only due to the pain, but also because he knew exactly what he was about to see. He scanned the top sheet, the routing code, the cover header, and the redacted signature. But when he reached the protocol string, something inside him awakened. Not visibly. Just a slight tightening of his mouth, a flicker of recognition of what it all meant.

Then he turned the page, and there it was—a name—Dorsey.

He stared at the name without blinking.

Merrit moved closer to the bed. "You knew him...Dorsey?"

"Not knew," Teddy said in a gravelly-thin voice. "Served under him. Indirectly." He rested his hand on the page. "Major General Franklin Dorsey never got his hands dirty. He operated three layers removed from the rest of us. Strategic Planning, Defense Intelligence Agency. But he had a footprint. His funding approvals always came through with too many backdoors. We all knew there was something off—but if you asked questions, you didn't get answers. You got reassigned. Or worse. I heard rumors that he blackmailed senators to get his financial backing, even to the point of threatening to kill their families, and generals who didn't agree with him or his methods wound up either under JAG investigation or six feet under at Arlington."

"He was the one who pulled the trigger?" Cross asked from the corner of the room.

"No," Teddy said. "He never pulled anything. Too entrenched in high-level politics. He had people for that. Experts in making it look natural. But he authorized Operation Firelight. He pushed it through under VESTIGE, accusing General Montgomery of embezzlement to hide the financing. Gave us a green light with no intention of extraction. When we finished the job, they tried to silence us."

He lowered his hand to the blanket, curling his fingers around it. "Kohrs was his cleaner. CIA liaison. What some call a 'wet boy' and most term an assassin. Compartmented all internal reporting—gave it just enough legitimacy to pass a desk check, but no oversight. By the time the mission went sideways, the operation didn't officially exist. We were expendable."

Merrit didn't leave right away. She hovered at the edge of the room for a moment, then reached into her briefcase and pulled out a slim folder marked with a restricted access band. "There's something else you should see. We found it in Dunning's compartmentalized case log. Not part of the official Firelight file. It was buried in an off-grid index in a basement file room awaiting destruction at Fort Belvoir—paper only. No log entry in the Army computer network or any Pentagon file."

She opened the folder and handed him a single document.

A diagonal red slash ran across the page. The header read—

TOP SECRET – EYES ONLY
OPERATIONAL CONTAINMENT DIRECTIVE
SABLE PROTOCOL
Clearance Code: 731-X5
Handler: DUNNING / OCN-7017
Issued via: Task Group D-7 // SAD-L

Teddy didn't speak as he scanned the lines, his brow tightening upon reading what amounted to an execution order. The weight of that revelation pressed behind his ribs like a bruise being hit repeatedly. "This isn't retaliation," he said. "This was built in. From the start." He lowered the page slowly, his eyes hard now. "They didn't burn us after it went wrong. These assholes planned to burn us before the mission even started."

"I know that now, and it explains what has been going on here," Merrit stated.

Eli muttered something unintelligible, low and filled with anger, under his breath.

"So we were sacrificial lambs led to slaughter the second we landed in Laos," Jack said, bitterness in his voice.

"Yes," Teddy said. "They needed deniability. And when we survived, they needed the myth—the rogue unit, the massacre of innocent civilians, the court-martial—to cover up what really happened."

"Why didn't you bring this forward before now?" Merrit asked

Teddy turned to her. "To who? The same operational structure that let Dorsey disappear into a think tank? The same system that shredded every order copy and buried my team under false charges? There was no one to bring it to. Not then." He looked back at the file, rubbing his thumb across the microfilm sleeve. "But now it's different. Now they came for me openly. And now I'm not the only one holding the thread that leads directly to Dorsey."

He glanced at each of them in turn. "You want to stop this? You burn it down from the top. Dorsey's still moving pieces. That means this isn't over. And if we don't stop him, whatever he's rebuilding now—whatever this thing has become—it'll be worse than what we walked away from during Operation Firelight. I didn't bury it to protect them. I buried it because there was no one left to listen. No command-level officers I could trust. No court wanted to hear the truth. I thought surviving would be enough. I was wrong."

The room stayed quiet.

But something had changed.

For the first time, all five of them understood the same truth.

This wasn't about vindication. It was about preventing what came next.

1759 Hours
January 29, 1984
JAG Operations Wing
Office of Lt. Colonel Merrit
Fort Bragg, NC

The office was silent, the kind of quiet that came with locked doors, late hours, and a lack of trust in the chain of command. Merrit sat behind her desk, the surface cleared except for one item—a thick manila envelope marked with her initials, an internal tracking code, and no external routing numbers. It would never be mailed. It was meant to be hand-delivered when this transitioned from a quiet investigation to an active prosecution.

Cross stood by the window, his back straight and hands clasped behind his back, watching the orangish-red hues of dusk spread across the compound. He hadn't said much since finishing the last page of the field orders. "You're not going to get this through standard channels. You know that."

"I'm not trying to." Merrit draped her jacket over the back of her chair, rolled up her sleeves, and sat at her desk. She began typing and didn't look up from the document as she spoke. "This isn't about convictions. Not yet. It's about leverage. I'm building a back door into the system."

"Do you really think one memo will stop a powerful man like Dorsey?"

"This isn't a memo. It's a lifeline." She finished the paragraph and pressed print three times because she needed this in triplicate. The daisy wheel printer on the file cabinet sprang to life with a metallic clatter as the carriage retracted. "If I send this packet to the Oversight Office at Langley, it disappears. If I bring it to the Senate Defense Subcommittee, Select Committee on Intelligence, or the Armed Services Committee under sealed evidentiary review, it gets buried for years under a mound of red tape and closed-door hearings. But if I prepare an evidentiary summary and quietly deliver it to Senator Taggart, off the record—"

Cross turned to face her. "Do you really think he'll touch this?"

"I don't care if he does. I care if he knows it exists. He's been on the Senate Armed Services Committee since '79. He's very old school, doesn't like covert funding structures or unauthorized field actions. He's been waiting for a nail big enough to hang someone with, and this might be it."

"And what if it isn't?"

"Then at least, we make it impossible to pretend Operation Firelight and what occurred afterward didn't happen. Because once it's in the bloodstream, Dorsey can't control the narrative anymore."

Merrit stood up, walked to the printer, pulled out the page, and read it aloud. "Unredacted field orders recovered from off-site location confirm existence of covert compartment under protocol string VST-714. Documented routing through Strategic Planning (DIA) suggests Major General Franklin A. Dorsey authorized a black-world funding initiative, Operation Firelight, later sanitized under Operation VESTIGE. Associated financials indicate the use of off-ledger transfers and shell corporations. Initial evidence supports allegations of falsified charges against Colonel Theodore Roosevelt IV and all associated personnel."

She set the page down—less than half a page of printing, but each word carried weight—and looked at Cross. "If I go through JAG, they block me. If I go public, they kill Colonel Roosevelt. So we do both—quietly. We build a case airtight enough to be undeniable while the others close the gap on Dorsey directly."

Cross shook his head. "Do you think this is winnable?"

"No, not entirely, but I think it's survivable—if we move first." She slid the paper into the prepared manila envelope, sealed it, and leaned back in her chair. "If we get this to the right people before they realize what we have, it keeps them reactive. They can't strike first if they're scrambling to cover their tracks."

Cross rested his hand on his sidearm holstered on his hip. "You do know what comes next, right?"

"I do."

"Then say it."

Merrit held up the manila envelope. "This puts Colonel Roosevelt right in the crosshairs, but we're not investigating anymore. We're building an air-tight case. And if we're lucky—we make them run from the confrontation before they shoot again."

CHAPTER 26

0630 Hours
January 30, 1984
Private Room 512
Womack Army Medical Center
Fort Bragg, NC

The room was still and silent except for the low hum of equipment as Teddy pushed himself higher in his bed, trying to find a more comfortable position. The pain was quieter now. Not gone—but dulled to a distant throb, like the echo of something trying to remind him that he wasn't out of the woods yet.

He didn't need the reminder that he'd been cut open, stitched up, drugged, and kept under guard for two weeks. For most of that time, he lived with the knowledge that death was imminent—not just as a fleeting thought, but as a certainty. No one could tempt fate as often as he had and remain among the living for long.

But today felt different. The silence this morning was of a different kind. Not the hollow, tense quiet that had hung over the room for days—where every creak in the hallway made his body tense involuntarily, where the hum of machines seemed to count down to something he couldn't see. No. This was something else. Stillness, but with weight. Not fear. Not dread. Something quieter. A pause that didn't feel like it was holding its breath.

The lighting was dim, casting a soft amber glow from the corner lamp instead of the harsh overhead fluorescent lights. The flow rate on his oxygen line had been reduced from ten to five liters through a nasal cannula. Only one IV bag of normal saline remained, half empty. The heart monitor beeped in a slow, steady rhythm. No one hovered over him, poking, prodding, and taking his vital signs every fifteen minutes, preventing him from getting any rest. No voices whispered outside the door. Even the air felt less vigilant.

Teddy blinked, gazing up at the ceiling and breathing slowly, every muscle urging him to remain still. The shadowy men of his past hadn't returned. Someone or something out there had caused them to pause their attempts on his life. The legacy protocol?

152

He moved ever so carefully, with his muscles resisting every movement and each stitch along with every dull ache layered beneath the bandages. Even repositioning his hand to a more comfortable spot on the sheet was enough to induce pain. But it wasn't sharp now. It didn't feel like his body was coming apart at every stitched or stapled seam—just soreness. And that word—healing—had seemed so far away for so long that he hadn't dared to believe it might actually begin.

Teddy thought about Merrit and Cross—two people who had started as his handlers and jailers. Now they were something different, standing beside him and risking their careers, perhaps even more. Cross had pulled the trigger to save his life. Merrit had buried a legal hammer inside an envelope meant to break Dorsey and his black world operation wide open.

And Jack and Eli…God, he hadn't known if they would show up. He wouldn't have blamed them if they hadn't. But they did. And they moved like the team they once were—quick, quiet, and decisive. But without him.

He gazed at the dim light of dawn filtering through the window slats. The room remained the same. The bedside table still stood to his right, the IV bag still hung to his left, and the monitors continued to beep in a steady rhythm. Yet something had changed.

The room wasn't guarded openly—at least not by force.

The two MPs outside the door had been rotated—he could hear them, faint conversations, but their tone was relaxed. Not careless, just not tense. That hadn't happened since the first night. Since the second surgery. Since they realized someone had entered this place with murder in their hands.

His body still felt like it belonged to someone else—heavy and uncooperative. The long line of stitches across his side throbbed in time with his heartbeat with every breath. But now there was clarity too. A calm that had nothing to do with medication and everything to do with what he hadn't felt since the moment they put him in that cage.

Control. He didn't have it completely. Not yet. But it was returning—through Merrit, who had finally stopped thinking like a prosecutor, pushing past her Army training, and started thinking like a field officer. Through Cross, who no longer viewed him as a fugitive but as a man whose testimony might uncover the truth of something even he hadn't anticipated.

And, most importantly, through Jack and Eli. They were out there now, moving like quiet, deadly professionals. They were doing what they had always done best—turning the enemy's structure into a weapon against itself.

For the first time since the knife attack, since the pain began in the jail cell, and since they dragged him into that first freezing hallway, Teddy allowed himself to breathe—not just reflexively but with purpose. He closed his eyes again and let the sound of the monitor fade into the background. His body ached, and his muscles twitched with exhaustion. But something deeper had eased.

He was no longer alone.

For the first time in years, that meant something.

Today, he felt safe enough to let his body relax, even if just for a moment.

And the war was finally turning back toward those who started it.

```
2345 Hours
January 30, 1984
Near the Wardman Club
Southwest Waterfront
Washington, D.C.
```

The waterfront had changed over the last ten years. New money had arrived, constructing condos with private marinas and restaurants serving twenty-dollar cocktails on recycled wood menus. Yet not everything was shiny. The wooden piers still had rough edges and splinters that could cut deep. Shadowy figures continued to gather in places where no security cameras pointed, and the right kind of men still passed through unnoticed.

Eli parked their borrowed, plain black sedan three blocks away in a side alley near the loading docks. Jack rode shotgun, dressed in an expensive three-piece suit, looking like he had just come from a lobbying dinner but without the arrogance. He carried himself in a way that suggested he preferred not to be remembered.

They remained silent as they exited the car.

The Wardman Club resembled any other old-money retreat nestled within a historic building—polished marble floors, leather chairs by the fire, and dark wood bookshelves filled with volumes of leather-bound classic books that no one read. It was a place designed for discretion, for those who no longer needed to seek permission.

Jack and Eli entered under assumed names—*Liam Foster* and *Kimo Walker*. They were clean-shaven and dressed in suits, registered as corporate security consultants with a late dinner reservation. The fake IDs were legitimate, vetted by Merrit and Cross. Nothing about them would raise any red flags. They were positioned just high enough in the hierarchy to blend in with this crowd and low enough to go unnoticed.

Dorsey wasn't there. Not yet. But his aide sat at the back near the bar, drinking and laughing with two men Jack recognized from the Washington, D.C. society pages—men who secured contracts with defense contractors and had never worn a uniform in their lives.

Their mark—Rudy Trask—was exactly the kind of man Jack remembered from Southeast Asia, a former enlisted soldier turned private logistics operator. No paper trail existed for him after '77, but his name had shown up twice on billing records linked to defense contracts that lacked movement logs. Jack had noticed it, the kind of detail you only caught if you were trained to spot lies in the margins. Something he learned while debriefing two East German defectors in 1969 during his time as an interrogator with U.S. Army Intelligence.

Rudy spent his days managing fleet transportation for a consulting firm serving three clients, all of whom were shell companies linked to Dorsey. He still smoked clove cigarettes and carried a switchblade knife, even when he wasn't expecting trouble.

Eli leaned in closer to Jack. "Are you sure this is the right guy?"

"Yes. He signs off on Dorsey's travel schedules. If we track him, we track the General." Jack sipped his club soda. "We don't push. We let him talk."

The bait was already set. A former NSA analyst, now moonlighting as a disgraced contractor, had been leaking "anonymized data sets" into the defense gossip chain—Jack made sure of that. The aide had already taken the bait. He just didn't know it yet.

When Trask entered the alcove next to the restroom to take a call on the pay phone, Jack and Eli followed him, staying close enough to hear the important parts.

"Yeah, I heard it too. That name came up again—Roosevelt, the Rough Rider. Can you believe that? I thought they shut that door in '72..."

Eli tensed up, clearly not happy with the conversation.

Jack remained still. His undercover intelligence training taught him to ignore those types of emotional triggers or distractions.

"No. He's not dead. Not yet. But there's movement, and Kohrs isn't answering calls anymore." Trask began to pace nervously, limping across the floor to the end of the phone cord because of a combat injury to his hip. Sweat dripped onto his collar—the kind that came when secrets were in flux and no one was in control.

Jack shared a fleeting glance with Eli.

The game had changed. Time to improvise.

They waited until he finished his call and returned to his friends. While he paid his tab by handing cash to the bartender, Eli and Jack moved toward the exit, watching from the phone booth across the street.

As Trask walked to his car parked nearby, Eli and Jack followed a short distance behind him.

Jack allowed him to take five steps into the alley before stepping off the sidewalk to join him. "Rudy Trask."

The man froze.

"Jesus Christ," Trask yelled, turning to face him. "You can't just—who in the hell are you?"

Jack smiled, not wide or friendly. "Let's say I used to run certain types of errands for a man you still work for. A man with silver hair and too many enemies."

Trask opened his mouth then closed it again. He reached for his coat pocket but stopped short. Not out of fear, but out of consideration for the odds. He still wasn't sure where the threat was coming from.

Jack didn't let him figure it out. "You have worked on Dorsey's itineraries for six years. I'm not asking how many flights you booked. I'm asking what you've been cleaning up for him since Kohrs disappeared."

That hit home.

Trask's breath caught—just barely—but Jack noticed it.

"I don't know what you're talking about," Trask said.

"Yes, you do," Jack said. "Because Dorsey doesn't keep people around unless they're good at making things disappear. Schedules. Records. Witnesses."

Eli stepped out of the shadows, cracking his massive knuckles. "You make the wrong call right now, and you don't walk away."

Trask raised his hands slowly. "I'm not stupid."

"No," Jack said. "Just scared. And smart enough to know something's changed." He moved closer now. Not threatening—just making his presence known, along with the .357 Magnum in his concealed shoulder holster, pulling it out just enough for Trask to see it. "Here's what's going to happen. You're going to give me his next movement window. Not a lie or a dummy trail. The real one. Where Dorsey will be. Who is he meeting? You're going to do that because if you don't, what's coming for Dorsey is going to land on you first.

Trask hesitated for a moment before nodding once. "Okay."

Jack smiled again. "That's better."

CHAPTER 27

0845 Hours
January 31, 1984
Private Room 512
Womack Army Medical Center
Fort Bragg, NC

The knock on the door was soft, not a warning or a request—just enough to maintain the rhythm of the place. Teddy didn't answer. He didn't need to. Whoever was there would eventually come in. A few seconds later, the door opened halfway, and Merrit stepped inside. Cross followed her into the room.

They didn't rush in, stand at attention, or ask if he was awake. They simply entered, understanding the weight it now carried. The hospital room was no longer just for recovery. It had become their de facto headquarters—ground zero—a war room equipped with a heart monitor and morphine drips.

Teddy nodded to acknowledge their presence. He didn't try to sit up—his body still punished him for that. The stitches along his side pulled with every movement, and he knew the color hadn't returned to his face. But his mind was clear now.

Merrit placed the folder at the foot of the bed and sat in the chair closest to him. Cross remained standing, one hand resting on the backrest and the other at his side. Both of them shared the same look in their eyes—steady yet taut with more than urgency.

They'd found something.

"You're either about to bring me good news or put a bullet in me," Teddy said, trying to lighten the mood.

Merrit didn't smile, clearly not amused by his poor attempt at levity. "We've got real movement. Jack and Eli locked in Dorsey's next appearance—Quantico, at the logistics annex in a closed-door meeting. No aides. Minimal security."

Cross nodded. "It's not on any official itinerary. We confirmed all the information through his private travel coordinator. It's a secure site, but not currently assigned to the military—he's using it like a fallback. Probably thinks it's quiet enough to talk off-the-books."

Teddy pushed himself higher in the bed. "He's not wrong. It's smart."

"He's careful, but not cautious. That's the crack in his armor. He doesn't know we're watching the legal side too." Merrit opened the folder, turning it so he could see the top page. It wasn't long—barely three typed paragraphs. The language was precise, exhibiting a clarity that could only come from someone who had spent years wielding bureaucracy and the legal system like a scalpel.

Teddy read every word without interruption.

His hand lay still against the top page, palm half-curled, fingertips brushing the crease. His hand trembled—not from fear, but from the effort it took to remain still while every line of that summary pressed deeper into old wounds he had long stopped touching.

He reached the line referencing Dorsey and paused.

Then again, regarding Kaufman's name.

And once again, when he read the final paragraph. *Three attempts on Colonel Roosevelt's life while in custody...*

He didn't speak. Not yet.

[CONFIDENTIAL SUMMARY – CLASSIFIED APPENDIX | Prepared by LTC Sarah Merrit, U.S. Army JAG Corps]
Reference ID: VST-714-AZ9/OR5
Subject: Unacknowledged Operation Involving Colonel Theodore Roosevelt IV – Laos, 1972

SUMMARY:
This document summarizes preliminary findings from the recovery of primary-source field orders and financial routing related to a covert, unacknowledged operation conducted during the Vietnam War. The materials, verified through forensic inspection and internal cross-referencing, are believed to be the only surviving documentation of a DIA/CIA-sanctioned top-secret mission compartmentalized under protocol string VST-714-AZ9/OR5—a legacy black-world designation not recorded in standard oversight archives.

The documents refer to a direct-action raid called Operation Firelight (codename redacted from surviving copies) targeting enemy-held financial infrastructure in North Vietnam, conducted by a Special Forces team (codename Shadow Lance) led by Colonel Theodore Roosevelt IV, operating at that time under authority relayed through DIA Strategic Planning.

Signature fields on all recovered orders were chemically redacted in accordance with the decommissioning protocols established to sanitize sensitive operations during 1972–73. However, the accompanying authorizations adopt a format exclusive to Major General Franklin A. Dorsey who served as the Assistant Director of Strategic Planning at the DIA. The authorization protocol string aligns with a known, compartmented funding stream traced to three offshore holding fronts.

Orion Five Ltd. (United States)
Dynstar Solutions (Panama)
Redleaf Export Co. (Vancouver)

These corporations are connected to Cold War contingency fund distributions used for covert operations throughout Southeast Asia. All three entities were quietly dissolved between 1973 and 1976.

Additionally, recovered materials include a microfilm reel containing an unsigned mission debrief by Lt. Cmdr. Nathan Kaufman (Naval Intelligence, listed MIA 1973) which supports Colonel Roosevelt's account of the mission's intent and execution. Kaufman's report identifies Colonel Martin Kohrs (CIA Task Group D-7) as the internal operations U.S. Army liaison responsible for managing post-mission fallout.

FINDINGS:
1. The recovered orders and supporting financial records directly contradict the official account that resulted in Colonel Roosevelt's arrest and conviction.
2. Evidence supports the conclusion that Operation Firelight was authorized, funded, and deliberately disavowed after its completion.
3. Leadership associated with the compartment (Dorsey) remains active in the private national defense sector and may still impact classified infrastructure.
4. The risk of ongoing retaliatory activity is considered high. Three attempts on Colonel Roosevelt's life while in custody indicate that active containment efforts are still in progress.

RECOMMENDATION:
Seal this document under Level 4 clearance pending a complete review. Prepare an unredacted evidentiary brief for off-channel delivery to the Senate Armed Services Committee through a vetted conduit (recommended: Sen. Thomas Taggart, R-VT). Priority objective: isolate living architects, secure their testimony, and prevent additional operational cover-ups.

The heart monitor behind him ticked in a steady rhythm but quickened—enough that Merrit didn't look up from her seat, though from her expression, she noticed the change. Cross remained at the foot of the bed, arms now folded, watching him with the patience of a man who had witnessed operations go wrong and understood how little comfort after-action reports provided to the survivors.

Teddy looked up from the page. "You wrote this yourself."

Merrit nodded. "Every word."

He slowly turned the page back, convinced the letters might change if he moved too quickly. "It's surgical. Not dramatic. Just the truth—carved down to the bone."

"That's how you get someone like Taggart to read past the first sentence," Merrit replied.

"I don't care about Taggart." Teddy let the page fall closed again. "I care that someone finally called it what it was." He looked up at her—not as a broken man or even one still recovering. Just a man who had waited too long to hear something honest from anyone in a U.S. Army uniform.

"They told the world I went rogue. That we killed innocent civilians, then we ran. They made us into something disposable. Something vile in the eyes of the American public. But this…" Teddy tapped the page once. "This is proof we were never the problem. Only the victims."

Merrit didn't reply. She didn't need to. Everything on the page pointed to her convictions.

Cross took a slow, steady step forward. "Are you ready to move on this?"

Teddy looked at both of them. "I've been ready for ten years." He closed his eyes, and when they opened again, they were focused. "Send the brief. Give Senator Taggart what he needs. Just don't wait for him to act. Because the moment this gets close to Dorsey, he's going to do what men like him always do—burn the trail and take out the witnesses."

"We'll be ready," Merrit said.

"You'd better be. Because I'm done hiding."

"Good. That is my hope for writing this summary brief. Unredacted field orders, protocol ID tied to Dorsey's office through Strategic Planning. We've tracked the funding—three offshore shells with post-war cleanup fingerprints. The moment we confirm the voice logs on that microfilm, we name him."

"And Kohrs?" Teddy asked.

"Gone," Cross said. "No public sightings since '76. He might still be out there. Might not. Probably dead, another one checked off the cleanup list. But everything points to Dorsey still pulling the strings."

Teddy finished the page and placed it on the blanket. His fingers didn't tremble, but the heart monitor behind him ticked a little faster. Not out of fear, but because he was concentrating on this moment.

"And you trust Senator Taggart?" he asked, looking at Merrit.

"I don't need to trust him. I need him to see it. Once this hits his hands, Dorsey doesn't get to operate in silence anymore. But to answer your question, yes, I trust him. He's always been a straight shooter on the hill."

Cross stepped forward. "You give the word, Teddy, and we move on this. We've got the legal knife halfway in. Stratton and Red Horse are ready to bring pressure from the other side."

Teddy didn't speak for a long moment. He stared at the folder, at the ceiling, and then finally at the two of them. "Then we finish it. But we need to do it clean. No bloodshed unless it has to be spilled. Killing without recourse or need makes us no different than them. Dorsey goes down in broad daylight. Not from a bullet. From the truth."

Merrit gave a single, quiet nod.

And the war moved forward.

```
1000 Hours
January 31, 1984
Private Room 512
Womack Army Medical Center
Fort Bragg, NC
```

The hallway outside the recovery ward had taken on a different shape over the last twenty-four hours. It wasn't just the guards on duty or the fact that the nurses moved more quietly now—it was in the silence itself, the tension that clung to the walls. Something had changed. The threat hadn't disappeared, but the hospital no longer felt like a waiting room for death.

Jack and Eli headed to the second checkpoint with quiet determination, not speaking to anyone. Their starched U.S. Army OD-green fatigues were understated, borrowed from a logistics unit on the other side of the base—just enough to navigate the building without attracting unwanted attention. They weren't flashy or loud with awards and badges. Instead, they were neat and efficient.

Jack handed over the forged visitor badge without flinching. The young corporal behind the plexiglass barely glanced up from his clipboard as he buzzed them through. Eli followed, his field jacket zipped up and his head down. They used different aliases this time, *Noah Bennett* and *Nashoba Grey*, just to be safe.

They took the stairs instead of the elevator, and neither of them said a word until they reached the upper corridor. The lighting here was soft, filtered through blinds that hadn't been adjusted since before sunrise. Jack noticed it immediately—no change in the angle of the slats, no morning updates. That meant no one had breached the wing overnight. It also meant Teddy had gotten several hours of much-needed sleep.

"We need to move fast," he said.

Eli nodded, his hands tucked into his pockets. "I agree."

Colonel Cross was already waiting for them at the far end of the hallway in the recovery wing, seated on a bench outside the restricted room. With his elbows on his knees, he read a typed briefing sheet marked with red ink notations along the margins. He appeared tired—the kind of tired that didn't show on his face but settled deep into his posture—with slumped shoulders and his head down, gazing at them through hooded eyes.

When he stood up to meet them, there was no ceremony—only an unspoken understanding that time was measured differently now. "Report?"

"Trask broke," Jack said, mimicking a breaking motion with his hands. "We have a forty-eight-hour window. Dorsey is attending a closed-door private briefing in Quantico. No press or aides in attendance. One driver. He's being careful, but not careful enough."

Colonel Cross creased and folded the page in his hand. Although his expression didn't change, something behind his eyes did. He moved closer, gesturing toward the vacant charting alcove by the window, positioning himself between them and the nearest nurse's station so they could talk in private.

"Where?" Cross asked.

"The old Logistics Annex," Eli said. "Used to be part of their procurement auditing unit. It's not listed on any official itinerary. That's the giveaway."

Cross frowned. "And he thinks it's secure?"

"Yes, but he's wrong," Jack said. "And if we move before the legal side goes public with their investigation, we can box him in—without alerting whoever's still protecting him."

"And Trask gave this up willingly?"

"He's not brave, think of him as a yellow-belly." Eli faked a punch at his face, stopping an inch from his nose. "Just scared of what's coming. Call it self-preservation."

Jack leaned back against the wall, arms crossed. "We told him Teddy was alive and that we had evidence. Enough to implicate Dorsey, maybe more. Trask didn't ask for proof. He believed it on instinct."

Cross looked at the closed door down the hall where Teddy still lay, recovering from his injuries.

Jack followed his gaze. "We do this right, we isolate Dorsey. Corner him before he disappears again, and we gain the upper hand."

"And if he runs?" Cross asked.

"Then we pull him into the light of day and hope he melts like a vampire," Jack said. "Whatever it takes."

Merrit emerged from the hallway, having overheard the last part of the conversation. "You found his window?"

"Forty-eight hours." Jack looked at his watch. "Thirty-six now."

"Then we don't wait. We're on the clock and it's already ticking." She glanced at Cross then back at Jack and Eli. "We take the shot. We've got nothing to lose."

CHAPTER 28

0200 Hours
February 1, 1984
Alexandria Safehouse
Alexandria, VA

The safehouse was silent except for the occasional creak of the old floorboards. It was a rowhouse built before World War II, purchased by someone with a long memory and deeper connections. No bugs, records, or nosy neighbors who would ask questions. The kind of place Teddy might have used twenty years earlier—and Jack had made sure of that before they walked in.

The room smelled of old wood and radiator heat, a quaint location you didn't rent but just knew how to ask for. Jack sat at the desk in the corner, which was covered with maps, hand-drawn building diagrams, two notepads, a thick personnel folder taken from Trask's personal satchel, and a shortwave radio tuned to base chatter from the Quantico range. Eli sat by the window, one boot on the sill, watching the street below through a gap in the blackout curtain.

Jack flipped through the final version of the personnel roster that Trask had given him. It listed four names—two drivers, one custodian, and one internal courier with low-level clearance. The briefing room was located in a secondary annex—no security cameras inside, no official sign-in logs, and no reason for it to exist unless someone wanted plausible deniability. Dorsey would be alone. By design.

Then he made a fourth pass through the entry protocols for the Quantico annex. Nothing computerized—just a laminated access badge with a red stripe across the top, temporarily issued and signed in ink by a department head Trask had worked under since '82. A matching clipboard sign-in sheet had his name written three lines from the bottom.

"Do you think he'll show?" Eli asked.

"He has to," Jack said. "This isn't a public face-to-face meeting. This is where he makes sure no paper trail survives. If he were going to disappear, he would have done it already. He's not hiding. Not yet. This is cleanup. He's closing doors, not running from them."

Eli nodded. "Then we hit it clean. Quiet."

"Exactly." Jack folded the roster and tucked it into the inside pocket of his jacket. "Trask's ID badge and access slip are in the folder. It will get me past the first two checkpoints if no one's looking too hard, and the desk sergeant doesn't ask why I'm delivering a sealed folder instead of using a certified courier service. If he does, then I'll have to improvise…but I'm good at doing that after slipping in and out of East Berlin like smoke."

Eli adjusted the angle of his chair. "Are you gonna be wearing a uniform?"

"No! Civilian contractor. Logistics jacket. Same one Trask wore last fall when he moved Dorsey through Norfolk without a single log entry. Already tailored to fit me and pressed."

Eli let out a grunt. "And me?"

"You'll be stationed in the service corridor using a janitorial pass borrowed from a warehouse detail at Bolling. You won't be seen unless I call for backup. No weapons need to be drawn unless necessary. We need eyes, ears, and confirmation, not a firefight with bodies scattered everywhere. That directive came from Teddy. He wants this done clean without any bloodshed."

"And if Dorsey smells the trap? What then?"

Jack smiled, using the innocent persona he had perfected through countless undercover intelligence operations within the Soviet bloc. "We make it look like we were never there, leaving no trace but the whispers of our shadows."

Silence lingered for a moment.

"And if we don't get him alone?" Eli asked.

Jack set down the clearance pass and looked straight at him. "Then we back off. We do it right and don't move on him until we get everything we need to bury him legally."

Eli's expression remained unchanged, but the tension in his shoulders eased as he leaned forward, resting his forearms on his knees. "And Teddy?"

"He knows what we're doing. But if this goes bad, he stays out of it. Teddy doesn't need another charge hanging over his head."

Eli nodded in silent agreement. They both knew it was a lie. Teddy wouldn't stay out of anything—not when it came to the mission, and not when it came to finishing what someone else had started.

Jack stood up, shrugged on his jacket, and checked his watch—a standard Army-issued timepiece, its crystal face scratched from some long-forgotten run in the Vietnam jungle. "Nine hours. You ready?"

Eli stood, cracking his knuckles. "Always. Let's move."

```
1000 Hours
February 1, 1984
Private Room 512
Womack Army Medical Center
Fort Bragg, NC
```

The room was quiet once more, but this time the silence was intentional. The lighting had been dimmed at Teddy's request, and the blinds were partially closed. A legal pad rested on his lap, its top page already half-filled with his distinctive block handwriting, a habit ingrained in him since his four years as a cadet at the United States Military Academy. His IV line remained in place, but the painkillers had been reduced. He needed clarity more than comfort now.

The pen felt heavy in his hand, not because of the effort, but because of what it represented.

He wasn't writing a confession or pleading for justice. He was documenting the truth in the written voice of someone who had lived it—names, dates, protocol strings, orders received through veiled channels, spoken in secure rooms, delivered without witnesses. He remembered all of it.

He wrote slowly, just as a man writes when he knows his words might be read in court—or at a funeral.

At the top of the page, he had written—

To whom it may concern—should I not survive what's coming next…

But he crossed it out.
Too formal. Too final.
He started again. This was something he had to do.

My name is Colonel Theodore Roosevelt IV, United States Army. I am writing this statement not to seek absolution but to document the truth. Everything that happened during Operation Firelight was real. The orders were authorized, and the operation was fully sanctioned. What occurred afterward—the betrayal, the cover-up—was not the work of a rogue team acting alone. It was orchestrated by a system designed to silence its own.

He paused, breathing through the dull, painful pressure in his side. Then he continued.

I preserved the evidence. I buried it only because, at the time, there was no one left willing or able to listen. If you are reading this now, it means someone finally did.

His hand stilled. The page waited.

Outside, footsteps passed by the door—faint, routine, a nurse making her regular rounds.

But deep down, Teddy's mind was focused on the war he had never stopped fighting—until now.

He completed his statement, set down the pen, and then signed his name.

1108 Hours
February 1, 1984
Quantico Logistics Annex
Quantico, VA

The Quantico logistics annex was located at the southeastern edge of the base—a low, squat concrete rectangle surrounded by 12-foot chain-link fencing topped with barbed wire, flanked by motor pools and low-slung service sheds on either side. On paper, it was still classified as an inactive U.S. Marine Corps records processing facility. In reality, it was exactly what Jack had expected—a private staging area for off-the-books meetings that no one wanted documented as having occurred.

The main checkpoint stood unguarded. A clipboard rested on a folding table next to a steel security door that lacked a keypad, featuring only a white button on the buzz-in intercom. Jack approached in a tan contractor's jacket zipped up to the collar, a plastic ID badge clipped to his breast pocket, and a tan canvas courier pouch slung under one arm.

The guard inside looked up through the narrow glass slit.

Jack tapped the clipboard, located Trask's name two rows from the bottom, and signed his cover identity, *Chuck Fedderson*, beneath it with steady precision. "Courier delivery—logistics control," he said, holding up the folder. "Priority handoff."

The guard checked the signature, gave a cursory glance at the badge, then buzzed the door open. No questions asked. Just muscle memory and apathy, weary of his meaningless job.

Inside, the corridors were narrow and lined with faded olive-green filing cabinets. The air felt stale, and the hum of the fluorescent lights filled the silence. Jack moved deliberately, never appearing to search—just walking like he belonged there.

Eli was already in position, down the hall near the utility alcove. He had entered through the back door with a borrowed maintenance badge and the perfect scowl of a man facing his fourth broken HVAC blower motor of the week. He stood with a mop handle in one hand and a clipboard in the other, blending in like a shadow cast by the building itself.

Jack walked past him, keeping his gaze focused ahead.

A minute later, the door at the end of the hall opened, and Dorsey emerged.

Jack continued walking, yet he observed everything.

Standing six feet tall with silver hair, movie star features, an expensive tailored dark gray suit, and a briefcase tucked under one arm, retired U.S. Army General Franklin A. Dorsey made a striking impression. There were no aides—just a solitary driver lingering outside, leaning against a government-issued black sedan. Dorsey muttered something under his breath to the man behind him then pointed at the inner office.

Jack counted to four, then to five seconds. He kept walking, turned the corner, slipped into a recessed mail alcove, and waited.

As soon as Dorsey entered the briefing room, Eli moved forward with a rag in one hand and discreetly attached a listening device to the back of the phone wall plate. Nothing flashy—just a suction cup microphone connected to a small battery-powered receiver/transmitter. Dependable.

They wouldn't move on him today without confirmation of his presence.

And now they had his voice.

CHAPTER 29

1130 Hours
February 1, 1984
Private Room 512
Womack Army Medical Center
Fort Bragg, NC

Merrit stood by the door for a long time before entering Colonel Roosevelt's room. The blinds were drawn again with soft light filtering through the slats. He was either asleep or close to it—eyes closed, head angled toward the wall, the corner of the legal pad still visible beneath one hand.

She crossed the room to the chair beside him.

The top page of the legal pad lay open. She glanced at the first few lines, intending only to glance at what Colonel Roosevelt had written. But she couldn't tear her eyes away from the words on the page.

The tone was not what she expected.

No anger. No cries for justice. Just the cold, precise clarity of someone who knew he had nothing left to prove—and everything to document.

She read in silence.

To whom it may concern—should I not survive what's coming next…

My name is Colonel Theodore Roosevelt IV, United States Army. I am writing this statement not to seek absolution but to document the truth. Everything that happened during Operation Firelight was real. The orders were authorized, and the operation was fully sanctioned. What occurred afterward—the betrayal, the cover-up—was not the work of a rogue team acting alone. It was orchestrated by a system designed to silence its own.

I preserved the evidence. I buried it only because, at that time, there was no one left willing or able to listen. If you are reading this now, it means someone finally did.

My team was deployed under false pretenses to execute a classified mission that no official would ever acknowledge or admit even existed. The target was a rural area inside Laos, near suspected Chinese smuggling routes along the Ho Chi Minh Trail. Our mission objective was to gather intelligence on alleged arms trafficking—at least, that's what we were told. In truth, it was a false flag operation designed to create evidence of foreign-backed atrocities that could justify expanded U.S. intervention in Southeast Asia. Villages were destroyed, the people murdered, not by enemy hands, but by covert CIA-backed strike teams operating through Task Group D-7.

Instructions were relayed verbally through secure intermediaries. We operated under strict blackout conditions—no exfiltration support, no aerial reconnaissance, and no official oversight.

We were informed that the orders originated from DIA Strategic Planning and were operationally routed through our CIA liaison, U.S. Army Colonel Martin Kohrs, associated with Task Group D-7. We received precise coordinates, entry protocols, a time window, and little else aside from the implicit threat of repercussions if we questioned our orders or asked the wrong questions.

We executed the mission exactly as directed and completed the objectives precisely. However, once it was over, no recovery team arrived, no return signal was issued, and no acknowledgment ever came. Instead, my team was deliberately scattered, our records altered, charges fabricated, and our identities erased.

They claimed Operation Firelight never existed, labeling it a rogue operation. But I carried the original authorization in my vest, even as I realized they planned to erase every last one of us. I made a decision that day—to bury the truth—not out of cowardice, but out of survival. Exposing it then would have led directly to the deaths of my men, and the truth would have died with them. I chose to live with their lie, not to save myself, but because I knew that one day someone might come looking for answers—and they would need something concrete to find.

I kept the documents, the original orders, and the financial paper trail. I held onto them because someone had to. And now, if you're reading this, it means I didn't die fast enough for the men who tried to bury us.

If you seek justice, start with Major General Franklin A. Dorsey. Ask him what "VST-714" means. Question him about what happened to the others who knew the truth. And if you manage to find Kohrs, ask him who personally signed the final fallback orders.

This isn't about clearing my name. It's about ending theirs.

Respectfully,

Theodore Roosevelt IV

Colonel Theodore Roosevelt IV
United States Army

Her hand tightened around the edge of the pad. These were not the last words of a soldier.

It was an officer's final act of command—a map drawn in words for those left standing.

Merrit closed the pad, being careful not to wake him, then sat back in the chair with her arms crossed, her eyes fixed on the slow rise and fall of his chest.

She didn't say a word. But in that moment, Rachel Merrit no longer viewed him as a convict recovering from multiple surgeries. She saw the man who had survived when the system tried to erase him—and realized she would follow him into whatever came next, even straight into the fires of hell.

1245 Hours
February 1, 1984
Private Room 512
Womack Army Medical Center
Fort Bragg, NC

Merrit sat in the chair beside Colonel Roosevelt's bed, as still as stone, with the legal pad resting across her knees. One hand gripped the top corner while the other hovered above the margin, her thumb frozen on a line halfway down the page.

If you seek justice, start with Major General Franklin A. Dorsey…

Her brow was furrowed, but not in disbelief. No part of her doubted the contents now—not after seeing the orders, the protocol string, the microfilm, everything. What caught her off guard was the restraint in it— the precision. Colonel Roosevelt hadn't written it to prove a point. He'd written to leave a record. The language wasn't defensive. It wasn't even angry. It was...tactical. A weapon designed to cut quietly once it was in the right hands.

"Do you always read other people's last words out loud?" Colonel Roosevelt's voice sliced through the silence like a match struck in a quiet room—low, dry, and distinctly awake.

Merrit looked up, suppressing a smile at the small joke since she hadn't made a sound.

Colonel Roosevelt's eyes were open. Not wide, not filled with challenge—just observing her with the same cool detachment she'd noticed when he was bleeding out on a gurney, giving orders between gasps. But now there was something softer. Not weakness. Something else. Something measured.

"I didn't think you'd wake up this soon," she said.

"I never really sleep," he replied, moving under the blanket with a grimace. "Old habit to stay alive."

She placed the pad on the bedside table. "It's not a last will. I know that."

"Good. Because I'm not done yet."

Merrit leaned forward, her elbows resting on her knees and her hands loosely clasped in front of her. "It's clear. Clean. You name the players, lay out the operation, and you back it with a timeline that matches everything Jack and Eli brought in. That kind of testimony, paired with the recovered orders? If we move fast—it'll crack open legal doors inside Congress and the intelligence community I didn't think I'd ever get near."

"You're still going to need leverage," Teddy said.

"Already working on it. Taggart gets the brief tonight. Discreetly. No official delivery. I'll be there when he opens it."

He watched her for a moment. There was no triumph in his eyes. No smugness—just exhaustion and a quiet calculation behind every word. "They're not going to fold. Dorsey won't run. He's a tactician. He'll counterstrike. He's got infrastructure left—people we haven't seen yet. Kohrs may be long dead and buried, but someone else is keeping the lights on. Dorsey will burn everything before he lets it surface."

"I know. And I'm not naïve enough to think this ends with a subpoena or an arrest warrant." Merrit paused and looked him square in the eyes.

"But I believe you. Not just because of what I read. Because I see how much of your life you've built around making sure it survives."

"You asked me once why I never went public. Why I waited this long." Merrit nodded. "Yes."

Teddy looked past her, toward the far wall. "There's a kind of damage the truth does when it comes too soon. If I'd pushed this in '73, '74...it wouldn't have just gotten me killed. It would've gotten the rest of them hunted down. Jack. Eli. Maybe even Cross, back then." He turned back to her. "So I waited. Until the right people were watching. Until the wrong ones got too comfortable. And now?" He gave her the faintest smile. "Now they're the ones looking over their shoulder."

2042 Hours
February 1, 1984
Senate Office Building
Washington, D.C.

The halls of the Senate in the United States Capitol building were nearly empty at this hour. Just a few aides working late, a handful of security personnel rotating shifts, and the soft hum of vacuums echoed from somewhere on the lower floors as the janitorial staff cleaned the offices.

Merrit moved quietly, her coat draped over her arm and the locked leather briefcase in her hand. Her heels didn't echo as she walked, like someone who belonged. She felt a little stiff after the hour-long flight from Pope Army Airfield in a Learjet 23 borrowed from General Bulhalter, Ft. Bragg's commanding officer.

Senator Thomas Taggart's office remained illuminated. No receptionist occupied the desk in the outer office—the inner door stood slightly ajar, a habit that had not changed since his time as Chairman of the Armed Services Subcommittee.

Merrit knocked once and stepped inside the inner office.

Taggart glanced up from a folder of base realignment requests and blinked in surprise. "Colonel Merrit. To what do I owe the pleasure of your unannounced visit?"

"You're working late," she said.

"I'm old. I wake up early and stay up late. It's where the good information resides. Again, why are you here?"

She placed the briefcase on his desk, unlocked it, and lifted the lid.

"Is this official?" Taggart asked.

"No. Which is why I'm handing it to you and not your staff. What's inside doesn't exist yet. But it will—if you want it to." She handed him the unsealed manila envelope.

He opened it, pulled out the packet, and scanned the top sheet. "Where'd you locate this particular protocol string?"

"Keep reading."

"Major General Franklin Dorsey is connected with this?"

"Yes, sir."

Taggart remained silent for a long while. When he finally spoke, his voice was softer than usual. "Where did you get this information?"

"Recovered by Colonel Roosevelt's team. Orders. Routing paths. Financial chain. There's microfilm too. And a firsthand statement. It's clean, tied to Dorsey, and completely admissible in court—if you back it."

Taggart looked up at her, and the weight behind his expression wasn't confusion. It was recognition. He knew the name, the signature pattern, and the game. "Colonel Roosevelt, huh? I thought this operation was buried under compartmentalized classifications in '72."

"It was," Merrit said in a steady tone. "But the fire didn't finish the job."

Taggart leaned back in his chair and tapped one finger on the cover sheet. "This is the kind of thing that gets people killed or forced to commit suicide in disgrace like General Montgomery."

Merrit didn't flinch, knowing that statement was made to shock her. "That's already happened. And there have been three attempts on Colonel Roosevelt's life to this point. He almost didn't make it on every one of those tries. He's currently protected in a secure wing at Womack Army Medical Center."

He nodded, his brow furrowing in thought. "Then I guess we'd better make sure it doesn't happen again. And keep him alive. I will need a credible witness for the Oversight Committee."

CHAPTER 30

2107 Hours
February 1, 1984
Surveillance Van
Quantico Logistics Annex
Quantico, VA

Jack sat behind the open case of an old portable reel-to-reel tape deck, headphones over his ears, as the monitor light cast a dim green hue across the dashboard. Eli sat in front, watching the annex through tinted windows, his hands gripping the wheel but not turning it.

Inside the annex, the audio pickup was clear. Dorsey's voice came through with such clarity that Jack could almost imagine him sitting in the next seat.

"We should have shut it down in '72. But Kohrs swore they wouldn't make it out. Colonel Roosevelt's team was supposed to die in Laos. That was the deal."

Jack froze. Now he heard the threat come from the man who had tried to kill them. That made this even more real.

"But now he's alive, and someone recovered the orders. If that protocol string resurfaces…we're not just talking about Colonel Roosevelt. We're talking about operational collapse. I want the last of those files gone. Everything Kohrs held onto. Every last trace of VESTIGE."

Eli gripped the steering wheel so tightly his knuckles turned white.

"If we move fast, we can still contain it. But if Colonel Roosevelt testifies…if it gets to the Senate Oversight Committee—then we all burn," Dorsey said in a voice cold enough to freeze on contact. A few seconds later, the door clicked shut, marking his exit from the room.

Jack removed the headphones. "Got it…all on tape."

Eli kept looking straight ahead through the windshield. "Good. We end this."

2131 Hours
February 1, 1984
Surveillance Van
Quantico Logistics Annex
Quantico, VA

Jack leaned forward and flipped the switch to duplicate the reel-to-reel recording onto a cassette tape. The old machine whirred as it worked. He labeled the tape by hand—*DORSEY – 02/01/84, CONFIRMATION*, using a black magic marker.

Eli watched the annex exit through narrowed eyes, his arms crossed over his chest. "He's leaving."

Jack glanced out the window. Dorsey emerged from the side entrance without a coat and a briefcase in hand. His driver opened the rear passenger door without a word. They were smooth—too smooth. There was no urgency or indication in their mannerisms that they knew they had been overheard. That made it worse.

"He knows time's running out," Jack said. "He just doesn't know how fast."

Eli glanced at him. "Do you want to take him out tonight?"

Jack shook his head. "Not here. Not dirty. We go in loud, fists flying and guns blazing, innocent people will get hurt or killed, and they will bury us with it in both the press and the courts. We do this Teddy's way— clean, deliberate, and out in the open, then people will listen to the truth." He tucked the cassette into a padded pouch and zipped it shut. "Tomorrow, we move first before Dorsey does, and he slips through our fingers."

CHAPTER 31

0643 Hours
February 2, 1984
Private Room 512
Womack Army Medical Center
Fort Bragg, NC

The morning light streamed through the blinds as Teddy opened his eyes. For a moment, he felt disoriented—not from pain or medication, but because the silence around him was calm and controlled, not tense.

Merrit was already there. She sat beside him in the same chair as before, her shoulders straight and her expression unreadable. On the bedside table was a standard black tape recorder, its buttons worn smooth, with a cassette tape beside it.

Teddy raised an eyebrow. "You brought me a mixtape?"

Merrit didn't smile. Instead, she inserted the cassette into the open deck, closed it, and pressed play, the soft whir of the machine filling the intervening silence.

Dorsey's voice resonated in the air between them. "We should've shut it down in '72...Kohrs swore they wouldn't make it out. Colonel Roosevelt's team was supposed to die in Laos..."

Teddy didn't move or blink. He sat on the bed, listening to the man who planned to kill him and his men.

"If Colonel Roosevelt testifies...if it gets to the Senate Oversight Committee—then we all burn."

When the tape produced only static, Merrit pressed the stop button.

No one spoke for several seconds.

"That's it," Teddy said, concealing the turmoil inside beneath his calm facade.

"It is," Merrit said.

"He's not just guilty. He's scared."

"Yes."

"And that makes him unpredictable."

Merrit nodded. "That's why Jack and Eli are prepping to intercept him the next time he shows up at the annex. They're not going in alone. We've looped in Colonel Cross. He'll be there. Logistics and Marine Corps security are already tightening movement around the annex. Senator

Taggart's going to stall anything Dorsey tries to rush through formal channels to block our efforts to arrest him."

Teddy pushed himself higher on his pillows, his breath catching from the pressure in his side. "You got an extra blank tape like that for me?"

Merrit tilted her head. "For what? Why do you need one?"

He met her eyes. "I'm not going to that briefing in person. But my voice is. You want the truth on record? You're going to get it. And so will Dorsey, loud and clear."

0728 Hours
February 2, 1984
Private Room 512
Womack Army Medical Center
Fort Bragg, NC

The room had been cleared. The nurses were excused. The guard rotation was delayed for the next two hours. The door was locked from the inside, not for secrecy, but so Teddy could speak without interruption.

He sat upright in the hospital bed with extreme effort, one arm protectively cradled against his side where the stitches still burned. Merrit helped him lean forward, sliding several pillows behind his back and adjusting the bedside table to keep the tape recorder and microphone within his reach. The small black cassette unit sat there now, a blank tape loaded and waiting. A legal pad lay open to one side, filled with notes he hadn't needed to reference even once.

Cross stood in the corner, arms crossed, silent and listening.

Merrit pressed the record button.

The red light clicked on.

For a few moments, the only sounds were the hum of the oxygen feed to the cannula under his nose and the steady beeping of the heart monitor.

Teddy cleared his throat.

"This is Colonel Theodore Roosevelt IV, United States Army. I'm recording this statement voluntarily, as official testimony regarding my role in a covert operation designated Operation Firelight, classified internally under protocol string VST-714. This mission has since been shrouded in false records and official denials, publicly described as an unauthorized rogue action. Let me be clear, the mission was real. It was officially authorized. And it was deliberately buried. I led that mission, and I've lived with the consequences for over a decade."

His voice remained steady and calm, each word chosen carefully and without hesitation. He did not raise his tone, but the clarity and conviction behind his words were unmistakable. This was not a plea, an excuse, or a justification. It was a surgical incision—precise and purposeful.

"We were deployed under full operational blackout conditions. Initially, we believed we were on a reconnaissance mission to observe Chinese supply routes along the Ho Chi Minh trail. In truth, it was a staged operation designed to fabricate evidence of Chinese-backed atrocities and provoke U.S. escalation in Laos and, by extension, Cambodia. The atrocities themselves were real, but they were carried out by CIA-directed assets, not enemy forces. We had no extraction contingency and no recognized chain of command in the field. Funding for Operation Firelight was funneled through offshore shell entities specifically set up for deniable operations. Our orders disappeared from official records the moment they were authorized. The man who authorized that operation is Major General Franklin Dorsey—then assigned to DIA Strategic Planning. The man responsible for managing the cover-up was Colonel Martin Kohrs, CIA liaison for Task Group D-7. The reason I survived to tell you this is simple—I never stopped expecting the day they would return to finish what they started."

He paused, drawing a shallow breath, careful not to let his voice waver. Anyone else might have mistaken that brief hesitation for pain or fatigue, but those who truly knew Colonel Theodore Roosevelt IV understood what it was—controlled precision, a measured pace, and clarity that came from years of waiting.

"I preserved the orders. I retained the financial trail, the documented approvals, and the final mission debrief authored by Naval Intelligence officer Nathan Kaufman—written exactly one week before his disappearance. I safeguarded every piece of evidence because no one else could or would. And now, if you're hearing this, it means someone finally gave a damn."

He looked directly at Merrit as he spoke the next part. "If I don't make it through this…then let this statement be entered into the record. Let it be played before any tribunal, oversight committee, or federal court brave enough to take it. Let it stand as proof that my team was not rogue. We were soldiers. And we followed orders that never should have been given."

He paused again, a brief silence underscoring the seriousness of what was to follow.

"This isn't about redemption. It's about accountability."

He reached over and pressed the stop button.

The red light faded.

No one moved.

Merrit wrote a title on the cassette label, *Colonel Theodore Roosevelt IV – STATEMENT, VST-714*, and handed it to Colonel Cross, who had a plane waiting at Pope Army Airfield to take him to Quantico.

Then Teddy leaned back against the pillow and closed his eyes. His job was done. Now it was time to rest until the next phase of the plan began.

CHAPTER 32

1144 Hours
February 2, 1984
Quantico Logistics Annex
Quantico, VA

The logistics annex looked unchanged from the outside—weather-stained concrete, two long windows obscured by old aluminum blinds, and a narrow, cracked concrete walkway leading to a reinforced side entrance.

However, the building's rhythm had changed. Jack sensed it in the parking lot, evident in the subtle uptick in activity. Since sunrise, two new black sedans with government plates had appeared. A man in a civilian suit stood by the entry kiosk with a clipboard tucked under his arm. Another man circled the perimeter without ever glancing at the parked vehicles nearby.

They weren't ordinary minimum wage security guards or Army MPs, but watchers—highly paid, experienced mercenaries hired by Dorsey.

Inside the surveillance van parked across the street, Cross sat behind the wheel, binoculars resting against his thigh and a half-folded topographic map laid out on the dashboard. He wasn't in uniform—no name tag or insignia—just an old, faded Vietnam-era U.S. Army field jacket and the quiet intensity of a man who had decided this time he wasn't going to miss the shot.

Eli moved silently across the annex, creeping behind the maintenance ramp with calculated, slow steps to remain in the shadows cast by the structure's low east-facing wall. The service door had no cameras or guards—only a mechanical lock that Trask had described in detail. It would take him less than ten seconds to bypass, if necessary, but he didn't intend to break in. Not yet, unless the situation demanded it.

Jack stood alone at the entrance of the public corridor, wearing the same contractor's jacket from the night before, with a leather portfolio tucked under one arm. In his other hand, he held a compact tape player—an old military-issue model with a manual counter and a red record stripe worn smooth along the edges. Inside, a cassette was labeled in clear block print. *Colonel Theodore Roosevelt IV – STATEMENT, VST-714.*

At 1151 hours, he watched Dorsey's car pull into the lot, its tires gliding into the second-to-last space. The driver never exited the vehicle. Dorsey emerged alone, his overcoat draped over one arm and his briefcase swinging effortlessly in his hand. He didn't look around or pause, just moved straight toward the annex doors, exuding the confidence of a man who had spent his entire career making people disappear—on paper, in reality, and into history.

Jack waited for the general to disappear into the hallway before crossing the lot himself. He didn't rush or hesitate. The portfolio under his arm wasn't merely a prop—it contained a second copy of Teddy's statement, typewritten and signed, meant for the Senate Oversight Committee in case everything else failed. The cassette was the actual delivery.

Inside the lobby, a civilian clerk manned the admin desk, glancing up with practiced boredom.

Jack approached without slowing down, reached into the portfolio, and pulled out the envelope. "This is sealed evidence, from a senior U.S. Army JAG officer. It's to be delivered directly to General Dorsey and played in his presence."

The clerk blinked, surprised by the formality of it. "Is this...already cleared by security?"

"Yes." Jack offered the envelope and cassette together. "It's part of a pending testimony package for the Senate Oversight Committee. You'll want to start playback immediately." He didn't wait for a response, turned, walked back toward the side corridor, and vanished through the door leading to the maintenance access hall—where Eli was already waiting.

Ten seconds later, the red light on the annex's internal playback console illuminated.

And Teddy's voice resonated throughout the room.

1158 Hours
February 2, 1984
Quantico Logistics Annex
Quantico, VA

The cassette was already rolling when Dorsey entered the room, though he didn't notice it at first. The machine sat on the long briefing table next to a stack of defense procurement folders and an untouched legal pad. The aide sent ahead to prepare the space was nowhere to be found. For a brief moment, the room felt almost too quiet.

Then the voice started.

"This is Colonel Theodore Roosevelt IV, United States Army."

Dorsey stopped. His hand paused halfway to the back of the chair.

The voice was unmistakable—calm, controlled, and measured in both cadence and volume, yet sharp enough to break glass.

"I'm recording this statement voluntarily, as official testimony regarding my role in a covert operation designated Operation Firelight, classified internally under protocol string VST-714..."

Dorsey turned slowly, hoping the tape would disappear if he moved too quickly. But it didn't and kept playing.

"...the mission was real. It was officially authorized. And it was deliberately buried."

His throat tightened. The room hadn't been swept for surveillance—not today. No uniformed staff were present. The door clicked shut behind him, locked from the outside. He was alone with the voice of the man he'd ordered erased.

"The man who authorized that operation is Major General Franklin Dorsey—then assigned to DIA Strategic Planning..."

Dorsey reached for the cassette player to stop it—but hesitated. His fingers hovered over the eject button, trembling. He knew this wasn't just a tape. It was a message, meant to inform him that the other shoe had dropped, courtesy of the perpetual thorn in his side, Colonel Roosevelt IV.

If he destroyed it, someone else would have one, two, three, or more copies.

If he let it play, he risked everything he had built over the past decade falling apart.

And either way, they were already too close. It was the endgame now.

1203 Hours
February 2, 1984
Private Room 512
Womack Army Medical Center
Fort Bragg, NC

The noon sun crept across the floor tiles, slowly crawling toward the far wall. Teddy hadn't moved. He sat upright against the pillows, his arms resting at his sides, and his gaze fixed on the blank screen of the small television across the room.

He wasn't watching. He was listening. For something that hadn't yet arrived. Confirmation.

Merrit paced behind the curtained partition, a phone pressed to her ear, speaking softly into the receiver so as not to disturb him.

But Teddy remained still. He didn't ask for news or check the time. He could picture Dorsey's reaction—the exact moment his voice came through the tape, the tightening of the shoulders, the flicker of panic just behind the eyes. Men like Dorsey didn't break at the sight of a weapon. They broke at the sound of their own name spoken aloud.

He leaned back into the pillows, a faint grimace tightening his jaw from the strain on his side. The pain persisted and would continue for a long time. But that wasn't what he was waiting for.

The real pain had not yet begun. But it was on its way.

And this time, it wouldn't be his to carry.

1211 Hours
February 2, 1984
Quantico Logistics Annex
Quantico, VA

Dorsey didn't waste any time once the tape ended. He yanked the cassette from the player with a sharp, metallic click and shoved it into his coat pocket. His hands trembled, but he willed them to be still. The hallway outside the briefing room was empty—no aides or secretaries in sight. Even the clerk at the front desk had stepped away, likely drawn by the same quiet machinery that had slipped this message under his nose.

He wasn't sure how it had reached him—not completely. But he knew what it meant. Colonel Roosevelt's men were close, maybe even in the building. He moved quickly now, cutting through the side corridor toward the staff exit. The usual waiting car wasn't parked in the driveway. He'd signaled the backup detail on a secure channel five minutes earlier using a code phrase intended for only one situation—Extraction without protocol.

If they were on schedule, a second vehicle would be waiting outside the east fence line, two blocks from the annex. As he reached the rear door, he pulled it open and came to an abrupt halt.

Eli Red Horse stood on the other side of the threshold, arms crossed, completely blocking the doorway. His expression reminded Dorsey of the fierce Native American warriors in all the old Westerns as they scalped their victims. Instead of making an accusation, Red Horse didn't say a word. He just stood there cracking his knuckles.

Dorsey froze for a split second—then turned and ran back toward the hallway—where he found Colonel Cross already waiting ten feet away, a

Colt .45 caliber pistol holstered on his hip and a JAG-issued arrest warrant in his hand.

"You're under arrest, General Dorsey," Cross said.

"This is an unauthorized operation. You have no jurisdiction. I order you…" Dorsey's voice cracked like flint against steel.

Jack appeared at the far end of the corridor, calm and composed, holding a duplicate cassette in his hand. "Your orders don't work here. You heard the tape. So did your secretary. So will a federal oversight panel. You've got two options. Walk out of here now, under control, or wait for the press to show up with your name and picture already printed under the front page banner headline *Cover-Up in Washington*. There is a third option." He drew his .357 Magnum revolver from his shoulder holster and spun the cylinder.

Dorsey clenched his jaw but remained still, wondering if Stratton was bluffing. Then he remembered, Stratton was a highly trained undercover intelligence operative capable of killing without remorse and had done so on many occasions.

Cross unfolded the arrest warrant with a quiet finality. "You authorized a mission. You erased your own team and ordered the massacre of innocent civilians in Laos. And now we have your voice confirming it. No more shadows, sir. No more disappearing files. No more deaths. You're under arrest for crimes against the United States government, three counts of attempted murder, war crimes, and treason. I'm sure additional charges will follow."

Eli stepped in behind him now, as silent as a stone wall.

Dorsey glanced between the three men. Then—slowly—he reached into his coat, pulled out the tape, and held it out.

Jack didn't take it, smiling like he'd won the lottery. "You're not in charge anymore."

Cross stepped forward and placed a firm hand on Dorsey's shoulder, holding a set of handcuffs in his other hand. "This time, you answer to the people you buried. Franklin A. Dorsey, you have the right to remain silent…"

CHAPTER 33

1306 Hours
February 2, 1984
JAG Operations Wing
Office of Lt. Colonel Merrit
Fort Bragg, NC

Merrit stood at her desk, one hand resting on the back of her chair while the other held the still-warm phone receiver to her ear. The hallway outside was quiet with the blinds drawn against the midday sun. Her computer monitor glowed behind her, displaying an open document.

"Yes," she said, her voice calm. "I want the certified audio tape transferred to the DOJ office on 17th Street—sealed chain of custody, no military routing. And I want a statement ready for the Senate Oversight Committee by this afternoon about the prosecution of General Franklin Dorsey. If anyone pushes back, you tell them it's from me—and it's supported by recovered operations material flagged as legacy black-world."

"Yes, ma'am," her law clerk, Sergeant Delaney, replied. "I'll handle it personally."

"Good. Keep me posted." She hung up the phone in a smooth, practiced motion and turned toward her desk.

The exoneration brief remained open on the screen.

Four pages drafted the night before included every detail she hadn't been ready to write until now—the false charges, the forged signatures, and the sealed orders. She reached for her pen, made two final notes, and circled the line in her handwritten notes where the summary began.

Subject: Roosevelt IV, Theodore — Request for Immediate Legal Review and Full Exoneration

She didn't feel triumphant.

Not yet.

But she felt a sense of forward motion—like halted momentum finally breaking free after years of resistance, and rolling toward finality. There were still hearings to navigate and layers of classified sludge to burn through. Yet Dorsey's arrest marked a turning point.

She picked up the packet and slid it into the delivery pouch marked for federal review.

The system had buried Colonel Theodore Roosevelt IV.

Now it was going to dig him back up.

```
1338 Hours
February 2, 1984
Private Room 512
Womack Army Medical Center
Fort Bragg, NC
```

Teddy sat up straight when Colonel "Iron Vince" Cross entered the room. There was no warning or knock—just the soft click of the door followed by the sound of boots on the tile. Teddy turned his head to see who it was before reaching for the remote to raise the hospital bed's incline a few inches to ease the painful strain on his abdomen.

Cross walked over and stopped at the foot of the bed. "Dorsey is in custody. Official. Clean. No resistance. He's cooling his heels in the same cell you occupied a few weeks ago, except with a few more guards and working security cameras to ensure his...safety."

Teddy didn't smile. He let his head fall back onto the pillows, knowing that the word *safety* meant preventing Dorsey from being killed by someone in the shadowy black world. "The tape?"

"Jack delivered it personally."

"And the brief?"

"Merrit has already filed the motion for review. The DOJ will receive it before the end of the day. Senator Taggart is supporting it—quietly for now."

Silence hung in the air for a long moment.

Teddy smiled at the good news. "That's one ghost down."

Cross hesitated before reaching into the inside pocket of his coat. His hand emerged with a sealed envelope—standard government stationery, the kind used for internal court notices and classified routing orders. There were no markings on the front, just Colonel Theodore Roosevelt IV, typed and centered.

Cross held it out without ceremony. "For you."

Teddy took it with a slow, deliberate motion. His grip wasn't steady yet—pain still shot through his side with every movement—but his fingers held firm as he broke the seal and slid the single sheet free.

The paper was thick, watermarked, and official.

He scanned the top line.

UNITED STATES DISTRICT COURT – CLASSIFIED PROTECTIVE NOTICE

Then the language revealed itself to him, clear yet unmistakable.

Effective immediately, Colonel Theodore Roosevelt IV, United States Army, is designated as a material witness under protected status pending exoneration proceedings. Any further detention, transfer, or interrogation must be subject to federal judicial oversight. Actions taken outside approved legal channels will be considered obstruction.

He paused at the next paragraph where a name had been hand-signed in black ink.

Judith A Myles

The Honorable Judith A. Myles, Eastern District of North Carolina

Teddy read it again.

This was neither a pardon nor a vindication.

But it was something rare—leverage backed by the law, not by shadows or figures determining his fate in a dark room. A document that declared, for the first time in a decade, that the government couldn't make him disappear without anyone noticing.

He let the paper rest against his chest, its weight feeling more symbolic than literal. It signified that they knew who he was—and no longer pretended otherwise.

Cross stepped back. "Senator Taggart called in a favor. Judge Myles signed it herself. It doesn't clear your name, but it guarantees you stay alive until we do."

We? Teddy stayed quiet. He locked eyes with Cross—and this time, there was no suspicion in them, no distance, just an acknowledgment of the facts.

This war hadn't ended, but the battlefield had finally changed to the courtroom, and this time, he had the advantage of the truth and the evidence to back it up.

Cross stood there a moment longer, watching the man who had once been hunted across half the world by his own government, now lying motionless on a bed they had tried to turn into a grave. "You're not cleared yet."

Teddy nodded. "No, but I'm not planning on leaving anytime soon."

Cross nodded. "You're not alone anymore."

1642 Hours
February 2, 1984
JAG Operations Wing
Office of Lt. Colonel Merrit
Fort Bragg, NC

The late afternoon sun streamed across Merrit's desk, casting long shadows through the half-closed blinds. The office around her was quiet. Most of her staff had gone home for the day. Yet she remained, still in uniform, her sleeves rolled up to her elbows and her jacket draped over the chair behind her.

The phone buzzed once on her direct line.

She picked it up. "Lieutenant Colonel Merrit."

"Colonel Merrit," said the male voice on the other end of the line. "The Department of Justice has reviewed your submission. The affidavit and operational material were authenticated through the Senate Oversight Committee Liaison Office this morning. Effective at 1700 hours, Colonel Theodore Roosevelt's conviction in absentia is officially under motion for vacatur pending a federal court hearing."

This was good news. Merrit held the receiver steady. "And the record?"

"Sealed during review. Colonel Roosevelt is listed as a protected federal witness, status 3-A. The Senate Oversight Committee has issued a temporary injunction against any further prosecution or internal detention until the formal hearing date is set."

The tension in her shoulders eased—slightly, but it was still present. "Do I have a written confirmation?"

"Already signed. You'll receive it via fax in under an hour. The original will be delivered to your office via courier by eight o'clock tomorrow morning."

She hung up the phone, stood, and walked over to the filing cabinet by the window. She pulled out a red folder—*ROOSEVELT IV, THEODORE – CLOSED CASE 1972*—and dropped it into the burn bin without a moment's hesitation.

The truth had not only been spoken.

It was now officially entered into the system.

1815 Hours
February 2, 1984
Private Room 512
Womack Army Medical Center
Fort Bragg, NC

The knock on the door was soft yet deliberate, unlike a nurse's tap or a medic's check-in.

Teddy turned his head on the pillows. His body remained stiff beneath the dull weight of recovery. His eyes narrowed at the sound, already half-expecting who would come in before the door opened.

Jack entered first, wearing a simple black suit coat over a white dress shirt—no tie, just clean lines and quiet eyes. His hair was slightly longer than it had been the last time Teddy saw him in daylight.

Eli followed closely behind, his broad frame nearly filling the doorway. He wore a faded brown leather bomber jacket and blue jeans, and his expression revealed little until he stepped fully into the room.

They remained silent at first.

Jack let the door click shut behind him and walked toward the bed. He pulled up a chair without asking. Eli didn't sit—he stood near the corner, arms crossed, watching his friend like a soldier observing a man who has fought too long alone.

Teddy glanced between them then let out the closest thing he'd had to a laugh in days—a breath that caught in his chest and made his side ache but still came out with something like warmth. "You boys took your sweet time."

Jack smiled. "You always did have a flair for the dramatic."

Eli moved closer and set a folded brown paper bag on the rolling bedside table. "For you."

Teddy glanced at it, raising an eyebrow. "What did you bring me?"

"From that place in Fayetteville, Smoking Joes," Eli said, "the one with the ribs."

Teddy blinked, grinning from ear to ear. "Damn. You really do love me."

Jack leaned back in the chair, exhaling like a man who'd been holding it in since the end of the Vietnam War. "They're not chasing you anymore. The DOJ is actually listening. Taggart's got your back. Merrit burned the case file."

Teddy let the words hang in the air for a long moment. "It's not over."

"No," Jack said. "But this time, it's on *our* terms."

The room grew silent once again.

Not too heavy, just consistent.

The kind of quiet that men like them earned through blood, sweat, sacrifice, and honor.

CHAPTER 34

1530 Hours
February 9, 1984
Private Room 512
Womack Army Medical Center
Fort Bragg, NC

The hospital room was quiet, bathed in late afternoon light that filtered through the blinds in golden hues and pale shadows. A gentle breeze whispered through the half-open window, stirring the edge of a discharge folder and post-hospital instructions left on the tray table. The monitors were silent now—disconnected and unnecessary. The IV line had been removed that morning, and the bandages were smaller and thinner. The pain was still present but manageable.

Teddy sat in the chair by the window, dressed in a white shirt and black tie with a gray suit coat draped over his shoulders, black slacks neatly pressed, and polished dress shoes. He wasn't in a hurry to leave. He hadn't felt rushed since the order came down—DOJ confirmation, protective status locked into the system, and the exoneration hearing soon to be scheduled. The wheels were turning, and this time, they weren't meant to grind him beneath the heavy stones of fake justice.

He cradled a cup of coffee in both hands, allowing the warmth to seep into his fingers. His posture was straighter than it had been all week, although the scar on his side still tugged if he turned too far. He was healing—not just physically.

There was one good thing about being stuck in bed for weeks—his left leg didn't ache. The time off did it a world of good, allowing the titanium rod in his tibia to stabilize and the microfractures to calcify.

The door swung open.

Jack stepped in first, neither in disguise nor in a U.S. Army uniform—just Jack "Ghost" Stratton, sharp-eyed in a soft gray wool cardigan and tan slacks, with a messenger bag hanging at his hip. Behind him came Eli, dressed in a charcoal sweatshirt and faded blue jeans, his hands in his front pockets, as quiet as ever. They both stopped when they saw him sitting there—not with worry, but with recognition. Teddy wasn't just alive. He was back.

Jack offered a faint, lopsided smile. "Are you ready?"

Teddy raised an eyebrow. "To sit in a courtroom for six hours while the government debates whether they ruined my life on purpose? I can hardly wait."

Eli grunted as he stepped forward and set a brown paper bag on the bedside table.

Jack raised an eyebrow. "More ribs?"

"Better ones," Eli said. "From the joint down off Pershing, Pitmaster's Paradise. You remember it. We closed the place for the night, eating every bit of their inventory and drinking all the beer after a training mission."

Teddy nodded. "I sure do. I always remember the good ribs."

They didn't rush him. They never did. The silence that followed as they ate wasn't empty—it was filled with years of friendship, missions, and loyalty that never wavered, even when the world did.

Merrit appeared a minute later, holding a file folder in one hand and her class A uniform jacket still buttoned. She looked tired but satisfied. When she saw the three of them together, her expression changed—less business, and more...something older. Respect, perhaps. Recognition.

"The hearing date is confirmed and entered into the docket," she said. "Federal courtroom, closed session. One week from Friday. I'll be there as your lawyer."

Teddy pointed at her. "You'll need to be. I wasn't about to accept *no* for an answer."

She stepped forward, placed the folder next to the bag of ribs, and rested her hand on the edge of the table. "You won't need to. They're not ready for you."

"No," he agreed. "They never were."

Eli crossed his arms and remained quiet.

Jack leaned back against the wall.

The moment lingered—not as an ending, but as a breath held before something greater.

Teddy glanced out the window once more. Below, the world carried on, oblivious to the weight of the moment. Nurses completed their rounds with practiced efficiency. MPs changed shifts with a mix of vigilance and routine. Paperwork passed from hand to hand, a constant flow of bureaucracy that seemed to contrast sharply with the stillness inside.

But in this room, everything had come to a halt for the first time in a long while.

Not in surrender, but in readiness, as if the air itself were charged with unspoken resolve, waiting for the next move in a life-or-death game that had been played for too long.

1000 Hours
February 17, 1984
U.S. District Court
Eastern District of North Carolina
300 Green Street
Fayetteville, NC 28301

The courtroom was small, designed more for function than for spectacle. The walls were paneled in dark oak, the ceiling was low, and fluorescent lights hummed overhead. A single American flag stood behind the bench with the seal of the United States embossed in the wood below it. The gallery was sparse—four pew-style benches on each side, only half-filled. There were no press or TV cameras, just legal observers, a federal clerk, a stenographer, two U.S. Marshals, and the weight of a lie that had lingered too long in silence.

Teddy sat at the defense table—neither handcuffed nor escorted by a federal law enforcement agent. He wore a tailored dark gray suit, a black tie, and dress shoes—a straightforward, conservative choice for the courtroom. Given the betrayal by his superiors, he chose not to wear his U.S. Army class A dress uniform and green beret, as it felt inappropriate for the occasion. The scar across his right side was hidden beneath the fabric. Every movement he made showed the careful precision of a man managing pain. He wasn't there to put on a show. He was there to listen.

Merrit sat beside him, her class A uniform crisp and neat, adorned with ribbons that signified her achievements and dedication. Folders were arranged in front of her like weapons she didn't need to draw, each one a testament to her dedication and readiness. Cross sat directly behind them, hands folded in his lap, dressed in his class A uniform. Jack and Eli occupied the far left corner of the gallery, also dressed in traditional black suits and ties.

At 1001 hours, the door behind the bench opened, and Judge Judith A. Myles walked in.

"All rise," the bailiff said, standing beside the bench.

Everyone in the room stood up.

Judge Myles took a seat, prompting the rest of the room to do the same.

"This hearing is now in session," Judge Myles said, her voice calm and measured. "Case number 72-5417, United States v. Colonel Theodore Roosevelt IV, regarding motion for post-conviction relief, review of sealed wartime records, and consideration of vacatur."

Judge Myles glanced at the prosecution table—empty except for a DOJ representative seated alone with a sealed brief in front of him. "Mr. Klein, have you reviewed the materials submitted by Lieutenant Colonel Merrit?"

"Yes, Your Honor," Klein replied. "We've examined all declassified orders, corroborated the recovered field materials, and authenticated the subject's personal statement as well as the taped recording of Major General Dorsey."

"And your recommendation?"

Klein rested his hands on the file. "The Department of Justice withdraws all objections. We support full vacatur of the conviction."

Whispers arose behind them in the gallery. Some supported the decision, while others, louder and more forceful, questioned the DOJ's judgment, urging Judge Myles to ignore the recommendation.

Judge Myles raised her hand to silence them. "Let the record show that the Department of Justice acknowledges the events surrounding Operation Firelight, under Operation VESTIGE, were authorized by high-level command structures, including former officers within the United States Army, DIA, and CIA. The court recognizes that Colonel Theodore Roosevelt IV did not act independently, unlawfully, or in violation of his oath. That the charges of the murder of innocent civilians, listed as war crimes, desertion, and conspiracy, were made under false pretenses and supported by suppressed evidence."

She turned toward Teddy—not harshly, but without formality. "Colonel Roosevelt, do you wish to speak before I proceed with my ruling on your case?"

Teddy stood up carefully to minimize the pain in his side. He didn't glance at the naysayers in the gallery. "I've waited twelve years to hear this institution speak the truth. I won't waste more of its time asking for anything else."

Myles nodded. "Understood." She picked up the gavel—not as a symbol of authority, but as the final step in a process too long denied. "It is the ruling of this court that the conviction of Colonel Theodore Roosevelt IV be formally vacated. That his record be cleared of all related charges. That any restrictions on his movement, employment, and status as an officer of the United States Army be lifted immediately and without prejudice."

The gavel struck down on a wooden block.

The sound may have been subtle in the room, but it carried a sense of finality as the echo faded away.

Judge Myles stood. "Court is adjourned."

The room seemed to exhale, holding its breath in reverence for the moment that had just passed. Teddy sat in his chair, resting his hand on the edge of the table. Merrit leaned toward him just enough for him to hear her voice over the commotion behind them. "It's done."

"No," he said. "It's finally started. I got my life back…and I'm finally home." Before she could stand to put her folders in her briefcase, Teddy placed a hand on her arm. "I have something for you."

"What?" she asked.

"We all have call signs or nicknames. Mine on the covert side is Rough Rider, after my great-uncle, President Roosevelt. In the Army, it was Bull or Bull Moose, also tied to my uncle, but more due to the way I charge into battle. It's time you received one." He placed a Special Forces pin on the table, the motto *De Oppresso Liber*, Latin for *To Free the Oppressed*, seemed appropriate. "This is for you. Today, yours is Valkyrie."

"Why?"

Teddy laughed. "It's from Norse mythology. Valkyries are divine warrior maidens who serve Odin, choosing those who may live or die in battle. They guide the souls of fallen warriors to Valhalla, where the heroes prepare for Ragnarok. Valkyries are often depicted as fierce and noble, embodying the ideals of bravery and honor. Their name translates as 'choosers of the slain,' highlighting their critical role in Norse warrior culture. By helping to keep me alive, you made an honorable and brave choice like a Valkyrie."

Merrit smiled. "Thank you, but only if you call me Rachel, not Merrit, Colonel, or ma'am."

Teddy extended his right hand. "Welcome to the club, Rachel."

She offered him a firm handshake. "I accept, Rough Rider."

1100 Hours
February 17, 1984
U.S. District Court
Eastern District of North Carolina
300 Green Street
Fayetteville, NC 28301

The sidewalk outside the courthouse was quiet, set back from the main road and partially shaded by a row of old elms. No cameras or TV reporters were present. The court proceedings had been closed to the public—

strictly need-to-know, buried under layers of jurisdiction and military discretion.

Teddy stood at the bottom of the concrete steps, his suit coat unbuttoned and flapping in the breeze, shoulders back with that upright posture that had never left him, not even in a hospital bed. The muscles in his side still flared when he breathed too deeply, but he didn't favor it. Not here. Not now. He wanted to project an air of calm defiance in the face of what had happened to him.

Jack leaned against the railing to his left, arms crossed, his white dress shirt unbuttoned at the collar, suit coat draped over one shoulder, and a dossier tucked under one arm. Eli stood just beyond him, scanning the passing cars discreetly, always alert for the tail that never arrived.

They weren't wearing uniforms, yet they carried the burden of them.

"So," Jack said, "what now? Do we book a week's vacation in the Keys with our back pay? Let the brass catch up with resurrecting us on paper? I can already hear the sound of the waves drowning out all the noise that's sure to come our way once the press finds out."

Teddy chuckled, shaking his head. "As tempting as that sounds, I think we both know that's not our style." He glanced at the thin manila envelope that Merrit had handed him just before they left the courtroom. The moment Merrit passed it to him, she had said only one thing. "This came from Langley. Unrequested. Black seal. Someone remembers you."

Now it rested, unopened and folded, in the inner pocket of his coat, feeling heavier than it should have been.

Eli inched closer. "Is that what Colonel Merrit gave you about that Dorsey cleanup crew?"

"Maybe," Teddy said. "Or maybe it's the next one. We stirred the pot. Someone's probably watching to see what spills out."

Jack didn't smile, but his eyes were sharp. "You thinking what I'm thinking?"

"I'm thinking," Teddy said, "that if they tried this hard to bury one op, there's more out there they haven't unearthed yet."

Eli let out a soft grunt. "Then we go digging, trying to figure out who else they screwed. Whatever they're hiding, it's worth the risk."

Teddy looked at both of them, his gaze steady and clear. "Not yet. They wanted us gone. And we're still standing. So we don't disappear. We stay right where they can see us."

Jack pushed off the rail. "Does that mean we're staying in the system? In the United States Army?"

"For now," Teddy said. "Until we decide whether to burn it down or take it back."

Eli opened the driver's door of their white Ford conversion van as Jack walked around to the passenger side. Merrit, after extensive legal wrangling, successfully retrieved it from the police impound in Arizona and had it shipped to Fort Bragg via C-130.

Teddy paused for a moment longer. Then he turned toward the road, reached into his coat, and took out the envelope.

Inside was a single page.

No identifying header or official seal.

A simple line of coordinates—*18S UJ 23394 06571.*

Beneath it, four words, typed as a declaration of warning. Of what? Teddy didn't know.

They never shut it down.

He stared at the coordinates for a long moment. MGRS (Military Grid Reference System)—ten digits. He didn't need a map. That square had been etched in his memory for over a decade, back when red-flagged facilities were built on American soil, hidden within urban sprawl where no one would think to look.

It was Baltimore, near the old harbor industrial loop. A decommissioned Army engineering site had once been used for urban counter-sabotage drills but was shut down in 1978. The buildings remained condemned on paper, yet real estate records showed no demolition—only a transfer of ownership to a holding company that no one had ever heard of. He recalled the place, not for what had happened there, but for what they weren't allowed to do. The site had been taken off the books before Operation Firelight—quietly condemned, buried under property transfers and shell companies, the kind of black-world location no one ever reopened.

Until now.

Teddy folded the page and tucked it back into the inner pocket of his suit coat before climbing into the van.

They stayed silent as the engine started, already moving toward the future.

The van's engine rumbled beneath them, steady and familiar. Teddy sat in the front passenger seat, his body angled to relieve the lingering pull in his side.

Eli adjusted the rearview mirror. Jack glanced at him but didn't ask. Their movements were unhurried, characterized by a lack of sudden calls to action. It was simply a quiet readiness, the kind that comes after years of living under the long shadow of a war that never truly ended for them.

The city outside drifted past the windows as they headed for Fort Belvoir, awaiting confirmation of their U.S. Army status. Low buildings lined the road, and cracked sidewalks stretched beneath their weary feet. People walked with their heads down, the world continuing on, unaware that the story unfolding in the white conversion van had changed more than just three lives.

"I used to think," Teddy said, "that if the truth ever came out, that'd be the end of it. That we could stop running. Let it go."

Neither Jack nor Eli interrupted him.

"But it doesn't end," Teddy went on. "It just moves deeper. Changes shape. And the next time it surfaces, it doesn't send orders—it sends shadows." He turned to look out the window, resting one hand on the dashboard. "They didn't clear our names because we were innocent. They did it because they were afraid of what else we might prove."

Eli grunted in agreement, while Jack stayed silent.

The van reached the edge of the city, gliding onto the quiet highway with barely a ripple. The buildings thinned, and the space widened. Yet no one spoke. There was no need to ask what came next. The piece of paper in Teddy's coat pocket had already revealed it—another buried operation, another lie waiting to be exposed. This time, they wouldn't wait to be hunted.

They would go in first with a carefully devised plan—something the remnants of the black world wouldn't anticipate.

The wind pressed against the windows as their speed picked up.

Teddy leaned back in his seat, closed his eyes for a moment, and allowed the silence to envelop him. It wasn't peace. It wasn't closure. But it was clarity.

And that, for now, was enough.

CHAPTER 35

1030 Hours
February 20, 1984
Temporary Housing
Fort Belvoir, VA

The house was simple and quiet, nestled behind a stand of old cedar trees, a mile from the administrative offices at Fort Belvoir. It wasn't designed for long stays—just a peaceful holding space for officers awaiting clearance, review, or transition. The furniture was government-issued, the kind that creaked if you sat on it the wrong way. But the air was fresh, the air conditioner worked well, and the power was reliable. The curtains were rough, and the carpets didn't quite match the size of the floors. Yet the place was clean, secure, and silent. After years of living on the run, it felt almost alien.

It wasn't the barracks, but it also wasn't freedom. The Army referred to it as transitional quarters. Teddy had seen enough of these to know what it truly meant—limbo with furniture.

Jack hadn't sat down since the package arrived. He stood near the back door with his arms crossed, sleeves rolled up, and the top button of his shirt undone, watching the shadows shift across the grass outside through the screen door. He looked like a man waiting for a verdict he already knew was coming.

Eli sat in the corner armchair, hands steepled, elbows resting on his knees, and his jaw tense. No one had spoken for the last few minutes.

Teddy stood near the front window with the curtains drawn halfway closed. Outside, the trees swayed in the morning breeze, their branches casting shadows that glided slowly across the sidewalk and front lawn. His unbuttoned coat hung loosely around his frame. He had lost a great deal of weight in the hospital. The stiffness in his side had faded to a manageable ache, but he still favored his left hip when he turned. Old habits. Old wounds. He hadn't asked for updates. The system was in motion now, and when it moved, it brought answers whether you wanted them or not.

On the coffee table behind him lay a folder—Army brown, thick paper, sealed with a single white sticker and bearing his name and rank. Colonel Theodore Roosevelt IV, typed in black ink and centered on the front of the folder. No apology. Just the acknowledgment of a status that had never truly been revoked—only ignored.

The courier who delivered it twenty minutes ago was already gone—no ceremony, no rank insignia, just wearing a plain civilian suit and the brisk rhythm of someone delivering orders too classified to be sent through normal channels. He waited just long enough to ensure it reached Teddy's hands then left without a backward glance.

They all knew what was coming.

Teddy turned away from the window and approached the table. He picked up the folder, ran his thumb along the edge of the seal, and broke it cleanly. Inside, he found a single typed sheet of textured military-grade paper. There was no seal at the top, no unit insignia—only neatly typed text.

Colonel Theodore Roosevelt IV, Captain Jack Stratton, and Master Sergeant Eli Red Horse – you remain under U.S. Army commission.

Your records are now under final review. As of 0800 hours this morning, your status has been reactivated under Tier Four provisional clearance, Office of Covert Operations (OCO). Pending formalization of full exoneration, you are authorized to resume your duties in either an advisory or operational capacity at your discretion.

If accepted, your initial briefing is scheduled. Enclosed are the grid coordinates and arrival protocol. Additional details are classified and will be provided in person.

This assignment is discretionary.

You may decline.

Additional directives are classified. Coordinates attached.

Beneath the printed lines sat two words handwritten in black ink.

Request accepted.

No signature or agency of origin—just the facts and a set of MGRS coordinates typed on the lower half of the page—*18S UJ 23394 06571*. They matched those in the letter Merrit had given him at the courthouse. Teddy read it twice before laying the page flat on the table.

"They're not wasting time giving us a mission," Teddy said. "These coordinates are in southern Baltimore, near the old wargame grounds. The place was officially shut down but continued operating, unofficially going dark in '78. I remember the file. Red-stamped, no debrief, no demolition record. Just a line drawn through the access registry."

Eli grunted. "So why bring it back now?"

Teddy didn't answer right away. He pressed his palms flat against the counter and stared at the envelope. "They're trying to tie up the rest of the loose ends. Not the mess we exposed—whatever's still hiding under it. They never cleared the files. They just changed the locks. Now someone's opened the door again, and they want us to walk through it."

Jack picked up the letter. "Do you think this is bait?"

"No," Teddy said. "I think it's a test. Or a cleanup job someone doesn't want traced to them. Either way, they didn't pick us to close the loop. They picked us because we're the last ones who know what that loop looks like. And I think we're the only ones who remember where the bodies are buried."

Eli raised an eyebrow. "Are you gonna tell them *yes*?"

"Yes, I am." Teddy's reply came without pause. "We're not going in blind. We check the files. We trace the ownership. Then we hit it fast—our way." He took the letter from Jack and reread the final paragraph—a single line of text.

You may decline.

It wasn't an invitation but the U.S. Army's way of pretending they hadn't spent the last twelve years trying to forget him.

"It's just the three of us. And whoever left that site warm after all these years is going to learn what happens when you try to rebuild something that should've stayed buried," Teddy said.

Eli leaned forward in his chair, his hands resting on his knees. "Do you trust what's in that letter?"

"I trust the message," Teddy replied. "I don't trust the sender. They think we'll walk in because we're grateful. Like we owe them something for finally pulling the knife out of our backs."

Jack walked over to the table and examined the letter. "It's not an offer. It's a door."

"Exactly," Teddy replied.

"And we're walking through it?" Eli asked.

Teddy didn't answer right away. He stood with one hand resting on the back of the chair, his eyes still on the page. "They want us to go quiet. But we don't go quiet this time. We don't crawl back under the rug just because the Army found a use for us again."

Jack nodded. "So what do we do?"

Teddy looked up, his gaze steady. "We show up. But we write the terms into our contract that benefit us, not them. No masks or lies. No shadows or handlers. We do the job. We expose what's left. And when this thing ends—if it ends—it won't be in some back hallway with a bullet in our backs. It'll be where everyone can see it. But we don't take orders. If they want a clean-up crew, they can call someone else. If they want the truth uncovered before it kills the next man in line…" He looked at them both, his voice even. "Then we walk through that door and make sure it doesn't happen again. And if this leads where I think it does—we finish it. All of it. Pack light. We move on this before the brass has a chance to change their minds."

No one needed to say anything more. No one questioned his decision.

Eli stood up, grabbed his field bag from the floor, and slung it over one shoulder.

Jack reached for his coat. "I'll call in two throwaway mobile phones and a car. We'll be off-post in thirty."

And just like that, the decision was made—not with ceremony, not with fanfare, but with the same quiet, exact force that had kept them alive this long.

Teddy folded the letter and slid it into the inner pocket of his coat, pausing for a moment longer. The silence no longer felt like waiting.

It felt like a choice. They weren't being pulled back or reactivated.

They were returning of their own free will—because the war wasn't over yet.

This time, they would be going in first.

Not to clean up someone else's mess.

They were going in to finish the job on their terms.

2000 Hours
February 20, 1984
519th Intelligence Battalion
Fort Bragg, NC

The office was quiet, the lights dim. Colonel Vincent Cross stood by the window, field uniform sleeves rolled up to his elbows and hands relaxed at his sides, gazing out into the night beyond the glass. The post appeared peaceful under sodium floodlights—rows of vehicles, vacant buildings, and a lone MP patrolling on foot across the south parking lot. However, Cross didn't notice the stillness. He sensed the pressure building beneath it.

The message came through at 1930 sharp.

No questions or requests for his input—just a single flag in the secure system.

Tier Four OCO activation: Acknowledged
Roosevelt, Stratton, Red Horse—status: Operational
Deployment grid: Pending

He hadn't even received a phone call.

They had been cleared for official movement without him.

Behind him, the desk was cluttered with folders he hadn't touched—after-action reports from a dozen unrelated units, a field packet on a SOUTHCOM intercept in Honduras, and a half-read memo on domestic intel restructuring. None of it mattered anymore.

What mattered was what was missing from the system.

He walked over to the file cabinet in the corner and opened the drawer labeled *CLASSIFIED: JAG HOLD*. It was nearly empty now. Merrit had taken most of the physical files for the federal audit after the hearing. What remained were fragments—redacted directives, unsigned protocols, and one old manifest from an unnamed operation, showing only a date and a transport record out of Aberdeen in 1973.

Cargo: Unknown
Personnel: Classified
Destination: Redacted

Cross stared at it for a long moment before sliding it back. This wasn't just cleanup. It was an ignition point. He had spent years pursuing Colonel

Theodore "Bull Moose" Roosevelt, convincing himself that the man was a rogue, unpredictable, and dangerous. And he'd been right about one thing.

The Rough Rider was dangerous.

Not because he defied orders, but because he understood how they were written and the dangers of following them without question.

Cross returned to the window, watching the tree line and his own reflection in the glass. He was no longer an outsider. He was no longer a step removed or merely an observer. Somewhere between the testimony, the bruises, and the truth that Merrit had unearthed, he had stopped hunting them and started protecting them.

And now they were stepping into something that no one else had the clearance—or the courage—to touch.

He didn't envy them. Still, he knew one thing with absolute clarity. If the U.S. Army was willing to hand the keys back to Colonel Theodore Roosevelt IV, then whatever lay behind that door was worse than anyone wanted to admit.

0600 Hours
February 21, 1984
G-2 Annex Briefing Room
Building 259
Fort Belvoir, VA

The room wasn't designed for comfort. The concrete wall, made of pale cinder blocks, met a strip of green industrial carpet that fell short at every corner. It displayed typical workmanship by a lowly private or PFC. A long conference table dominated the space, surrounded by upright chairs with metal frames and government upholstery—gray, stiff, and scratchy. Fluorescent lights buzzed overhead like a warning.

Fort Belvoir's old G-2 annex had long served as a storage area for excess paperwork and classified briefings. It had no windows, only a single entrance, with two uniformed MPs stationed on either side of the door.

Teddy sat at the end of the table, his posture straight despite the lingering discomfort in his side. His coat was draped over the back of the chair, and his boots were planted flat on the tile. Across from him, Jack leaned back with his ankle hooked over a knee, idly spinning a pen between his fingers. Eli sat to Teddy's right, his forearms resting on the edge of the table with an unopened manila folder in front of him.

Major Gaeta, dressed in a class A uniform, stood at the front of the room, flanked by two staff members and a portable chalkboard brought in from storage. He looked young for his rank—too smooth around the eyes—but his voice conveyed authority.

"This is a Tier Four classified orientation under Directive Foxtrot-Four-Six. You are not here as detainees. You are not here as fugitives. You are here under reinstated commission, subject to field operational discretion under the Office of Covert Operations. You will not be publicly acknowledged. You will not be officially listed on any roster. But as of 0900 this morning, you are once again soldiers."

He removed the cover from the chalkboard.

Three names were handwritten in block printing at the top.

ROOSEVELT IV, THEODORE COL. O-6
STRATTON, JACK A. CAPT. O-3
RED HORSE, ELI MSG E-8

Beneath them, two stenciled words.

ACTIVE: OCO

Major Gaeta turned back and gestured at the folders laid out in front of each man. "You'll find your non-disclosure agreements inside. One page. Standard black-tier language. You'll sign it. You'll keep a copy. And if this legal agreement ever sees light outside this room, you'll be recalled under Article 106A of the UCMJ and disappear so far down the chain you won't see daylight again. Questions?"

"I do," Teddy said. "Since the brass invoked Directive Foxtrot Four-Six, are we assets, soldiers, or just fire-and-forget? We're just useful again. And if it all goes to hell, they'll swear we exceeded our orders and throw us in prison again—no trial, no questions."

"You're soldiers, Colonel Roosevelt," Major Gaeta said. "Uniformed, armed, and unacknowledged. The kind of men they call when the mission matters more than the aftermath. And if it goes to hell, it won't be like last time. You won't be disavowed, abandoned, or left behind. We will get you out no matter the cost. But you and everything that happened will be buried under so many layers of classification that anyone looking will need a map and a miracle to find you. That's the nature of the work. You knew that walking in."

"Good enough." Teddy nodded at Eli and Jack.

Jack flipped open his folder. His brow arched at the wording, but he didn't say anything. Eli read more slowly, clenching his jaw. Teddy opened his folder and read silently.

UNITED STATES ARMY – OCO / DIRECTIVE FOXTROT FOUR-SIX NON-DISCLOSURE AGREEMENT

By signing below, I acknowledge that I have been granted provisional access to materials, operations, or personnel classified under Tier Four/Black-level clearance.
I agree:
1. To reveal no operational details, whether past or present, without explicit written authorization.
2. To report any unauthorized disclosures or security breaches within 24 hours.
3. To accept the consequences of a breach as outlined in Article 106a (Espionage) and the applicable provisions of the UCMJ.
4. That no acknowledgement of my service, participation, or actions under this directive will be made public without declassification.

Signed: _____ Date: _____
      Colonel Theodore Roosevelt IV

Teddy picked up the pen from the table and signed his name with slow, deliberate strokes before setting the folder aside.

The major gathered the papers in silence. "You are now under formal orders. No medals or commendations will be formally issued except under compartmentalized status. Only the President can change these orders, and, given time and your excellent records of service, that will probably happen in the near future. But your actions have been recognized—quietly, and at the highest level. The Secretary of the Army sends his appreciation. Off the record."

Eli let out a soft grunt of satisfaction. Jack appeared as though he might smile, but he didn't.

As the room emptied, Teddy remained behind. He had something to take care of. Once the others left, he walked to the side door and entered a narrow communications room. The phone inside was hardwired and military green—the kind he hadn't seen since '72.

Teddy picked up the receiver and dialed the five-digit internal extension he had been given—10128.

"519th Intelligence Battalion, Sergeant Michaels speaking," a male voice said.

"Message for Colonel Vince Cross from Colonel Roosevelt," Teddy said.

"Go ahead."

"Tell him this. The Army finally remembered us. We're back in service. And this time—we're not the ones running." Teddy hung up, turned around, and walked out.

Outside, the morning sun rose over the treetops. The breeze carried the faint scent of wet pavement. Jack and Eli waited at the curb beside a tan Army sedan with the engine idling.

Teddy slipped on his coat, adjusted the collar, and joined them.

They weren't just soldiers again.

They were operational.

And this time, they were setting the terms.

CHAPTER 36

1000 Hours
February 22, 1984
Freighter in International Waters
North Atlantic Ocean

The freighter groaned in the icy waters of the North Atlantic, its hull slicing through swells beneath a gunmetal sky. The sea heaved dark and slow beneath the hull, an endless swell of winter-gray water creaking and groaning against the steel. Somewhere below the horizon, the moon tried and failed to break through the cloud cover. The sky was a single sheet of ash, and the wind off the waves struck like cold iron.

This particular ship was not listed on any civilian manifest. It hadn't docked at a commercial port in almost a month. Its registry numbers had been scraped, repainted, and covered multiple times with the lettering on the stern now barely legible under layers of corrosion.

Stacked steel cargo containers towered in rusted rows across the deck, each labeled with counterfeit export tags—old company logos, corroded clamps, and shipping numbers that led nowhere. The registry on the stern read *SEA LION*, although no such vessel existed in any international fleet. Below the name, the sandblasted outline of seven letters and a single digit remained. *Delilah 7.*

Deep in the lower decks, behind a steel bulkhead fitted with six-digit rotary locks and within a sealed maintenance compartment, the hum of a hidden communications terminal echoed against the insulated walls—Soviet-manufactured, vintage early '70s—rewired to operate on an internal generator and shielded from electromagnetic leakage. A strip of masking tape marked the edge of the terminal, displaying three words, handwritten in black magic marker.

DO NOT INITIATE

However, the order had already been given. The only factors delaying it were the failsafe timer and the final review of the documents.

Fluorescent lights flickered overhead. A solitary man sat cross-legged on a bolted steel bench in the room, reviewing the final pages of a burn folder filled with decades-old secrets.

Nero was middle-aged, lean, and unremarkable in appearance, wearing a faded knit cap pulled low over his ears, a black sweater, cargo pants, and a wool-lined peacoat typical of a merchant marine sailor. His boots were laced tightly but showed signs of wear at the toes, and their soles were nearly silent as he moved across the narrow steel floor.

The skin on his right palm was pale and ridged with acid burn scars. It was an unmistakable mark left by Legacy handlers after Rough Rider saved his life. It wasn't a badge but a promise.

The file in his hands had only one label.

LEGACY/BLACK – DORSEY NODE
TRIGGER CONFIRMED: DELTA-ONE-NINER-BLACK

He flipped to the last insert—a grayscale image printed from a Washington, D.C., security camera. Colonel Theodore Roosevelt IV was exiting his temporary Army quarters, alive and back in service with a Tier Four/Black-level clearance assignment with the OCO. The date stamp of February 22, 1984, confirmed what he already knew.

Target preserved.

Beneath it, new instructions—the order to complete the legacy protocol.

OBJECTIVE SHIFT: EXPOSE NODE. TERMINATE CLEAN-UP CHAIN

He folded the photo once and tucked it into the well-worn slot of the burn vault at his side. Then he stood up, walked over to the built-in console in the wall, and entered a seven-digit password from memory—1635289—on the keyboard.

The black screen flickered to life revealing a solitary green blinking cursor.

He typed beside the terminal's blinking green cursor, letter by letter, each keystroke firm and deliberate.

DELTA-ONE-NINER-BLACK

The terminal flickered. A hidden relay activated with a soft mechanical snap. The screen transformed—no menu, no prompt—just a single word in block capital letters.

PROTOCOL RECOGNIZED

Nero leaned back in the chair and exhaled. He reached beneath the terminal for a steel latch and pulled out a long, narrow, sealed black plastic waterproof case. Inside, he discovered four envelopes, each labeled with a different name and numeric code.

He selected only one—Rough Rider—D19B.

Then Nero stood, crossed the compartment to the narrow steel hatch, and knocked twice.

"North star?" a voice responded from the other side.

"Guides home," he replied.

The door swung open. Another man dressed in similar clothing stood there—armed with a holstered sidearm but appearing relaxed. He took the envelope silently and nodded. Then, he turned and disappeared down the darkened passageway, his footsteps fading into the cold steel labyrinth of the freighter.

Nero stayed behind and returned to the console, waiting for the failsafe timer on the wall to count down to zero. It was only a few seconds away.

When it beeped, he entered a command into the console.

SEND://PRIORITY-ZETA-K-7/GENEVA_CORE/NODE-DORSEY
>EXECUTE

Silence enveloped the area. No broadcast alert was heard. Just a pulse—a secure signal bouncing from a deep-sea relay to an orbital satellite, routed through cold server hubs in Austria, Cairo, and São Paulo before reaching a final node somewhere beneath the financial district of Geneva.

Nero knew what would happen next. Two minutes later, the Geneva server bank went offline.

In Luxembourg, a silent trigger was activated within a numbered holding company, prompting an automatic SEC reporting anomaly. In Zürich, bank regulators flagged three firms for irregular fund routing. At 4:17 AM local time, Swiss compliance authorities issued immediate seizure orders.

By sunrise, three shell corporations previously linked to Dorsey's black-world infrastructure were frozen under international fraud protocols and flagged for external audit.

Nero watched none of this unfold in real time. His work had reached its conclusion. He slid the burn folder into a lead-lined drawer, sealed it with a press, and turned off the chamber lights. The only sound now was the low, ceaseless, heartbeat-like thrum of the engines at the stern of the freighter.

He would never return to the United States. Yet the system he had served—a neglected black doctrine hidden beneath layers of denial—had moved one final time.

Legacy Protocol: Activated
Node: Burned
War: Concluded—quietly

Nero powered down the communications console, switch by switch, until only darkness remained. The ghost of a war that never officially occurred reached back across decades to erase the last traces of the men who tried to rewrite it.

His job, his work was complete.

0730 Hours
February 25, 1984
Officers Housing
Colonel Theodore Roosevelt IV
Fort Belvoir, VA

The early morning light seeped through the open curtains of the east-facing window, filtering through the last wisps of fog rising from the Virginia pine trees and casting a warm orange glow across the floorboards. The quarters assigned to Colonel Theodore Roosevelt IV weren't luxurious, but they were quiet, secure, and private—exactly what a black-world U.S. Army officer needed in the days following his reactivation.

The three-bedroom house was sparse and functional, furnished with typical drab military furniture, store-bought framed pictures, and linens. Yet, it lacked personal items, photographs, and knick-knacks—nothing to reflect a distinguished military career spanning over twenty-five years. Most of those items were scattered across the country in various storage facilities.

A worn Vietnam-era M1911A1 lay disassembled on a cleaning cloth next to a steaming mug of black coffee. On the edge of the desk rested a familiar tan folder labeled OCO-Tier Four.

Teddy sat at the desk wearing a white T-shirt, blue jeans, and sneakers, his eyes focused on the steel gray envelope in front of him. It had no stamp, return address, or seal of any kind.

The envelope hadn't been delivered by a courier—it simply appeared—tucked into the mail slot in the front door around 0300 hours, just after the shift change of the base perimeter security patrols. There were no footprints in the frost on the sidewalk leading up to the porch.

Across the room, Jack "Ghost" Stratton leaned against the doorframe leading from the kitchen, flipping through an open map case and scanning the old logistics routes that passed through Baltimore's eastern corridor. Eli "Stone" Red Horse sat on the couch, lacing up his black jump boots.

Duffel bags, footlockers, and various cardboard supply boxes were stacked against the wall in the entry hall, ready to be loaded into their assigned, completely off-the-books, nondescript black van. The Virginia plates traced back to an abandoned warehouse in the Richmond industrial district.

Teddy waited the mandatory five minutes before opening the envelope, aware of its contents—the final determination of the legacy protocol.

He pulled out a 4 x 6 white index card. It didn't have typed lettering but had embossed text burned cleanly into the page. Standard black-world procedure to wipe both prints and DNA from any document.

LEGACY/BLACK
DORSEY NODE: DISSOLVED
CLEAN-UP CHAIN: NEUTRALIZED
PROTOCOL CLOSED

A final line appeared below in a smaller font, almost like an afterthought.

Response not required. Witness not forgotten.

Teddy stared at the card for a long time, running his thumb along the edge. Its significance wasn't in the message—it was in what it didn't say. Slowly, he set the card down on the desk next to the disassembled M1911 slide. Outside, a bird sang in the cedar tree near the fence line before falling silent once more.

Jack crossed the room and looked over his shoulder at the note. "You didn't tell us that you pulled the trigger. So it's done?"

Teddy nodded. "Yes. The legacy protocol has been closed. Dorsey and the global machine he built have been terminated with extreme prejudice."

"And the others?" Eli asked.

Teddy glanced at the card again. "They took everything down and chewed out the roots." He slipped the card into the top desk drawer and closed it gently. It didn't matter if anyone else saw it. Only one person understood the message—him.

The war had never been about medals or revenge. It had always been about exposure. And now, at last, the shadowy world that had tried to erase them was gone—eliminated by a buried order made for moments just like this.

Then came the knock at the front door.

Teddy walked to the door and opened it. Standing at the threshold was a U.S. Army courier dressed in a class A dress uniform, but the uniform displayed no rank, no name, or ribbons—only a plastic identification card clipped to the pocket that read, *OCO Transmission, Temporary*.

"Message for Colonel Roosevelt," the man said, handing over a sealed white envelope.

Teddy took it. "Dismissed."

The courier stepped back and walked into the misty yard, disappearing behind the tree line where a plain black sedan idled with its engine running.

Teddy closed the door, broke the wax seal on the back of the envelope, and pulled out a sheet of paper with a printed message on it.

Protocol Confirmed – 04:23 Zulu
Northern Operator Asset Engaged
Phase Two Clearance Pending
Contact: Deep Coordination Cell – Eastern Division

And underneath it, in a neat block of text.

The match has been lit at 18S UJ 23394 06571. Your move.

Teddy stared at the clear movement order. "Jack!"

"Yeah." Jack walked over to him. "What's up?"

"We have our orders. Get me a line to the Eastern Division. Scrambled. We move at dusk." Teddy placed the letter on the desk, pulled an index card from the drawer, and wrote a note.

To: Colonel Vincent Cross
Another cell is awake. Watch your six.
Warn LTC Merrit.

He slipped the page into a separate envelope labeled *Colonel V. Cross, 519th Intelligence Battalion—Fort Bragg, NC,* and handed it to Jack. "Call a courier and get this delivered."

"Consider it done," Jack replied.

Eli stood up from the couch. "I'll get everything loaded, Colonel."

Outside, the fog had lifted. Inside, the war had started again.

However, this time Shadow Lance made the first move.

"Get your gear together," Teddy said. "We're not done. But this part—the chapter about Dorsey—is over."

Jack smiled. "Where to? Baltimore?"

Teddy picked up his cleaned M1911 pistol and reassembled it without looking. "Yes! When one legacy ends, you start something new. A Roosevelt climbs his own hill."

Glossary

Military and Intelligence Acronyms and Terms:

1. Army JAG (Judge Advocate General's Corps):
Legal branch of the U.S. Army that provides legal services to soldiers, including advice on military law, criminal defense, and legal assistance. JAG officers serve as attorneys and are involved in various legal matters, including court-martial proceedings and administrative law.

2. CIA (Central Intelligence Agency):
A U.S. government agency responsible for gathering and analyzing foreign intelligence to support national security. Established in 1947, it conducts intelligence operations, including covert actions, and provides critical information to policymakers.

3. CIA Task Group D-7:
A fictional covert subgroup under CIA management, specifically mentioned as responsible for oversight and subsequent cover-up of Operation Firelight. Used as the operational handler group for Firelight and Sable Protocol. Responsible for operational deception and asset disavowal.

4. CID (Criminal Investigation Division):
The branch of the U.S. Army responsible for investigating felony crimes, war crimes, and intelligence-related offenses within Army jurisdiction.

5. Confidential Informant (CI):
An individual who provides information to law enforcement agencies about criminal activity, often in exchange for some form of consideration, such as reduced charges, immunity, or financial compensation. CIs can be crucial in investigations, as they may have insider knowledge about criminal organizations, drug trafficking, or other illegal activities.

6. Cutout:
A third party or intermediary is used to relay information or orders between two parties. The purpose of using cutouts is to keep secrecy and lower the risk of direct contact between people involved in sensitive operations. By passing information through cutouts, identities are protected, and information is kept separate, making sure no single person has access to all parts of a sensitive operation. This method is used to improve operational security and reduce exposure.

7. DIA (Defense Intelligence Agency):
A combat support agency within the U.S. Department of Defense, providing military intelligence for strategic and operational purposes.

8. Joint Personnel Recovery Center (JPRC): A task force within the Military Assistance Command, Vietnam (MACV) that operated from 1966 to 1973, focusing on the recovery of U.S. and allied personnel listed as Prisoners of War (POW) or Missing in Action (MIA) during the Vietnam War.

9. MACV-SOG (Military Assistance Command, Vietnam – Studies and Observations Group):
A highly classified, multi-service special operations unit during the Vietnam War that conducted reconnaissance, sabotage, and psychological warfare missions in Vietnam, Laos, and Cambodia. It executed covert operations in Laos, Cambodia, and North Vietnam from 1964 to 1972.

10. MGRS (Military Grid Reference System):
A standardized coordinate system utilized by NATO forces to provide precise map locations by dividing the Earth into a grid. It is widely employed by ground forces to ensure operational precision.

11. SAD-L (Special Activities Division – Liaison):
A component of the CIA that focuses on covert operations and paramilitary activities. It is part of the CIA's Special Activities Center (SAC), which conducts a range of operations, including those that require a high degree of secrecy and deniability.

12. Special Forces (Green Berets):
An elite branch of the U.S. Army specializing in unconventional warfare, foreign internal defense, counterterrorism, direct action, and special reconnaissance. Known officially as the U.S. Army Special Forces, these units are highly trained for operations behind enemy lines, often working in small teams to train and support indigenous forces or carry out high-risk missions. Their distinctive green beret, authorized by President John F. Kennedy in 1961, symbolizes their autonomy, adaptability, and expertise in asymmetrical warfare.

Operation Names and Terms:

1. Directive Foxtrot-Four-Six:
A Tier Four classified directive authorizing the covert reinstatement of military personnel under the authority of the Office of Covert Operations. Individuals reinstated under this directive are not acknowledged publicly, do not appear on official rosters, and operate under deep-cover conditions. Used in exceptional circumstances where deniable, off-record action is sanctioned by upper-tier command structures.

2. Directive Seven-Two:
A classified fail-safe protocol maintained by Operation Subnet Echo. Invoked only when a buried or presumed-dead asset is reactivated in hostile threat space. Directive 72 authorizes the automatic exposure and dismantling of corrupted internal command structures by releasing controlled intelligence leaks, financial triggers, or asset-protection countermeasures. Unlike Legacy Protocol (activation) or Sable Protocol (containment/erasure), Directive 72 serves as the system's last firewall—intended to destroy the cover of any operation or individual that threatens to erase critical assets to protect its own existence. Known to have been invoked only once prior to the Roosevelt case. Classification status: Eyes Only.

3. Legacy Protocol:
A classified, fictional covert-action contingency procedure triggered by a specific code phrase ("delta-one-niner-black"). Once activated, dormant operatives eliminate covert assets or dismantle rogue intelligence networks threatening operational secrecy or integrity.
1) **Primary Function:** A deep black contingency plan reserved for deniable, last-resort self-defense by black-world assets who are being eliminated by their own system.
2) **Trigger Phrase:** *"Delta-One-Niner-Black"*
3) **Activation:** Occurs via a secured, hidden phone line or terminal known only to legacy operatives.
4) **Effects Shown in Story:**
   a) Triggers a sealed terminal in a hidden U.S. facility.
   b) Releases a ghost agent aboard a North Atlantic freighter.
   c) Dismantles Dorsey's covert infrastructure: financial collapse, international audit triggers, and server banks in Geneva go dark.

d) It is fully executed in the background while Roosevelt is recovering.
5) **Failsafe Mechanism:** The Legacy Protocol operates as a contingency plan, ensuring that certain operatives can be reactivated when traditional command structures are compromised or unwilling to act.
6) **Reactivation of Dormant Assets:** It facilitates the return of operatives who have been sidelined or disavowed, allowing them to resume operations under the radar of standard military or intelligence oversight.

4. Operation Firelight:

A fictional covert Vietnam-era operation involving MACV-SOG with CIA backing, officially intended to monitor Chinese arms-smuggling routes supplying the Khmer Rouge via covert Laotian villagers. Secretly, unknown to Colonel Roosevelt and his team, it was a CIA-backed false-flag operation intended to justify future U.S. military intervention in Laos to wipe out the Pathet Lao by planting evidence of Chinese atrocities. When Roosevelt uncovered this deception and attempted to halt the false-flag operation, his team was cut off, blamed for a massacre that wasn't theirs, and arrested upon return to Vietnam. Codename of the team for this operation: Shadow Lance.

5. Sable Protocol:

Clandestine intelligence containment and erasure directive designed to preemptively eliminate or discredit field assets in the event of compromised operations, especially when those operations violate international law or exceed formal chain-of-command authorization. It is not a failsafe for protection—it is a clean-up weapon used by high-level handlers to remove evidence, tie up loose ends, and ensure deniability at the executive level.

1) Deploy false documentation (forged orders, mission rewrites, amended communiqués).
2) Fabricate alternate narratives via planted witnesses or falsified signal traffic.
3) Blacklist or burn operatives associated with the operation.
4) If necessary, terminate witnesses or field assets under "containment clause" (similar to non-official cover disavowal).

6. VST-714:
A fictional protocol identifier associated internally with Operation Firelight. It was used in official classified records to obscure actual mission objectives.

Sable vs. Legacy Protocol

Feature	Sable Protocol	Legacy Protocol
Purpose	Disavowal & Discrediting	Protection & Counter-erasure
Used by	Handlers, Black-world planners	Field assets, ghost agents
Authorization	High-level (CIA, Joint Interagency Command)	Deep-access field operatives only
Trigger Mechanism	Embedded directive via handler command	Sealed phrase or hardline signal (Roosevelt's call)
Moral Orientation	Protective of the system, sacrificial to assets	Protective of the asset, destructive to the system

Key Characters and their Callsigns/Names:

1. Colonel Theodore "Teddy" Roosevelt IV ("Bull" or "Bull Moose"):
Main protagonist, decorated Special Forces officer, and distant relative of President Theodore Roosevelt. Known for leadership, strategic thinking, and loyalty. Family legacy in the military dating back to the Rough Riders. Graduate of West Point, class of 1955. Former Green Beret turned covert operations specialist. He earned the nickname Bull for his ability to charge through bureaucratic red tape and battlefield chaos alike. Involved in a classified reconnaissance advisory group operating along the Ho Chi Minh Trail. Additional call sign for covert operations – "Rough Rider."

2. Captain Jack Stratton ("Ghost"):
Former Army intelligence officer, linguist – fluent in multiple languages, master of disguise and covert infiltration. Silver-tongued former Army Intelligence officer. Grew up bouncing between foster homes in Southern California. Brilliant at infiltration, language, and psychological ops. Called "Ghost" for his ability to vanish into civilian populations by enemy lines and assume roles flawlessly then reappear with actionable intelligence. He served alongside Roosevelt in Laos.

3. Master Sergeant Eli Red Horse ("Stone"):
Oglala Lakota Sioux, demolition expert, close combat specialist, calm and composed under fire. Born on the Pine Ridge Reservation in South Dakota. Served with distinction as a heavy weapons and engineering specialist, also a hand-to-hand combat instructor. Towering build, soft-spoken, and deeply loyal. Called "Stone" for his calm, immovable presence under fire.

4. Colonel Vincent Cross ("Iron Vince"):
Former CID investigator turned Military Intelligence officer, pursued Roosevelt's team following the failed CIA-backed mission, eventually became a reluctant ally. Career military officer. Prides himself on duty and order. Stoic, skeptical, but ultimately loyal to justice. Called "Iron Vince," a name he earned for his unbending discipline in combat zones.

5. Lt. Colonel Rachel Merrit ("Valkyrie"):

JAG officer with a background in counterintelligence law, known for her unshakable integrity and precision. Leads the investigation that uncovers the truth behind Operation Firelight and becomes Roosevelt's key ally inside the system. Called Valkyrie by Colonel Roosevelt for her loyalty and adherence to her duty like the Valkyries of Nordic legend.

6. Major General Franklin A. Dorsey:

A fictional high-ranking officer who authorized Operation Firelight and oversaw the cover-up efforts post-operation.

7. Colonel Martin Kohrs:

CIA liaison responsible for the erasure and cover-up of Operation Firelight details and team records.

8. Nathan Kaufman:

Fictional Naval Intelligence officer involved in operational intelligence who disappeared under suspicious circumstances after Operation Firelight.

9. Andrew Dunning:

Fictional CIA operative associated with forged operational orders related to the village massacre used to implicate Roosevelt's team. SAD-L (Special Activities Division – Liaison)

10. Shadow Lance:

An off-the-books Special Forces team formed under MACV-SOG with covert CIA backing during the Vietnam War. Comprised of elite operatives drawn from Special Forces, Intelligence, and Indigenous Warfare units, Shadow Lance was officially never activated and never decommissioned. Their primary mission—Operation Firelight—was designed to monitor Chinese weapons trafficking through Laos and Cambodia, but was later exposed as a false-flag mission to fabricate justification for U.S. intervention. Betrayed and abandoned, Shadow Lance was framed for atrocities they didn't commit. Now reactivated under provisional Tier Four clearance, they operate with full autonomy under the Office of Covert Operations (OCO).

Related Operational Terms:

1. Black-World Operation (Black Ops):
Covert or clandestine operations conducted with extreme secrecy, often without official acknowledgment, plausible deniability, and minimal oversight. Fully deniable, undocumented government operations. Often kept off budgets and out of sight of congressional oversight.

2. Burn Folder/Burn Notice/Burn Vault:
A classified folder or communication used in covert operations that can be destroyed or disavowed instantly if compromised.
   a. Burn notice: an official disavowal of an agent.
   b. Burn vault: a secure chamber for destroying or sealing classified materials permanently.

3. Clearance Code:
A unique alphanumeric identifier denoting access level to specific classified information (e.g., "731-X5" used in the Sable Protocol document).

4. Containment Directive:
Classified or semi-classified operational order used primarily within intelligence, military, or national security contexts. It authorizes specific actions to isolate, control, or neutralize a sensitive threat—be it personnel, information, or operational fallout—to prevent wider exposure, damage, or compromise.
   1) Possible Orders Within a Containment Directive:
      a. Monitoring or isolating individuals involved in the mission.
      b. Freezing communication or records, scrubbing databases.
      c. Classifying or reclassifying materials at a higher level (e.g., Top Secret/SAP).
      d. Issuing false narratives (e.g., "Bank of Hanoi never existed").
      e. Authorizing neutralization (in extreme cases) if exposure risk is too great.
      f. Cutting off support, funding, or access to assets (e.g., "no extraction plan").

5. Delta-One-Niner-Black:
The legacy trigger phrase used to activate the Legacy Protocol. Likely hardcoded into buried systems with deep intel ties.

6. Exfil (Exfiltration):
The extraction of personnel from hostile or covert zones.

7. False-Flag Operation:
A covert action designed to appear as if carried out by someone other than those actually responsible, intended to mislead or manipulate perception for political or strategic gain.

8. Field Asset:
A trained operative used in live operations or a resource actively involved in gathering information or conducting operations in a specific location, often providing critical insights or support to intelligence efforts.

9. Ghost Entity / Ghost Funding:
Entities or accounts created on paper to funnel black money or provide operational cover. Often linked to shell companies.

10. NDA (Non-Disclosure Agreement):
A legal contract that establishes a confidential relationship between parties, prohibiting them from disclosing certain information shared during their collaboration.

11. Node (e.g., "Dorsey Node"):
Refers to a key point in a covert network or conspiracy. Destroying a node collapses part of the operational infrastructure.

12. Non-official cover (NOC):
An agent working without diplomatic immunity or official affiliation— like a fake job or private sector front. Mentioned in reference to Dunning's executive director's tie to Sable Protocol.

13. OCO – Office of Covert Operations:
The fictional arm of the U.S. military requesting Roosevelt's team's reactivation. Used as a pseudo-agency to mirror real-world entities like the DIA or JSOC.

14. Protocol String:

In the context of military or intelligence operations—especially black-world or highly classified projects—is a coded reference that:

1) Links an order or operation to a specific clearance level or compartment.
2) Indicates that the document is governed by restricted access rules.
3) May point to a particular program, mission tier, or security directive, without using plain language.
4) Is often untraceable unless one is within the very specific access channel it was written under.
5) In simpler terms, it is a secret passphrase or access ID embedded in official orders that tells a computer—or a person with proper clearance—*what box this mission belongs to, who can see it*, and *how deep the classification goes.*
6) (Fictionalized Example)
   Auth Protocol: OP/SEG-9/VESTIGE-3
   To an outsider, it means nothing. But to someone in the know:
   a. OP/SEG-9 might mean "Operations, Segment 9"—a black-cell oversight group.
   b. VESTIGE-3 might be a specific project or mission tier involving legacy covert action.
   c. It tells the reader: this is real, it's deeply buried, and it's locked down under a highly restricted compartmentalized access system.

15. Safehouse:

A secure and discreet location used to protect agents, informants, or sensitive operations from detection or harm. It serves as a temporary refuge where individuals can safely meet, communicate, or plan without the risk of being compromised or surveilled. Safehouses are often equipped with security measures to ensure confidentiality and safety. For example, the house at Fort Belvoir.

16. Tier Four Operational Classification:

Not a real-world label but used in this story to signal high-level covert status with deep deniability and minimal oversight. Implies compartmentalization and direct access to black-world handlers.

Medical Terms:

1. Appendicitis:
The inflammation of the appendix, a small, tube-like structure attached to the large intestine. It typically occurs when the appendix becomes blocked, often by stool, a foreign body, or cancer, leading to increased pressure, reduced blood flow, and bacterial growth. Common symptoms include: Abdominal pain, usually starting near the belly button then shifting to the lower right abdomen. Symptoms include:
1. Nausea and vomiting
2. Loss of appetite
3. Fever
4. Swelling in the abdomen

Appendicitis is considered a medical emergency, as a ruptured appendix can lead to serious complications, such as peritonitis. Treatment usually involves surgical removal of the appendix (appendectomy), which can be performed laparoscopically or through open surgery. Early diagnosis and treatment are crucial for a positive outcome.

2. Appendix:
A small, tube-like structure attached to the large intestine, specifically the cecum. It is often considered a vestigial organ, meaning it has lost much of its original function over the course of evolution. The appendix can become inflamed, leading to a condition known as appendicitis, which often requires surgical removal (appendectomy) if it becomes severe.

3. Beta-blockers (e.g., Propranolol):
Used to reduce heart rate and lower blood pressure after an adrenaline spike. Referenced during Roosevelt's adrenaline crash.

4. Morphine:
An opioid analgesic derived from the opium poppy, used primarily to treat moderate to severe pain. It works by binding to specific receptors in the brain and spinal cord, altering the perception of pain and producing feelings of euphoria. Its use is carefully regulated in medical settings. It can be administered in various forms, including oral tablets, injections, and controlled-release formulations.

5. Peritoneal Bleed:
Internal bleeding into the abdominal cavity often following surgical rupture. Hollis treats this post-attack on Roosevelt in the ICU.

6. Psoas Sign:
A clinical test used to assess for appendicitis or irritation of the psoas muscle. It is performed by having the patient lie on their back and then attempting to flex the hip against resistance. If this maneuver causes pain in the right lower abdomen, it may indicate inflammation of the appendix or irritation of the psoas muscle due to an underlying condition, such as appendicitis. A physical examination technique used to evaluate abdominal pain.

7. PDS (Polydioxanone):
A type of absorbable synthetic suture used in surgical procedures. It is known for its high tensile strength and long absorption time, making it suitable for closing deep tissues and areas where prolonged support is needed. The running technique is a suturing method where a continuous line of suture is placed through tissue, allowing for rapid closure of wounds or incisions. This technique involves passing the needle in and out of the tissue in a series of connected stitches which can save time and provide even tension along the closure.

8. Serosanguinous Fluid:
A mix of blood and clear fluid—often seen at surgical sites. A sign of trauma or potential internal bleeding.

9. Short-acting Sedative:
Administered to reduce heart rate, pain response, and stress post-trauma. Hollis uses one to stabilize Roosevelt after the third assassination attempt.

10. Suture Rupture:
Tearing of surgical stitches—life-threatening in abdominal surgery. Triggered in the story by stress or movement after an assassination attempt.

11. Toradol (Ketorolac):
Non-opioid pain medication is often used in post-op care to manage inflammation and reduce opioid dependence.

12. Vicryl:

A type of absorbable synthetic suture made from polyglactin 910. It is commonly used in surgical procedures for closing wounds and incisions. Vicryl sutures are known for their strength, flexibility, and ability to be absorbed by the body over time, eliminating the need for removal.

13. Wide-spectrum Antibiotic:

Broad-range antibiotics are effective against numerous types of bacteria, critical in combat-related or surgical infections.

Typical Postoperative Pain Management (1980s, U.S. Military Hospital):

1) **Medication:**
   a) Morphine sulfate, either IV push or via Patient-Controlled Analgesia (PCA) pump (just becoming common in the mid-80s).
   b) If PCA wasn't available, the nurse would administer morphine as needed, likely every 3–4 hours.
2) **Route:**
   a) Intravenous (IV) for fast onset.
   b) Possibly Intramuscular (IM) if IV access is limited or PCA unavailable.
3) **Dosage:**
   a) Usually 2.5–10 mg IV every 3–4 hours as needed, depending on body weight, pain level, and tolerance.
4) **Other details:**
   a) Colonel Roosevelt would also be receiving IV fluids, either normal saline or lactated Ringer's.
   b) Vital signs monitored closely, especially respiratory rate and blood pressure, because morphine can depress respiration.
   c) He might have a Foley catheter, especially after longer surgeries or if sedation was deeper.
   d) A sudden collapse given dozens of abdominal stitches, recent internal bleeding, two major surgeries in less than a week, and his body still recovering from post-op stress would be medically dangerous. An adrenaline spike could absolutely lead to serious consequences.

Here's what could realistically happen:

1. Physiological strain

An adrenaline dump causes:

    a. Increased heart rate and blood pressure.
    b. Rapid breathing.
    c. Tensed abdominal and core muscles (involuntary).
    d. Vasoconstriction that can slow healing.
    e. Disruption of blood flow to the surgical site.
    f. Potential to re-open sutures, especially internally, or cause further micro-tears in weakened tissue.

2. Secondary symptoms:

    a. Dizziness or near-syncope from sudden BP changes.
    b. Sharp increase in abdominal pain due to involuntary core tension.
    c. Cold sweats, shallow breathing, and muscle shaking.
    d. Possible nausea or vomiting, which is *especially dangerous* after abdominal surgery—retching alone could rupture stitches or worsen internal bleeding.

3. Medical response:

    a. A doctor or a trauma nurse would immediately check his vitals.
    b. He might be given a mild beta-blocker (common in the '80s: propranolol or labetalol) to lower the cardiac stress response.
    c. Antiemetics to prevent vomiting (e.g., promethazine).
    d. Possibly a mild sedative to force the body to slow down and allow healing.

www.ingramcontent.com/pod-product-compliance
Lightning Source LLC
Chambersburg PA
CBHW071901220626
47052CB00002B/158